MW01232933

ISBN: 979-8-218-70690-6

*"For I know the plans I have for you," declares the Lord,*
*"plans to prosper you and not to harm you,*
*plans to give you a hope and a future."*

**—Jeremiah 29:11 (NIV)**

**To my husband, Tony —**
*Your love pushed me to keep writing, even when it hurt.*
*You always believed in my gift, even when I doubted myself.*
*This book carries your strength.*

**To my parents —**
*Though you are no longer here, your love still covers me.*
*Your faith, your wisdom, and your sacrifices shaped the woman I've become.*
*Thank you for the foundation that carried me through.*

**To my son —**
*You are the reason I keep going.*
*The reason I choose to heal.*
*May you always know that your mother is walking in her purpose—*
*And that you were part of the reason she found it.*

# CONTENTS

# Acknowledgments

A huge thank you:

First, I give all glory to **God**—my strength, my guide, and the reason this story exists. Every word on these pages is a testimony of His grace and mercy.

**To my siblings**—Murf, Monica & Michele —
You are all my biggest cheerleaders. All we have is us. I love y'all.

**To every survivor** who sees themselves in this story—thank you for your courage. You are not alone, and your voice matters.

**To my readers**—thank you for opening your hearts to Divinity's journey. May this story remind you that even in the ruins, God is building something

## PROLOGUE

You don't start a story like mine with fairy tales. There's no once upon a time. No glass slipper. Just a girl. A name. A silence so loud it swallowed her whole.

*Divinity Renee Destiny Rivera.*

Black and Puerto Rican. Green eyes, deep dimples, caramel complexion. Long, thick waves of black hair that once made people call me "pretty" before they ever called me "worth saving." I was born in between places—between cultures, between languages, between love and loss. My mother gave me that name like a prayer. Like prophecy. But for a long time, it felt more like a warning.

Because I was never the girl people thought I was.

On the surface, I laughed too loud and dressed too bright. I was bold in the halls at thirteen. Quick with comebacks. Always the one with jokes. But inside? I was drowning. By the time I was eighteen, I had lived more lives than some people twice my age. Done too much. Seen too much. Carried things I never asked to hold. And it nearly killed me.

Before the testimonies. Before the stages. Before the "you're so strong" speeches, there was a couch I slept on that wasn't mine. A school I disappeared from without anyone asking why. A boyfriend who held my dreams hostage and said it was love. A baby I didn't think I could raise. A God I stopped believing was listening.

And still—somehow—I lived.

Not just breathing. Not just surviving.

Lived.

With cracked ribs and scraped knees and a voice that shook every time I tried to use it. But I used it anyway.

Because something in me refused to die.

So no, this story doesn't begin in light. It begins in the dark. Where shame bloomed. Where silence festered. Where a girl who thought she had nothing left slowly started to write again.

And what she wrote became this.

Not because she was ready.

But because she couldn't stay quiet any longer.

Not every story begins with light. Some begin in silence. Mine began with a name I dared not speak and a wound I wore like skin. I wasn't born brave. I wasn't born whole. I was born already breaking.

But I survived. When the world tried to crush me beneath shame, I went quiet. When pain made a home in my bones, I stayed still. Until silence became louder than the scream.

This is not a story about brokenness. This is a story about motion.

I ran.

I hid.

I bled.

But eventually—I rose.

And when God called, I answered. Not because I was strong. But because I was finally tired of dying quietly.

If you're reading this… Maybe you've been quiet too.

Let me tell you how I found my voice.

Let me show you what He did with the pieces.

This is my testimony.

This is Divinity in Motion.

# 1 THE BEGINNING

*"Before I formed you in the womb I knew you." – Jeremiah 1:5*

## 1996

The phone rang at 7:14 pm—like it always did when he called. She stared at it first, lying on top of her comforter in her bedroom, a book resting open beside her and the lamp casting a warm halo against the wall. The cordless phone sat on her nightstand, flashing like it was daring her to answer. She wiped her glasses on her shirt like the motion might steady her. Then she picked it up.

"Hello?"

Pause.

"Don't 'Hey' me like you just remembered I existed."

I stayed in the hallway, feet cold on the tile, heart thumping like it already knew.

"You're pathetic, you know that?" My mother's voice cracked but didn't break. "You think a phone call once a year makes you a father? You think that's enough for her?"

I wanted to plug my ears. Instead, I sat on the floor, back against the wall, knees pulled to my chest.

"Don't lie. Don't you dare lie to me—"

Thud. Something hit the floor. Maybe the book.

"I don't need you. We do not need you!" she yelled. "Keep doing what you've been doing the last thirteen years—absolutely nothing!"

Then came the slam. Not just the phone. Her whole body went with it. And just like that, the whole apartment went still—except for her breathing, jagged and loud, like grief had taken her lungs hostage.

I sat outside my bedroom door, knees hugged to my chest, listening to her cry and throw things. She said she didn't need him, but I knew better. I was thirteen—not naive. My mother worked two jobs just to keep the lights on and food on the table. She needed him. Needed him to be responsible. We needed him. I needed him—to show up, to care, to be the father I dreamed of. But he never did.

Every time he let her down, a piece of my hope crumbled. Still, my mother kept trying. I hated that she did—because every time she reached out, he cut her deeper. I hated that she couldn't see she deserved more than the scraps he tossed her.

He always had an excuse. Still, she kept trying—not just for the money, but for me. I loved her for that. I admired her for it. But I also wanted her to stop. It wasn't worth the pain.

Without realizing it, I stood up from the cold, hard parquet floor and padded quietly to her room. She lay sprawled across her queen-sized sleigh bed, one arm tossed over her forehead like she'd been caught mid-prayer. Her cream robe slipped open at the shoulder, revealing a constellation of freckles against skin the color of chestnut and brown sugar. Her hair was still pinned from work, but tendrils had escaped and curled around her cheek like they didn't want to leave her.

She looked like something out of a photograph. Still. Almost too still.

Her hazel-brown eyes, though swollen from crying, shimmered with a quiet strength I couldn't name. She had dimples, high cheekbones, and a figure most women would envy.

I stood in the doorway without speaking. My feet knew not to cross the line where the carpet met the wood. She hated when I saw her like this—when the weight she carried finally showed up on her body. But I couldn't look away.

Her chest rose and fell in uneven breaths. An empty bottle of Motrin sat on the nightstand beside a lipstick-stained mug of something cold. The air still smelled faintly of flat iron heat. A tiny sauce stain marked her robe sleeve—probably from the rush to get dinner on before her second shift.

She looked tired. Not sleepy tired—soul tired. The kind that comes from holding up two lives on one back for too long.

And still, she was beautiful. Not magazine beautiful. Not the kind of pretty people whispered about in grocery stores. This was the kind of beautiful that made me ache. Because the world had no idea what it had taken for her to still be here.

I wanted her to have someone who would take care of her. Protect her. Give her something my father never did. But she never dated seriously.

Men came around sometimes—usually coworkers or old friends from church. They'd laugh too loud at her jokes, compliment how her earrings matched her shoes. A few brought flowers. She always smiled, polite, and let them flirt for exactly ten minutes before saying, "Well, I got a daughter and a second job, so unless you're offering to babysit, you might want to get going."

Of course, she didn't mean it. She just wanted them gone.

And they always went.

I used to think it was strength. Maybe it was. But maybe it was protection. Maybe it hurt less to send them away before they had a chance to stay and disappoint her.

At school, girls talked about their mothers' boyfriends like side characters in a sitcom—"He snores too loud," or "He eats the last of the cereal." But my mother's love life was a locked room, and she was the only one with a key.

Some nights, I'd wake up for water and see her standing by the window, robe tied too tight, one hand on her hip, the other holding a mug she never finished. Just staring out like she was waiting for someone to come back.

She never said she was lonely. But the bed never had two pillows. And she never smiled when love songs came on the radio. She turned the station instead.

Sometimes I imagined what she really deserved.

Not this cramped second-floor apartment in a brownstone with chipping paint and leaky faucets. Not paper-thin walls that let us hear Mr. and Mrs. Logan fighting every other night, or that hissing radiator that sounded like it had something to say. Not two jobs that left her feet swollen and her back screaming, or a paycheck that vanished before she ever saw the bottom line.

She deserved a house with real quiet. A kitchen with soft yellow windows and a sink that didn't shake. A fireplace. Big rugs. Candles that didn't smell like dollar stores. Silk robes instead of the ones she bought on sale at Conway. Fresh-cut roses she didn't have to buy herself.

I used to dream of having enough money to give her all of that. I still do.

She always said, "It's not about things, baby. It's about peace." But even peace costs something.

Even though she told me that, she always made sure I had the best.

And Juan? He never paid a dime.

My father didn't show up to school plays or send birthday cards. He didn't call unless he needed something or felt guilty for being trash. And every time he called, it lit a fire in her that made the whole apartment feel smaller.

She'd yell. Cry. Slam the phone. Say she was done. Then do it all over again six months later.

She said she didn't need him.

I knew better.

She needed him to be a man—and he never was.

My father was her first love. They dated for four years, and just before college, she got pregnant with me. I was told it wasn't planned—wasn't even wanted—but my mother refused to abort or give me up. She gave up college instead. Meanwhile, he left for school, claiming it was for "all of us."

Three months after I was born, he decided he didn't want to be with her—or be a father. And just like that, her dream of a family ended. But the truth was, she still held onto hope. She still loved him.

I just wanted her to be happy. I wanted her to meet someone new, to fall in love again, to have the family she deserved—and maybe, I'd finally have the father I always dreamed of.

I stepped in without a sound. The carpet muffled each footfall like it was trying to protect her too. I climbed onto the bed slowly, careful not to shift the mattress too much, and lay beside her.

She didn't acknowledge me. But she didn't pull away either. She didn't want me to know she had been crying.

I curled toward her, forehead resting near her spine. After a long moment, she reached back blindly and pulled my hand into hers. No words. Just the warmth of her fingers squeezing mine—tight, then tighter, then still. Her breath was uneven, shaky in the quiet. Mine followed hers, until we were both breathing like one broken machine. Her thumb brushed over my knuckles once, then again. That was all.

We didn't need to speak. I understood everything she was saying. And for a little while, the silence wasn't heavy—it was home.

I woke to the sound of a skillet crackling and the alarm yelling. The light was soft through the window—early, still pale. My mother's side of the bed was empty. The pillow held the faint shape of her head, the sheets already cold. I lay there for a moment, staring at the ceiling, trying to hold onto the safety of last night.

Then came the smell.

Sausage. Cinnamon. Eggs.

I sat up slowly, stretched, and padded down the hall toward the kitchen.

She was already dressed for work, wearing her black skirt, white blouse, black blazer, and a pair of earrings that only matched if you didn't look too close. Her back was to me, one hand flipping sausage links while the other stirred something in a pan. Her scarf was tied tight—the kind of knot that meant business.

On the table, two plates. Grits, scrambled eggs, toast, and sausage. Everything arranged just right—down to the little honey pack for the toast.

I sat down without speaking.

She poured juice into a glass and placed it beside my plate. Then she sat across from me and started eating like this was just a normal Wednesday. It was the closest thing to an apology she'd ever give. And the most I ever needed.

We didn't talk. Just chewed. Sipped. Passed napkins back and forth when they weren't needed.

The food was good. Real good. But that wasn't what made me swallow hard.

It was how she'd woken up and decided to feed me joy, even if she couldn't serve it to herself.

And I ate every bite, like I was trying to say thank you without making her hear it out loud.

After breakfast I headed to my room to get dressed. Rummaging through my closet, I ran my fingers through my long, thick curls, trying to think. I settled on my blue Guess jeans, a pink Guess top, and my blue, white, and pink Nike Air Max. My mother struggled, but she always made sure I was fly. I would tell her she didn't have to buy me name-brand clothes. As long as it was cute, I'd wear it regardless. She didn't listen—and I sure didn't complain.

After a quick shower, I tied my hair up in a side ponytail and checked myself out in the mirror. I had the same caramel complexion, green eyes, and dimples like my father. My mom always said I looked just like him.

"He must be hella fine," I muttered, laughing to myself.

Backpack slung over my shoulder, I headed to the front door.

"Div, have a good day at school!" Mom called from the hallway. "I'm off to work. Be careful coming home. Love you!"

"Love you too, Mommy!"

My mom worked a lot, so I spent a lot of time home alone—which honestly didn't bother me. It gave me the freedom to do what I wanted.

I wasn't a bad kid.

But I wasn't perfect either.

I followed the rules—mostly. Curfews, chores, grades. I kept my mouth shut when I was supposed to and said "yes, ma'am" even when I didn't mean it. But there was a part of me that stayed restless, even in obedience.

Sometimes I wanted more than rules and routines. I wanted to make my own mistakes. Not hers. And even if I didn't say it out loud, I was already starting to test the shape of my voice.

As I stepped outside and locked the door behind me, I immediately saw Harmony—my best friend since forever. Harmony wasn't just my best friend. She was the friend. The kind that doesn't need an explanation to understand what's wrong—the kind that shows up before you even ask.

Our mothers were best friends long before we were born. Harmony and I came into the world three months apart, and from the moment we could walk, we were always in each other's pockets. Birthdays, holidays, scraped knees, broken braids—us.

She was calm where I spun. Steady where I worried.

We didn't fight. We didn't need to. We just... fit. Even when we didn't always agree, we had a way of circling back to each other like the end of a prayer.

She knew when to talk and when not to. And she never made me feel like I had to perform to be loved. I used to think I was lucky to have her. But the older I got, the more I realized—what we had wasn't luck. It was something planted by our mothers and watered by every moment they never let us feel alone.

Harmony wasn't just someone I could count on—she was someone I never had to question.

"Heyyyyyyyyyyy, Chica!" Harmony sang, her voice carrying from the bottom of the stairs as I stepped through the gate of our brownstone.

"What's up, Bonita!" I replied, throwing my arm around her shoulders, feeling the familiar weight of her presence.

"O.M.G., you look cauteeee!" I added, giving her outfit a playful once-over, the way we always did. Harmony had this effortless way of glowing—like she could light up a room just by being in it. She was a little shorter than me, but she had this magnetic energy that made people gravitate toward her. Her confidence was contagious, and in a way, she made me feel like I could be brave too. Like I could stand beside her and be seen.

Harmony flashed a grin, tilting her head like she always did when she was flattered. "Thank you, thank you! So do you!" she said, her voice full of that sweet sincerity only she could pull off.

I flicked the end of my ponytail. "I try," I said, and we both laughed, the sound easy and familiar.

"Sooooo, today's the big day, huh?" Harmony teased, giving me that sly look she always wore when she was up to something.

"Ummm, you talking about Chris?" I asked, side-eyeing her, not sure where this conversation was going.

"What else would I be talking about?" Harmony shot back, practically bouncing on her feet. "You two have a project together, and he's coming by your house today, right?" She raised an eyebrow like she knew something I didn't.

I couldn't help but roll my eyes. "Ohhh, yeah… the project." I tried to keep my tone light, but Harmony wasn't buying it. She had that knowing look on her face, the one she always wore when she was about to push me into something I wasn't ready for.

"You made it seem like I'm about to give it up or something. Geesh."

"Please! You know better!"

"I do know better… that doesn't mean I do better." I smirked.

Harmony gave me the side-eye. "You KNOW better."

"Okay, okay! You're right. Happy now?"

"Much. But you did ask your mom, right?"

"Uhhh… I forgot. But I'm sure it won't be a big deal. It's just schoolwork. We're not doing anything."

We laughed as we walked into Junior High School 258—David Ruggles Middle School in Brooklyn. Our footsteps echoed through the hallway. Same morning routine, kids shouting across the hall, backpacks slamming into lockers, teachers calling out late names.

The building was old, and it smelled like pencil shavings, Lysol, and cafeteria grease. The floors had that always-damp feel, like someone had just mopped but never quite finished.

Harmony and I cracked jokes about Chris and the "project" we both knew was a little more than that. But my mind kept drifting.

I wasn't into boys until junior high. Then suddenly, they started looking… interesting. It wasn't like I wanted to get married or anything. I just wanted someone to notice me. Look at me a little longer. Laugh a little harder when I said something funny.

Then came Chris.

Chris was in eighth grade, a year older. Somehow we ended up in the same history class. The first day he walked in, it felt like one of those cheesy slow-motion scenes from a teen movie. The room didn't go silent or anything, but my ears stopped working right.

He was Puerto Rican, with curly hair that bounced when he walked, and the warmest brown eyes I'd ever seen. They made me feel like he knew something about me I didn't know myself. His smile? Yeah, it was dangerous. Like, make-you-forget-your-name dangerous.

At first, I couldn't talk around him. Literally froze. My brain went into sleep mode. I kept my head down and pretended to focus on class. But he caught me staring once—and he smiled. That was all it took.

After that, I got back to myself. We flirted, nothing serious. Just enough to keep the butterflies active. I liked it that way. Fun. Light. No strings.

But Chris wasn't like the other boys who mumbled or joked their way through crushes. He was bold, but not pushy. Sweet, but not soft. And I knew my mom would absolutely lose her mind if she knew I was even thinking about a boy.

She had a plan, school, college, career. Boys came after.

And maybe she was right.

But Chris made the hallway feel less like a hallway and more like a possibility.

Harmony and I walked into our last class of the day, history. The second I stepped into the room, she nudged me and nodded toward Chris.

I gave her a look and tried to play it cool. I walked to my seat—right next to his—and smiled.

"Hey Chris, what's up?"

"Same ol', same ol'," he replied, flashing that smile. I had no idea what "same ol'" even meant, but I laughed anyway.

I took out my notebook and tried to act normal.

"We still on for our study date?" Chris asked.

My heart skipped. Did he just call it a date?

"Um... yeah... sure. After school?"

"Yeah, that's cool."

"Okay, then after this class," I giggled.

"Bet. You want to go to my house or yours?"

I hesitated. I knew better than to not be home when my mom called for one of her check-ins. And technically, boys weren't allowed at our house when she wasn't home.

"My place is fine," I said, trying to sound casual.

"Cool," he said just as Mr. Wilmore began class.

Even though history wasn't my favorite, I liked his class. He made it fun. Class flew by—too fast—and before I knew it, the bell rang.

I shoved my notebook into my backpack and turned to Chris. "Ready?"

"Yep. Lead the way."

We walked out together, Harmony trailing behind.

"Hey, Chris!" Harmony said way too enthusiastically.

"What's up, Harm," he laughed.

"I hope you don't mind me tagging along. My house is right next door."

"Why would I mind?"

"I don't know. Don't want to be a third wheel or anything," she said dramatically.

"Harm! It's just a school project, not a date," I said, shooting her a look.

"Well, I was hoping it could be both," Chris said, grinning at me.

Harmony gave me the girl, he wants you look. I tried not to smile.

"Um... okay," I mumbled. Great job, Divinity. So smooth.

We made it to my house, and I pulled out my keys as we walked up the steps to the brownstone.

"I'll text you," Harmony said with a smirk, heading toward her door.

"Okay," I replied.

We stepped inside. The second I shut the door, my Nokia 8110 buzzed. I fished it out of my pocket but didn't catch it in time. Voicemail.

"Don't do nothin' I wouldn't do," Harmony's voice teased in the message. I laughed and shook my head.

I might've been a little rebellious at times, but I wasn't dumb. I quickly dialed her pager number, sending back a brief message,

*I'm being good. Promise.*

Then I grabbed my bookbag and headed upstairs, my phone buzzing in my pocket. I unlocked the front door to our apartment, letting Chris in.

"The Livingroom's right there. Make yourself comfortable—I'll be back in a second," I told Chris.

I ran to my bedroom, tossed my jacket onto the bed, and checked the time. I had barely made it back when the house phone rang. I didn't even need to check the caller ID—I knew it was my mom.

"Hey, Mom!" I answered quickly.

"Hey, baby. Everything okay?"

"Yes, ma'am. Oh—and I forgot to tell you, I have a history project due. My partner had to come over, so he's here now."

Silence.

I held my breath.

"Divinity Renee Destiny Rivera." That full-name tone. The she's-pissed tone. "You know the rules—no boys in the house without adult supervision. I get off in an hour. Tell that boy to come back in two hours."

"But, Ma—" I started.

"Don't 'but, Ma' me. Divinity, you heard me."

"Yes, ma'am."

"One hour. Love you."

"Love you too."

I hung up and walked back into the living room, hands on my hips.

"Sorry, but… you gotta go," I said.

Chris looked confused. "What do you mean I just got here?"

"I'm not allowed to have boys in the house alone. My mom's not playing that. You can come back in two hours."

He grabbed his bookbag and headed for the door without another word.

"You coming back? We still got a project to finish."

"I don't know. If I do, you'll see me," he said before walking out.

I leaned against the door, groaning. He's not coming back, I thought.

I trudged upstairs and threw myself onto my bed. If I was already in trouble, I might as well not be in double trouble. I pulled out my math book and started my homework.

"I hate math," I muttered.

Just as I started getting in the zone, the phone rang again. I looked at the caller ID, Puerto Rico.

I rolled my eyes. I already knew who it was.

I hesitated before answering. "Hello?"

"Baby girl?"

Pause. Two seconds. Three.

"My name is Divinity," I said coldly.

"Well, Divinity, you're my baby girl. This is your father."

"Father? I don't know what one of those is."

My voice was cold, but inside, I felt the sting of a hundred unsaid words. I wanted to scream at him. I wanted to ask, where were you when I needed you? Where were you when I was begging for you to love me?

But all that came out was the sharpness in my voice.

"I know I haven't been there, but I'm still your father. Show some respect," he said.

His words hit like a slap in the face. I was supposed to respect him? Respect the man who walked away when I was just a baby? The man who didn't care to show up? Who thought a few half-hearted phone calls could erase years of abandonment?

"Respect?" My voice shook now, and I didn't care. "I respect my mother—the one who raised me. The one who played both roles. You? I owe you nothing. Nothing."

I hung up before he could say anything else.

Even though I was angry, there was a part of me that wanted him to fight for me. But that part was small. And it wasn't enough to make me go back to him.

Right on cue, my mother walked into my room. "Who was that?" she asked.

I turned to her, still fuming. "The man who thinks he can call himself my father."

She walked closer. "What happened?"

"He just called me like everything's cool. Like we have a relationship. Called me 'baby girl.' Mommy, how can he even say that?"

"Honey, he is your father—"

"STOP DEFENDING HIM!" I screamed, my voice cracking like glass. The words came out sharper than I meant—too sharp, like knives.

She stood there, stunned, like I'd sliced something in her she didn't know was still tender. And maybe I had.

"I'm sorry," I whispered, but it didn't feel like enough. It wasn't enough. It would never be enough.

I never screamed at my mother. Ever.

She came over and wrapped me in her arms.

"Why doesn't he love me, Mommy?" I sobbed.

She stroked my hair. "He loves you in his own way. I know it's not how you want or deserve, but he does love you. And you have every right to feel the way you do."

The phone rang again. She glanced at the caller ID. "It's him. Do you want to talk to him?"

"No," I said, walking into the bathroom to wash my face.

She answered. "Yes, Juan?"

"Where is she?"

"In the bathroom. Washing her face."

"Did she tell you how she spoke to me? No respect." His accent heavy.

"Juan, what did you expect? A big 'Hi, Daddy'? She doesn't know you. That was your choice."

"I'm trying now. Doesn't that count?"

"She just asked me why you don't love her. Does that count for nothing? A few phone calls don't erase thirteen years. If this is you trying—try harder."

She hung up.

When I came out, she hugged me again.

"I'm so sorry you have to go through this. If I could make it better, I would. You'll always have me. Always."

"I know, Mommy," I whispered.

"Now... did you finish your homework?"

"Almost. Just a little math left."

"Okay. I'm going to change and start dinner. Is your friend coming back?"

"I don't know. He didn't seem too happy."

"And whose fault is that?" She raised a brow. "You know the rules. No boys home alone. No puppy dog eyes."

I nodded. "I know."

A few minutes later, the phone rang again. I picked up, expecting a telemarketer or maybe another check-in from Mom.

"Hello?"

"Yo, it's me. Is it safe to come by now?" Chris asked.

"Yeah. My mom's here," I said.

"Aight, on my way."

I brushed my teeth, fixed my hair, and headed up front just as Mom entered the kitchen.

"Ma, what's for dinner?" I asked, even though I already knew.

She smiled. "You ask me every Thursday. You already know it's smothered pork chops with mashed potatoes and peas."

"I just like hearing you say it," I laughed.

"Get your homework done."

"Oh, I'm done. Chris is coming back so we can finish the project."

"When were you going to tell me?"

"I just found out. He called me."

"Next time, give me a heads-up. Don't be a smart-aleck, Div. That'll get you in a world of trouble."

"Yes, ma'am."

The doorbell rang. I went downstairs.

"Who is it?"

"It's Chris."

I let him in. We went upstairs.

My mother walked over, composed but curious.

"Hello, Chris. I'm Divinity's mom."

"Nice to meet you, ma'am," he said, shaking her hand nervously.

"Will you be staying for dinner? We're having Div's favorite."

"I'd love to, thank you."

I gave him a look, trying not to laugh as I led him to the living room. We set up our project materials and actually got some work done. We laughed, researched, and had fun. It didn't feel like schoolwork at all.

Then my mom called us for dinner.

Chris pulled out both of our chairs. My mom looked pleasantly surprised.

"Wow. Did your father teach you to do that?" she asked.

"Yes, ma'am. He always said women are queens, girls are princesses and should be treated as such."

"Well, he raised you right," she said with a nod. "Let's bow our heads."

My mom always prayed before meals. I didn't always understand it, but I respected it.

After grace, we ate. She asked Chris a million questions—about his family, school, goals—you name it.

When it was time for him to leave, I walked him to the door.

"Thanks for coming back. Didn't want to fail that project," I smiled.

"Nah, I was coming back anyway. You think your mom would let me come over sometime? Like… just to chill?" He whispered.

I blushed. "She seemed to like you, but I'll ask."

He checked his phone. 7:45 p.m.

"I gotta run. See you tomorrow, Div."

He took off. I closed the door and turned around—to find my mom standing there.

"So… you like that boy, don't you?" she asked.

I hesitated. "I think I do. But we're just friends."

"You're too young for a boyfriend. Focus on your studies."

"But, Mom—he's sweet. And I know you like him."

"He is a nice young man. But I don't want you making the same mistakes I did. Focus now. The boys will come later."

I didn't respond. I knew what that meant, no to Chris chilling.

I washed the dishes, went to my room, and closed my door. That was the start of my secret relationship with Chris.

I wasn't going to make the same mistakes she did with my dad.

And even though I hated lying to my mother—I wasn't her. I was my own person.

## 2  THE END OF US

*"I loved you louder than I listened to myself. That will never happen again." –*
*Divinity's journal*

**MAY, 1997**

This was it—the year I'd finally graduate from junior high. I couldn't wait. High school was just around the corner, and the best part? I'd be going to the same one as Chris.

Yes, I said I wasn't gonna be like my mother—and I meant it. I liked Chris, sure. But I wasn't about to ruin my life for him. We'd been together since the first day he came over. We made out here and there, but it never went further. And of course, my mother still had no idea.

Chris had already graduated last year. Now, in just two more months, it would be my turn. Everything was looking up.

At school, I felt different. More seen. I walked through the halls of J.H.S. 258 like I had been born to rule them. Not in a mean girl way—I wasn't cruel—but people noticed me now. Girls whispered about my outfits. Boys tried to catch my eye. Teachers stopped calling on me just to embarrass me. I was, finally, somebody.

Lunchtime was the highlight. Harmony and I sat at our regular table near the windows, surrounded by noise and energy. Our spot was prime real estate. Girls from other cliques drifted over to ask if we liked their new haircuts or who we were crushing on this week. Harmony loved the attention. I liked watching her light up when she told a joke that made half the table double over.

Today, though, the energy shifted when Savon slid into the seat across from me without asking. Two boys followed and stood behind him like backup dancers.

"Divinity," he said, dragging my name out like a pickup line. "Why you playin' so hard to get?"

I didn't even look up from my sandwich. "I'm not playing. I'm just

17

not interested."

One of the boys snorted, but Savon leaned in like he thought I was bluffing.

"For real, though, what does Chris got that I don't?"

I looked up slowly and gave him the kind of stare that makes people back up. "Boundaries."

That got a few Oooohs from the table. Savon blinked, surprised.

Harmony choked on her soda. "Dang, Div," she muttered, grinning.

Savon put his hands up. "Aight. That's cold. But I respect it."

"Do you, though?" I asked sweetly, tilting my head. "Because you're still sitting here."

He laughed like I was flirting. I wasn't.

Eventually he left, but not before saying, "Tomorrow, I'm bringing you a Honey Bun. Everybody got a weakness."

I rolled my eyes so hard I nearly saw last week. "And yours is rejection," I muttered.

Harmony clapped the table. "You're getting too smooth. I love it."

After lunch, as I walked to science class, I passed the music room and caught a glimpse of a guitar case propped open inside. The sight stopped me cold.

Chris used to bring his guitar everywhere.

We weren't supposed to hang out at the park near my house after dark, but he'd show up sometimes anyway, guitar slung over his shoulder, acting like he was in a movie.

One night a few months ago, I remember sneaking out just for ten minutes—sweatpants under my coat, hair tied back in a scarf. He was sitting on the swings with his guitar in his lap and two grape sodas waiting.

"You came," he said with a half-smile.

"Barely. I'm risking my life out here."

He laughed. "It's just ten minutes. I missed you."

I remember sitting next to him on the swing. His arm wrapped around my shoulder, warm through the fabric. He played this slow, clumsy melody—not good, not terrible—but he kept sneaking glances at me while he played like I was the only thing in the world he wanted to see.

Then he said something I've never forgotten.

"I don't like when you act like you're hard to love," he told me. "You're not. You're easy."

At the time, it felt like a miracle. Like someone saw me, really saw me. No performance. No pressure. Just me.

18

I hadn't thought about that night in months. But now, remembering it, it stung like touching something that used to be warm but had gone cold.

I pressed my hand against my locker and closed my eyes. I didn't want to think about the good parts anymore. They just made everything hurt worse. Chris had been acting weird lately. Different. I could sense something was wrong I just couldn't put my finger on it.

Harmony reached her house first.

"See you later, girl," she said with a wave.

I waved back—then stopped cold.

Chris was standing on my front steps.

I smiled—but inside, panic flared. He knew he wasn't supposed to be here.

I hurried up, unlocked the door, and pulled him inside before any neighbors outside could get to gawking. As soon as we were alone, I gave him a quick hug and got straight to the point.

"Not that I'm not happy to see you… but what are you doing here?"

"I haven't seen you in three days, Div," he said, not meeting my eyes. "What's going on?"

"You know I can't always get away. I have to wait for my mom to let me out. And we've been talking on the phone."

"Yeah… but still."

He looked away. Something shifted in the air—heavy and tense.

"Chris," I said slowly. "Why are you really here?"

He exhaled like he'd been holding his breath for weeks.

"Look, you know how I feel about you. But… I've got needs, Div. And you're not willing to fulfill them."

I blinked. Once. Twice.

"Say that again?" My voice was flat with disbelief.

He shrugged, like what he was saying made sense. "Don't get me wrong—I really like you. But we've been together for a year, and we haven't taken that next step."

There was a silence so thick it made the room feel smaller.

"Then go find someone who will," I said. My voice didn't even crack. "I'm thirteen, Chris. I'm not losing my virginity just to keep a boy. I deserve more than that. More than this."

The words felt like stones dropping from my mouth. Each one hit something deep inside me on the way out.

He didn't say anything. He just stood there, shame barely creeping into the edge of his face.

"So you can leave," I said, stepping back. "Right now."

He looked like he might say something. But he didn't.

He left.

I shut the door behind him, the click of the lock sounding final.

I stood there a moment, then slid down to the floor. The hardwood pressed into my palms as I buried my face in my hands. My body shook. Tears hit hard and fast. Not soft, cinematic ones—real ones. Ugly ones. Gut-punch sobs that made me feel like I might never stop.

I had believed in him. I thought it meant something. That we meant something.

Turns out, he was just like the others. Just like Mom said. Superficial. If you didn't give boys what they wanted, they left.

But I wasn't gonna compromise my worth. My mother raised me better than that.

I wiped my face, dragged myself off the floor, and forced myself into routine. Lock the second door. Picked up the phone. Time for the check-in call.

"Hey, Mommy," I said, trying to sound normal.

"Hi, honey! I'm glad you made it home safe."

"Yeah. I'm just getting ready to do my homework."

"You okay? You sound tired."

"Yeah, just a long day."

"You sure it's nothing else?"

"Promise."

"Well, how about we go out for dinner? Give me a break from cooking."

"Thanks, but… maybe another night."

"Alright. I'll bring home takeout. See you in two hours. Love you."

"Love you too."

Just then, the phone buzzed.

Harmony.

I answered.

"Hey, Chica… did I just see Chris leave your house?"

I let out a breath I didn't realize I was holding.

"Yeah. That was him."

My voice cracked as I told her what happened, and I didn't even try to hide it.

Harmony didn't say anything at first. She let the silence stretch, like she was giving me space to fall apart without judgment.

"I'm here," she said finally. "You don't have to hold it in."

"I didn't think it would feel like this," I said, curling tighter into myself. "I thought I was doing the right thing, you know?"

"You were doing the right thing."

"Then why does it feel like I just gave something away? Like... like I lost a piece of myself just by saying no."

There was a pause, then Harmony's voice softened.

"I remember when I told Shawn I didn't want to do anything past kissing," she said. "He told me I was 'childish.' That he thought I was different, but I was just like all the 'scared girls.'"

I sat up. "Shawn? You never told me that."

"Yeah. Well. It was before you and Chris even got together. It wasn't serious. But it still messed with my head for a while. Made me wonder if I was childish."

"You're not."

"And neither are you."

The words settled into me like warm tea.

"I feel so stupid," I whispered.

"You're not. You're just... human. You trusted someone who didn't know how to value you. That's on him."

"Maybe. But I still miss him."

"I know." She paused, then added gently, "Even the trash ones leave holes."

I let out a little laugh through my tears. "That's messed up."

"But true," she said, and I could practically hear her smirking.

"I really do love you, Harm."

"I love you too. You don't have to go through anything alone, okay? You hear me?"

"Yeah."

"I'm right next door. Call me, knock on the wall, whatever. I'll come."

I closed my eyes. "Thanks. I think I'm gonna try and finish my homework."

"That's how I know you're lying," she said, and we both laughed.

"Alright. Love you."

"Love you more."

The next thing I knew, I was being gently shaken awake.

"Div... Div..."

My mom's voice.

I blinked open my swollen eyes and looked up.

"Yeah?" My voice came out rough, like I'd swallowed sandpaper.

Her brow creased. "Are you okay?"

21

"Yes, Mommy. I'm fine." I lied. Sat up like I hadn't just cried myself to sleep. Opened my notebook like I hadn't been out cold for an hour. I knew she'd come back to check again. She always did.

Later that night, I curled up on the couch in my hoodie, head buried, TV on mute.

She walked into the room, looked at me for a long moment, then sat down beside me.

"You've barely said a word since I got home," she said softly. "What's going on, Div?"

I shook my head, eyes still locked on the screen. She reached over and placed a hand on my knee.

"Baby. Talk to me."

I sighed and finally looked up. Her eyes were warm—but knowing.

"It's Chris," I said quietly.

Her brows lifted just slightly. "What about him?"

I hesitated. "He broke up with me."

Silence.

She stared at me—shock flickering across her face, followed by something else. Hurt.

She muted the TV.

"You and Chris were dating?"

I nodded slowly, bracing myself. "For a year, Mom."

She didn't speak. Just studied me, like she was trying to read past the words, deep into whatever I wasn't saying.

Then her jaw tightened. "A year? And you never told me?"

"I didn't want to hide it," I said, voice small. "But I knew your rule. No dating. And you always said you didn't trust him."

She stood and started pacing. "You didn't think that was something I should know? Divinity, you lied to me."

"I didn't want to disappoint you," I whispered. "I didn't want to mess up. And… I didn't want you to think I was turning into you."

That last part slipped out before I could stop it.

She froze.

Her back was to me. For a long second, she didn't move. Then slowly, she turned around. Her eyes weren't angry anymore—just tired.

"I'm not mad that you had feelings for him," she said. "I'm mad that you felt like you couldn't come to me. That you didn't trust me enough to be part of your life."

"I didn't know how."

She sat back down, closer this time. Her voice dropped to almost a whisper. "I was young once too. I remember what it's like to want love so bad you ignore everything else. But baby... no one who truly cares about you will ever ask you to trade your boundaries for their comfort."

I looked at her—really looked at her. Her eyes were soft, shining just a little. Her shoulders still tense, but her heart right there, open.

"I'm sorry, Mom," I said.

She wrapped her arms around me and pulled me close. "You're strong, Div. So strong. But you don't have to carry everything alone."

Her heartbeat was steady against my ear. She rubbed slow circles on my arm. I let myself lean into her warmth, let the silence between us heal a little bit of the crack I didn't even know had formed.

The ache from the breakup didn't vanish overnight. But it dulled. Life kept moving—school, friends, the countdown to graduation. The promise of high school just beyond the horizon gave me something to look forward to.

And my mom? She was already talking about prom.

The Saturday before graduation, we went shopping for my dress. Days like that didn't come often—no bills waiting, no second shift calling my mom's name, no rush. Just me and Mommy, walking through the mall like we were two regular people with time and money to burn.

Well... not burn. But at least pretend.

From the moment we walked in, she was already on a mission. "This is it," she said, her voice bright. "This is the start of everything."

She darted between racks like it was her prom, not mine.

"Ooh! Div, look at this one—lace and rhinestones! A two-for-one!"

"Mommy, I am not wearing something that looks like a disco ball exploded on it."

She laughed so loud people turned to look. "Girl, you're no fun."

We tried on everything. Peach satin that made me look like a melting creamsicle. A stiff blue number that scratched my ribs every time I moved. One dress was so tight I couldn't sit down, and another was so poofy I had to duck going through the dressing room door.

She took pictures anyway.

"Stop laughing!" I said through the curtain.

"But your face in this one—" she giggled. "You look like you're being attacked by the fabric!"

I peeked out. "I was."

At one point, a saleslady gave us side-eye when we pulled a few dresses off the "final clearance" rack. I saw it. So did Mommy.

She looked that woman straight in the face, then turned to me and said loud enough for the whole store to hear, "Baby, we decide what's in style."

We spent three full hours in that store. By the end, my feet hurt and my arms were sore from holding hangers, but I didn't want it to end.

When I stepped out in the blush pink off-shoulder dress—the one— I didn't even have to ask.

My mother gasped. Her eyes filled instantly.

"There she is," she whispered. "My baby girl."

I turned slowly in the mirror, letting the soft fabric swirl around me. For the first time in weeks, I felt... not broken.

Just whole.


The night of prom arrived, and everything felt surreal.

My room smelled like a mix of shea butter, flat iron heat, and that sweet lavender body spray I only used on special occasions. My mother was buzzing around, making last-minute adjustments to everything— even things that didn't need adjusting. I could feel her energy pulsing like static in the air: joy, nerves, maybe even a little sadness.

I was sitting at my vanity, carefully applying soft makeup—just enough blush, a little mascara, lip gloss that shimmered in the light. I'd practiced this routine at least a dozen times on school nights when I was supposed to be asleep.

When I turned to tell my mother I was almost ready, I saw her standing in the doorway, her eyes already glassy.

"I haven't even put the dress on yet," I teased, smiling.

She laughed and sniffled at the same time. "I know. But it's hitting me. My baby girl is going to prom."

When I slipped into the soft blush pink dress, it felt like something out of a dream. The satin was smooth and shiny, hugging what little curves I had without being tight. The off-shoulder neckline made me feel grown in the best way, showing off my collarbones. Tiny pearl beads scattered across the bodice sparkled every time I moved, catching the light like stars blinking awake.

But the skirt—oh, the skirt. Layers of soft tulle floated beneath the satin, giving it just enough fullness without making me feel like I was drowning in fabric. When I spun, the dress moved like it had a life of its own, shifting colors from pink to cream to soft gold under the lights.

I slid on the silver shoes we picked out together, nothing too fancy, just enough shine. Then I fastened the delicate bracelet Mom gave me—

a thin silver chain with a tiny heart charm. She told me it had been hers in high school, and that her mom gave it to her before her first big dance.

That made me pause.

She helped me pin up my hair into a simple, elegant updo, the kind of hairstyle that looked easy but wasn't. "Turn," she said softly, adjusting a bobby pin. "Just one more..."

When I looked in the mirror, I hardly recognized myself. I was still me—same eyes, same freckles—but something had shifted. I looked taller. Not in height, but in presence.

"You look so grown," my mother whispered, her hands pressed to her mouth like she was afraid saying it too loud would make time speed up.

I smiled, but there was a knot forming in my chest. A good one. A proud one. The kind that makes you realize something important is happening, even if you don't have the words for it yet.

She stood behind me as I adjusted the straps of my dress, her hand resting gently on my shoulder. Her voice cracked just a little when she said, "You're stunning, Divinity. I couldn't be prouder of the young woman you've become."

I turned toward her and hugged her tightly, careful not to mess up my makeup. "Thanks, Mom."

Before I left, I stood in front of the full-length mirror one last time.

I adjusted the dress again, even though nothing was out of place. Smoothed my hair. Turned sideways. Smiled. Then stopped.

It hit me—not the dress or the corsage or the sparkle—but the fact that this was one of those moments grown people talk about when they say, "I remember my prom night like it was yesterday."

I wondered if I would.

Would I remember how the satin felt on my arms? The way my mother's eyes shone? The sound of her praying?

Would tonight be one of the stories I told someday?

I reached for my journal on the dresser and quickly scribbled in the corner of a page,

*Don't forget this feeling.*

I snapped the book shut. Took a breath.

My heart was racing—not from fear. From knowing. That I was stepping into something new. Something mine.

She wiped the corner of her eye, then practically shoved me toward the stairs. "Alright, let's get these pictures before I completely fall apart."

She took pictures from every angle—on the stairs, by the front door, out on the stoop next to the flowers she'd planted in plastic pots last spring. She made me pose with the corsage three different times because the first two "weren't cute enough."

"Mom, it's fine."

"No, no, this one's going in the photo album and getting mailed to your aunties. Turn your wrist like this."

I rolled my eyes. "I'm not doing wrist modeling."

She grinned, holding the camera up. "You are tonight."

I posed again.

She beamed like I was walking into something sacred.

As I stepped back inside, I paused in the front doorway, letting the moment stretch. The light from the hallway cast a glow over her face. She looked at me like I was magic. Like maybe she had done one thing right in a life full of hard choices.

"You look like a princess," she whispered.

I laughed softly, heart swelling. "You're just saying that."

"I'm not. You are."

Then she reached out and took my hands in hers.

"Wait," she said, her tone shifting. "Before you go."

She bowed her head.

I knew what was coming.

We prayed before anything big—a test, a job interview, getting on the road. But this prayer? This one felt different.

"Lord, I come to you tonight to say thank you," she began, voice thick with emotion. "Thank you for a wonderful and beautiful daughter. I could not have asked for a better child. You knew what I needed when you created her. She saved me. I ask that you stay with her throughout her life, protect her from any harm that may come her way. Keep her safe tonight as she has fun with her friends. In Jesus name, Amen."

By the end, tears were running down her face.

I opened my eyes and stared at her. "Mommy... thank you," I said, almost in tears myself. "You are a wonderful mother, and I love you."

She smiled—this wide, tearful, glowing smile—and kissed my forehead. "I love you too. Go enjoy your night, baby."

My mom followed me to the door like she didn't really want to open it.

"You have everything?" she asked.

"Yep."

"Phone charged?"

"Full battery."

"Lip gloss?"

I opened my purse and showed her. "Front pocket."

She smiled and brushed a piece of lint off my shoulder like it meant something. Then she leaned in close and whispered, "If they start playing anything slow, don't be afraid to let somebody lead and not too close."

I raised an eyebrow. "Mommy…"

She laughed. "I'm just saying—be open to the moment."

Her voice turned serious again. "But not too open. And if any boy gets handsy—"

"I know, I know. Knee to the groin, then call you."

"Exactly."

She pulled me in for a tight hug, held me there for a few seconds longer than usual.

"You be safe," she said, her voice muffled by my hair. "And have so much fun."

"I will."

I stepped out into the night, the air cool against my skin, the weight of her love still wrapped around my shoulders like a shawl.

## 3  GONE

*"The Lord is close to the brokenhearted." – Psalm 34:18*

**Graduation day arrived like a whirlwind—**
But not the chaotic kind.

It was the kind of whirlwind that made everything feel just a little too bright, a little too fast, a little too big.

The sun was out, no clouds in the sky, just that perfect June heat curling around my cap and gown. Birds were chirping like they were in on the celebration, and the whole schoolyard buzzed with excitement— kids straightening their gowns, parents waving from the bleachers, the smell of hair grease, perfume, and someone's auntie's coconut oil hanging in the air.

I stood in line with my class, sweaty hands clenching the edge of my gown, heart thudding like a drum inside my chest. My name was somewhere in the middle of the list. I kept checking the program in my lap like it might have changed since they printed it. Harmony sat beside me, practically bouncing in her seat.

"You nervous?" she whispered.

I shook my head. "Not really. You?"

"I'm sweating through my dress. Don't tell nobody."

I snorted and bumped her shoulder. "Your secret's safe."

Then, the music started—the opening chords of "Pomp and Circumstance" echoing through the speakers like something sacred— and my stomach did a backflip.

We rose together, row by row, and marched in slow, measured steps across the field and toward the makeshift stage. I looked out into the sea of folding chairs and saw her—my mother—front row, center, standing up already with her disposable Kodak camera halfway to her eye, like she didn't want to miss a single second.

When my name was finally called, it didn't feel real.

28

"Divinity Rivera!"

My ears rang. My body moved before my mind caught up. I stepped forward, heels careful on the temporary wooden platform, knees locked tight so I wouldn't wobble.

"Go ahead, baby!" my mom's voice cut through the crowd—loud and proud. "That's my girl!"

I heard clapping, but all I could feel was the tight pull in my throat and the way the corners of my mouth refused to come down. I was smiling so hard my cheeks hurt.

The principal handed me a rolled-up paper tied with a blue ribbon—more ceremonial than official—but I held it like it was the key to everything. He said "Congratulations," and I nodded, barely hearing him.

When I turned back toward the seats, I found my mom again—tears now running down her cheeks, both hands clapping so hard I could see the sting in her palms.

My gown swished around my ankles as I walked back, holding that little diploma like a crown.

After the ceremony, the field turned into chaos. Laughter, hugs, people shouting names. Harmony's family wrapped her up before I could even say anything. I turned, and my mom was already moving toward me, arms wide.

She enveloped me in the kind of hug that erased everything else. She smelled like cocoa butter and laundry detergent and a little bit of sweat. Her cheek was pressed to the side of my face, and I could feel her breath catch.

"You did it," she whispered. "I knew you would. I'm so proud of you, Divinity."

I didn't want to let go.

She pulled back just far enough to cup my face and kiss my forehead. "Look at you. My baby girl… growing into this amazing woman right before my eyes."

"I'm still just a girl in a polyester gown," I said.

"Maybe. But you're my girl. And you made it."

She handed me a tiny bouquet—three pink roses with a blue ribbon that matched my school colors.

I looked down at them, then back at her. "You didn't have to."

"I wanted to. Today's a big deal. And we celebrate big deals in this house."

I tucked the roses under my arm and leaned into her side. Her arm went around me without hesitation.

"You hungry?" she asked.

"Starving."

"I was thinking… pizza, then we pick out a movie."

I looked up at her. "Are you trying to bribe me into a sleepover?"

She laughed, loud and proud. "I'm trying to make a memory."

We walked home slowly, not because we were tired, but because neither of us wanted the day to end just yet.

I looked up at the clear sky, at the rows of houses and the familiar cracks in the sidewalk I knew by heart. Everything looked the same—but I felt different.

Lighter. Like something had finally clicked into place inside me.

And I remember thinking, *This is the start of everything.*

**Six months later.**
**December 26, 1997.**

It was cold outside, but inside our little apartment, everything felt warm. Not from the heat—we had to rattle the old radiator to get it to hiss right—but from the mood. The kind of warmth that only came from routine, from love, from being known.

We had planned a movie night. Just me and Mommy. No interruptions. Just thick blankets, fuzzy socks, and one of those worn-down VHS tapes that never quite played right but we still refused to throw out.

The living room smelled like laundry and lemon Pledge. The TV was already set up, remote waiting on the armrest. Our favorite quilt—the patchy one with random fabric squares she swore had "history"—was spread over the couch like it was sacred.

"Okay," my mom said, standing in the kitchen with her hands on her hips. "We have orange soda, old popcorn crumbs, and exactly three peppermints. So we're clearly living large."

I laughed from the hallway. "We had candy yesterday."

"Keyword,      had."

She opened the cabinet dramatically. "Who ate all the good snacks? Hmmm?"

"You're the only one who eats those Little Debbie brownies."

"I don't recall that."

She reached in, pulled out an empty box, and turned it over like it had betrayed her.

I walked in and leaned against the fridge, grinning. "We can survive one movie night without sugar."

"Maybe you can. I need popcorn. It's not a real movie without popcorn. And what happened to the strawberry ice cream?"

"We finished it last weekend. You said we'd get more."

She stared at me like I had just delivered a terrible betrayal. "You let me forget to buy it?"

"You were dancing in the frozen aisle to Mariah Carey. I was lucky to get you out of there without public embarrassment."

She gasped. "Excuse me, I was blessedly festive."

I laughed and rolled my eyes. "Okay, Mariah."

She grabbed her purse and slipped on her coat. "I'm going to the store."

"What? Mommy, it's late."

"I know, baby. But I want tonight to be perfect. We haven't had a night like this in a minute."

She wasn't wrong. Between work and bills and everything life had been throwing at her lately, we hadn't had many soft moments.

"I'll go tomorrow," I said. "We can do without."

She shook her head, already tying her scarf. "It won't feel the same tomorrow. I'll be right back."

She bent down and kissed my cheek. "I want to get it all. Popcorn, candy, and that good ice cream. The one with the little strawberry chunks."

"I can come with you."

She stopped in the doorway, hand on the knob.

"No. You stay here. Start the movie. Get the blanket warm. I won't be long, baby."

I hesitated. There was a weight in her voice I couldn't place—not heavy, just... final, somehow. But maybe that was hindsight.

She smiled over her shoulder, that soft little half-smile that always made me forgive her for everything. "I won't be long. Promise."

The door opened. Cold air snuck in like a whisper. Then the door closed.

I glanced at the clock.

6:57 p.m.

The opening credits were already rolling by the time I started wondering where she was.

At first, I didn't think anything of it. I was curled under the patchwork quilt, flipping channels with the remote even though the tape was already in the VCR. Just killing time. Half-watching. Half-listening.

The radiator hissed in the corner. The smell of lemon Pledge still hung in the air from earlier.

I glanced at the clock.

7:27 p.m.

Okay. She left at 6:57. Thirty minutes ago.

She probably just ran into someone. That always happened—especially at the corner store. She could never just buy milk without talking to at least two people who knew her from church, work, or childhood.

Still, I got up and went to the phone hanging on the wall.

Dialed her cell.

No answer.

That didn't surprise me—Mom hated picking up while she was walking. Said it made her feel like a robot with a leash.

I hung up, tried again five minutes later.

Still nothing.

I sat back down and crossed my arms over my chest.

7:43 p.m.

Forty-six minutes.

Okay. Maybe the line was long. Or she stopped at two places. Maybe she went to get the "good" strawberry ice cream—the one that only the fancy store carried.

That had to be it.

But my throat was tight.

I turned down the volume on the TV. The room got too quiet too fast. The hum of the radiator suddenly felt loud, like it was breathing in place of me.

I got up again. Opened the fridge. Closed it. Walked to the hallway window and looked out.

Same old street. Wet pavement. One person walking a dog. A streetlamp flickering like it always did when it was cold. Nothing unusual.

But something felt unusual.

I walked back to the phone and picked it up again. Dialed her number one more time.

Ring. Ring. Ring. Voicemail.

This time, I didn't leave a message. I just stood there with the receiver in my hand, staring at nothing, the cord curling between my fingers like a lifeline I didn't want to drop.

The panic didn't crash in like a wave.

It crept.

Soft steps across the floorboards of my chest.

My hands started to shake. Not badly. Just enough to make the phone rattle when I put it back in its cradle.

7:57 p.m.

Exactly one hour.

And she wasn't back.

I stared at the front door like it might open on its own. Like she'd walk in, bags rustling, keys jangling, apologizing for taking too long.

But the door stayed closed.

That's when I reached for the other phone, the cordless and called the only person I trusted enough to say the words out loud.

I didn't want to say the words out loud.

Calling Harmony made it real.

But I did it anyway. My fingers were cold, stiff as I dialed. My heartbeat was a slow, dull pound in my ears.

She picked up on the second ring.

"Hey, Chica—what's up?"

My voice barely came out. "Is Tia home?" Tia was what I called Harmony's mother because she was like a aunt to me.

"Yeah, she's right here. What's wrong?"

"I can't get ahold of my mom." The sentence felt thick in my throat. "She went to the store over an hour ago, and she's not back. Her phone keeps going to voicemail."

There was a pause. Then Harmony's voice softened, like she dropped her volume on instinct.

"Okay. Hold on."

I heard her moving, then muffled words. Tia's voice came through in the background, calm and direct, like always. The kind of voice that didn't panic unless she had to.

Then Harmony was back.

"We're coming over. Now."

I hung up and sat back down on the couch. The quilt was bunched beside me like a memory. The movie on the screen played on, but I couldn't even register what was happening. The characters might as well have been speaking another language.

I kept glancing at the door.

Listening.

Praying for keys in the lock. Footsteps. A voice calling, "I'm back!"

Instead—nothing.

I grabbed my oversized sweater and threw on my sneakers. I went downstairs and sat on the steps waiting for Tia and Harmony. I couldn't stay in that apartment another minute longer. A full five minutes crawled by before the knock came. I shot to the door so fast I nearly tripped over the rug.

It wasn't her.

It was Tia, dressed in a long brown coat, scarf still around her neck, face tight with concern. Harmony stood beside her, hoodie half-zipped, curls shoved into a puffball under her coat hood. Her eyes locked on mine and instantly filled with tears.

"Come in," I said, stepping back. My voice sounded hollow in my own ears.

They stepped inside quickly, closing the cold out behind them.

Tia took one look at my face and gently guided me toward the stairs. "Tell me everything."

I sat, fingers tangled in my lap. "She left at 6:57. Just for snacks. Popcorn, candy, ice cream—whatever she could grab. Said she'd be right back."

"And she hasn't called?"

"Her phone rings, then goes to voicemail."

Harmony sat beside me, her hand resting over mine. "She's probably fine. Maybe her phone died."

I nodded like I believed it.

Tia stayed standing. She was scanning the room like there might be answers hiding in the walls. "Which store does she usually go to?"

"Sometimes Key Food, sometimes the little corner bodega. Depends on what she wants."

"She has her ID with her? House keys?"

"Always."

Tia inhaled slowly. "Okay. There could be a dozen reasons for this. A delay. A long line. A detour. Let's not jump to conclusions."

Harmony's eyes were still locked on the door. She didn't say anything.

I tried to focus on Tia's logic—on her certainty—but the buzz in my head wouldn't let me.

I wanted to believe it was all a mistake. That she'd walk in, bags full, apologizing for the wait and telling us the register jammed or someone spilled orange soda on the floor or something ridiculous like that.

But I couldn't shake the quiet.

The kind of quiet that wasn't just silence—but absence.

Then—headlights swept across the wall.

I turned.

Not just headlights.

Red and blue.

The light pulsed through the glass door like it belonged to something bigger than all of us. Something final.

Tia's body tensed. Harmony let out the softest gasp.

We didn't speak.

We just sat there.

And waited for the knock.

There was a knock at the door.

Three knocks, firm. Not rushed. Not hesitant.

Deliberate.

Final.

Tia moved before anyone else. She didn't say anything—she just walked to the door with the calm that only grown women learn, the kind that makes you feel safe until it doesn't anymore.

I sat there frozen, heart caving in on itself. Harmony gripped my hand tighter, but I barely noticed.

I watched Tia unlock the chain, then slowly open the door.

Two uniformed officers stood on the other side. One was a woman with a clipboard held tight to her chest. The other was a tall man with gray at his temples and kindness in his eyes, which somehow made it worse.

"Is this Naomi Rivera residence?" he asked gently, his voice too soft for a stranger.

Tia nodded once. "Yes. I'm her sister—this is my niece, her daughter."

The moment he turned to look at me, my body reacted before my mind could catch up. My stomach flipped like I'd swallowed stone. My ears rang. My fingers went numb.

The female officer stepped slightly behind the man, as if even she didn't want to be the one to say it.

"Ma'am," the man began, "I'm... I'm sorry to inform you that Naomi Rivera was involved in a serious automobile accident this evening."

No.

No, no, no, no.

The room went silent. The air stopped moving. Even the radiator seemed to hold its breath.

The officer continued. "She was struck by another vehicle that ran a red light at high speed. Emergency responders arrived within minutes, but—" he hesitated, then finished, "they were unable to revive her."

I didn't hear the rest.

It became noise.

Like radio static under water. The kind of sound that doesn't have a shape. A hum that lives under your skin.

I felt my body tipping forward like something had unhooked my spine. Harmony was crying now, but I couldn't hear her. Just the sound of my own blood pounding through my head.

"She's not—" I tried to speak, but the words cracked apart like ice.

The officer lowered his gaze. "I'm truly sorry for your loss."

"You're lying," I whispered.

No one moved.

"She said she'd be right back," I said, louder. "She just went to the store."

Harmony stood, grabbing my hand. "Div—"

"DON'T TOUCH ME!" I shrieked, yanking away so hard I nearly fell.

Tia flinched but didn't try to stop me.

"She's not dead!" I shouted. "She's coming back! She said she'd be back!"

I stumbled to my feet, but my knees betrayed me. They buckled like paper. I dropped to the floor in a heap, my hands slapping the tile hard enough to sting.

I screamed.

Not words. Not anything anyone could understand. Just noise. Pain pulled inside out.

Harmony dropped beside me, crying as she reached out again. This time I didn't fight her. I collapsed into her arms, sobbing into her shoulder. I couldn't breathe. Couldn't stop shaking.

"She's gone," I gasped. "Oh my God. She's gone."

"I'm here," Harmony whispered, voice cracking. "I'm here. I got you."

I heard Tia's voice behind us, suddenly steel.

"What hospital?"

"Kings County," the officer answered. "She was declared at the scene, but she's been taken there."

Tia paused. Then quietly, "Do I need to identify her?"

"I'm afraid so."

She let out a slow breath. The kind that holds everything together when you're one second from falling apart. "Okay."

I didn't look at her. I couldn't.

I pressed my face into Harmony's jacket and let myself vanish inside the dark. Let the sobs take over. Let my body shake like it didn't belong to me.

Tia moved toward the stairs and went to our apartment without another word. She passed my mother's bedroom, then stopped in front of the landline. We followed her and I heard her pick up the receiver.

Her voice was low. Controlled. "I have to start making calls."

The calls that would break the world.

The ride to Kings County was silent.

No music. No static. Just the sound of the tires humming against wet pavement and Harmony sniffling quietly in the back seat.

I sat up front beside Tia, my hands folded tightly in my lap like they belonged to someone else. I stared out the window, eyes fixed on streetlights that blurred past like smudges on glass.

Tia gripped the steering wheel with both hands, her knuckles pale. She didn't speak the entire ride. Not once.

We pulled into the hospital parking lot just after 9:20 p.m.

The fluorescent lights made everything look washed out. The building loomed gray and square against the sky, too bright in some places, too shadowed in others. Like it didn't know how to feel about itself.

Inside, the smell hit me first—bleach, plastic, old coffee, and something else I couldn't name. The kind of smell that told you this was a place where lives ended as often as they began.

The woman at the desk didn't ask questions when Tia gave her our names. She just nodded grimly and made a call.

A nurse came to lead Tia down the corridor. She turned back to us before she followed.

"I want you two to stay here," she said, voice quiet but steady. "I'll be right back."

I didn't argue. I didn't move. Harmony sat beside me in the waiting room, our knees touching. Her fingers toyed with the string on her hoodie, twisting it so tight it looked like it might snap.

The room had a TV bolted in the corner playing something forgettable—news, maybe. The sound was muted. All I could hear was the squeak of shoes on linoleum and the occasional cough from somewhere down the hall.

Ten minutes passed. Maybe twenty.

Then Tia came back.

Her eyes were red. She didn't speak for a long moment. Just looked at me and shook her head, once.

"It's her," she whispered.

I already knew. But something about hearing it knocked the wind out of me all over again.

"I want to see her," I said.

Tia blinked. "Baby, I don't think that's——"

"I need to see her."

"She doesn't… she doesn't look like herself right now. It's not——" she paused, then softened. "It's not how you want to remember her."

"I don't care. Please."

She studied my face, then let out a slow breath.

"Okay," she said. "Just you and me."

Harmony reached for my hand again. I gave it one last squeeze before standing.

The nurse led us through the double doors and down a quiet hall. The walls were bare. Everything hummed faintly—lights, machines, silence.

Finally, we stopped in front of a room.

The nurse unlocked it, nodded once to Tia, and stepped aside.

I walked in.

The air was too cold.

The overhead lights buzzed softly, casting a pale yellow glow over the metal table where she lay, covered to her shoulders in a white sheet. Her head was tilted slightly to the side, like she'd fallen asleep mid-thought.

Her skin was gray at the edges. Lips a little too still. Hair flattened in the wrong places. But it was her.

It was Mommy.

I stood there, frozen.

Tia hovered behind me but didn't say a word.

My feet moved before I realized it.

I stepped closer.

Her hands were folded on her stomach. Someone had straightened her out, like she was a doll being prepared for display.

"Hi, Mommy," I whispered. My voice didn't echo. It barely existed.

I reached out slowly. My fingers brushed her hand.

Cold. So cold.

"I'm sorry," I said, tears welling again. "I should've told you I loved you more. I should've held on longer. I should've made you wait 'til morning. I should've——"

My voice cracked.

Tia walked forward and placed a hand on my shoulder, just enough pressure to remind me I wasn't alone.

"I'm gonna be okay," I whispered. "I'm gonna keep going. But I just wanted you to know—before I go—I love you. I love you so much."

A single tear slid down my cheek and landed on the edge of the sheet.

I wiped my face, leaned down, and kissed her forehead gently.

Then I turned away, the sound of my breath the only thing I could hear.

Tia walked me out, one hand resting at the center of my back.

We didn't look back.

The hallway seemed longer on the way out. Like the hospital had stretched itself just to keep us there. I walked with my arms crossed, holding my own elbows like it was the only thing keeping me together.

Outside, the air had turned bitter. The wind cut through my sweater and made my teeth clench.

The ride home was silent again.

Tia kept her eyes on the road. Her face was calm, but I could see her blinking more than usual. Wiping the corner of her eye like something kept getting caught there.

Harmony sat in the back, curled up in her coat, staring out the window like maybe she could will the night to undo itself.

I leaned my forehead against the cold glass and watched the city pass by. Storefronts with their gates halfway closed. A bus pulling away from the curb. Headlights moving like ghosts.

And I thought, *how dare the world keep moving? How could cars still drive, and stores stay open, and people laugh in taxis… when my mother was gone?*

Everything felt different now. Too sharp. Too loud. Too quiet.

We turned down our block. The streetlights flickered the way they always did. The same stoops. The same mailboxes.

But nothing felt like home anymore.

I closed my eyes, breathed in the grief, and held it there.

I knew I'd have to let it out eventually.

But not yet.

## 4  SAYING GOODBYE

*"Grief isn't just sorrow. It's a goodbye without a thank you." – Cassandra Wade*

**The silence woke me.**

For the first time in forever, there was no hum from the kitchen. No keys jingling. No smell of toast or hair grease. Just… air.

I blinked at the ceiling. The light was dull—early gray. It took a minute to remember why my chest felt like it had caved in.

Then it hit me again. Like it would keep hitting me, every time I opened my eyes.

She was gone.

I sat up slowly. Every movement felt like it belonged to someone else's body. The blanket slid off my lap and crumpled at my feet. My throat was dry. My hands were shaking.

I heard voices in the living room. Distant. Grown-up voices. Soft. Careful. The way people talk when they're afraid someone might shatter.

I didn't want to hear them. I didn't want to hear anything.

I stood up and walked to the bathroom like I was underwater. The mirror didn't show me. It showed some other girl in my clothes, with my eyes, but hollowed out.

I turned on the faucet. Let the water run. Didn't touch it.

Everything looked the same. But nothing was.

I finally started my way to the kitchen to see what was going on. The moment I passed my mother's room I froze. I almost went inside, looking for her. I felt the sobs gather in my chest again. I stared into the room, feeling hollow.

"Divinity!" My thoughts were interrupted by Aunt Erica's voice. I snapped back to reality and kept moving.

I never thought I'd be helping plan my mother's funeral. It was the worst thing to happen to me—ever. I always believed my mother would

40

be with me forever. I wasn't delusional—I knew she would die someday—but not like this, not this soon. I thought she'd be old. I thought she'd be there when I went to college, got married, and had my first child. I thought she'd live to become a grandmother.

This wasn't supposed to happen. I kept asking God if this was some sick joke. If it was, I wasn't laughing. If it was a lesson, I couldn't begin to understand what I was supposed to learn from it.

I was trapped inside my thoughts, sitting stiffly at the dining table while Tia and my aunt Erica went back and forth. Their voices sounded like muffled background noise, like one of those old Charlie Brown cartoons—wah wah wah wah wah. I couldn't absorb anything they said. My brain had checked out.

I glanced at my aunt. She looked like a lighter-skinned version of my mom, with similar almond-shaped eyes and high cheekbones, but she didn't have the warmth. She wasn't even trying to hide her annoyance.

On the other hand, Tia was doing her best to advocate for what my mother wanted. She was my mom's best friend, and she knew her wishes better than anyone. Mommy and Tia knew each other since high school. Tia was more of a sister to my mom than Aunt Erica ever was. But Aunt Erica was hell-bent on doing the opposite. Her tone was cold. Her heart seemed even colder.

The bickering only made the ache in my chest worse.

Then my aunt turned to me. "Divinity, what would your mother want? You'd know better than either of us."

I didn't answer.

"Divinity?" she said again, waving a hand in front of my face.

I blinked. "Huh?"

"Where's your head at, child? I said—what would your mother want?" Her voice was sharp, irritated.

I sat up straighter and answered without hesitation. "Tia told you what she'd want. She was her best friend. She knows better than any of us."

"Don't you roll your eyes at me," my aunt snapped.

"I just want this to be over," I said, trying to keep my voice calm. "I just want to know what's going to happen to me." Silence fell. That was the part no one wanted to talk about. My mother was gone. My father didn't want me. So… where would I go?

"I'm sorry, honey," my aunt said flatly, her voice cold and unfeeling. "But I can't take you in. I've got three kids of my own, and I'm barely making it."

Her words hit me like a punch in the gut. I stared at her, hoping she'd take it back, but there was nothing. Just the hard, cold truth that she wasn't willing to help. My chest tightened, and all I could do was nod, trying not to break down in front of her. My stomach dropped. I bit my lip hard, trying to keep the tears at bay.

I can't go into the system. I'd lose everything. My friends. My home. My life.

Tia placed a hand on my back. "Don't worry, Div. I've already started the process to foster you. I'm doing everything I can to make sure the state lets me keep you until you're eighteen."

I nodded, unable to speak. I trusted her, but the fear in my heart wouldn't let me exhale.

My aunt gave a half-hearted shrug, as if it didn't matter to her at all. Her indifference felt like a slap in the face. How could she be so cold at a time like this? But I couldn't find the words to tell her that. Instead, I just let the silence suffocate me.

The truth was, my mom missed her sister more than she'd ever admit—and now she'd never get the chance to say so. I thought about telling my aunt, but what was the point? She didn't deserve that peace.

I stood up abruptly, the anger and hurt swirling inside me like a storm. My heart was pounding in my chest as I walked out of the room, slamming my bedroom door behind me. I locked it, threw myself onto the floor, and for the first time, I let it all out. I cried harder than I ever had in my life, each sob tearing through me like I was unraveling.

How could they do this to me? How could they not see that I was drowning? My mother was gone, and no one was here to help me stay afloat.

It felt like I was in a nightmare I couldn't wake up from. My body trembled as I sobbed, hugging my knees to my chest. *What am I supposed to do now, Mommy?* I whispered in my head. *How am I supposed to do this without you?*

Just then, my phone chimed.

I ignored it at first. I hadn't answered any calls or pages in days. But something told me to check this one. Something felt different.

Sure enough—it was him.

My father.

He had been calling nonstop since the day my mom died. This time, I couldn't ignore it. I had to make it stop.

I wiped my face, picked up the phone, and answered without saying a word.

"Baby girl? Divinity? Are you there?" His voice came through fast, panicked, and full of emotion. I almost believed it.

"Yes," I said flatly.

"I've been trying to reach you for two days. I've been so worried."

"I'm fine," I replied with zero warmth.

"I know I'm the last person you want to talk to, but I'm your father, whether you like it or not. I'm flying to New York. I want to bring you back to Puerto Rico with me."

I blinked. "Are you crazy? I'm not going anywhere with someone I don't even know."

"Divinity, you're my daughter. Where else would you go? I've missed out on your life and now it's time I step up."

"Oh, now you want to step up? Now that Mommy's gone? Where were you before? You didn't want me then, so why want me now?"

"I understand you're upset and hurting, so I won't argue with how you're talking to me," he said, almost too calmly. "We'll talk when I arrive. I'm coming for the funeral."

"You're wasting your time. I'm staying with Harmony's family. I'm not going anywhere with you."

"I'll see you in two days. I love you."

I didn't respond. I pressed end call and immediately hurled the phone across the room. It hit the wall with a loud crack.

A scream tore out of me—loud, raw, and heartbreaking.

Within seconds, they were banging on my door.

"Div! What was that? Are you okay?" Tia yelled.

"Divinity, stop acting like a brat!" my aunt bellowed.

"Don't talk to her like that!" Tia snapped. "She just lost her mother! Her world just collapsed, and all you can do is criticize her?"

"I know what happened," my aunt shot back. "She'll have to get over it. Life goes on."

"I'm not letting you talk to her like this," Tia said, her voice firm and protective. "She's hurting in ways you can't even understand."

Her words hit me hard, but in a way that made me feel safe—like Tia was the only one who truly understood my pain. She always had my back, no matter what.

"You don't get to decide that."

"I do when it comes to Divinity," Tia said, steel in her voice.

She turned back to my door, and her voice softened.

"Div… I know you're hurting. I know none of this makes sense right now. But I'm here. I'm going to take care of you. You're not alone. You can trust me."

Later that night, after the fight, the phone call, and the storm of emotions, I curled up on my bed, wrapping my arms around a pillow like it could hold me together. My chest hurt. My eyes stung. It felt like grief had buried me alive.

I rolled over, clutching the blanket to my chest, and something hard jabbed me in the side.

I sat up slowly, reached beneath the pillow—and pulled out a soft, leather-bound journal.

My breath caught.

It was the journal my mother had given me this year on my birthday. I'd never written in it. I always said I would, but life got in the way. I opened the cover and gasped.

There was a letter folded neatly inside.

The paper was cream-colored, her handwriting smooth and looping like cursive poetry. The top of the page read,

*"To My Divinity—if you're ever reading this, it means you're hurting. So let me be your strength one more time."*

I clutched the page, my hands shaking so violently that the words blurred. I could feel her presence in every letter, every loop of her handwriting. It was like she was there, speaking to me, guiding me through the storm of grief. My chest tightened as I read her words—my mother's last gift to me.

*My Sweet Girl,*

*I may not always be here in person, but I will always be with you in spirit. You are my greatest gift—my miracle, my joy, my reason for fighting. I know life isn't fair. I've lived that truth. But I want more for you.*

*I want you to love yourself. I want you to chase your dreams—even if you have to chase them alone sometimes. I want you to laugh, to sing, to cry, and still get back up. I want you to know that your value doesn't come from anyone else—it comes from the God who created you with purpose.*

*Don't ever settle for "almost." Don't let the world convince you that you're not enough. Because you are. Baby, you are enough, just as you are. And when the day comes when I'm no longer here, I want you to remember this,*

*I loved you with every breath I had. I still do. I always will.*

*Love,*

*Mommy*

By the time I finished, my tears soaked the pages. But this time, it wasn't just pain. It was… something softer. Something almost warm beneath the ache.

I held the journal to my chest and whispered through sobs, "I love you too, Mommy. I love you so much."

The next day was a re-run of the day before. Tia and my aunt going back and forth about the funeral. Tia and my aunt were trying to handle the arrangements. And by trying, I mean fighting. Tia knew exactly what my mom wanted. Aunt Erica? She seemed determined to override every suggestion, even if she didn't have a better one.

"She never said she wanted a closed casket," Aunt Erica barked. "Why would we assume that?"

"She told me," Tia replied, clearly biting her tongue. "It was after her friend Angela passed. She said, 'If anything happens to me, just keep it simple and closed. Let people remember me alive.'"

Aunt Erica scoffed. "Well, I never heard her say that."

I snapped. "Of course you didn't—because you weren't around. Don't come in here acting like you knew my mother. You don't even really know me."

I pushed back from the table and stormed to my room. I felt like I was trapped in some twisted déjà vu—like grief had hit repeat and refused to stop.

I sat on my bed, clutching the letter my mom had left me, curling into myself until I felt like I could disappear. I just wanted her to come back. I wanted her arms, her voice, her scent in the hallway. But all I had was silence… and yelling.

Their arguing grew louder. Voices raised. Again. I couldn't take it anymore. I stood up, slammed my door open, and marched back into the room.

"THIS is not what my mother would have wanted!" I shouted, startling them both into silence. "She would've wanted something simple but beautiful—something that brought people together, not pushed them apart."

I looked at them, my voice cracking with every word. "Stop thinking about yourselves. Start thinking about her. Her favorite color was olive green. Her favorite dress was the white and olive one that is still hanging in her closet. She looked gorgeous in it. She loved with her whole heart. Can we please show that?"

Tears burned at the corners of my eyes. "Make it happen. And stop arguing. I can't take this." I turned and walked back to my room, slamming the door behind me. I threw myself back onto the bed, tears soaking into the pillow before I even realized I was crying.

I hated this. Hated all of it. I hated that people only showed up when someone died. I hated that my aunt thought she could waltz in after all these years and take over like she knew anything about my mother—like she ever cared. And I hated that my mom wasn't here to tell her off herself.

I reached for the journal again, flipping to the page with her letter, the one she left behind like she knew I would need it. I didn't read it this time—I just held it. Held it like it was the last piece of her I had. Because maybe it was.

The house finally grew quiet. Tia knocked gently on my door, but I didn't answer. I didn't want to talk anymore. She respected that. She always had. I must've cried myself to sleep because the next thing I knew, the sun was casting long shadows across my floor. The hallway was silent. Still. Like, even the house knew that the next few days would be the hardest days of my life.

The next few days melted into each other like wax on hot pavement. People came. People went. They brought casseroles and stories and weak hugs. They said things like "She's in a better place" and "You're so strong."

I wanted to scream. But I didn't.

I just nodded. Smiled when I had to. Folded my hands in my lap like I was supposed to.

Every room smelled like a different kind of sorrow. Fried fish. Lemon Lysol. Cheap perfume. All of it clinging to the curtains, the furniture, my skin.

I remember Tia bringing me a plate—macaroni and cheese, string beans, some kind of baked chicken. I ate three bites and left it on the table. Harmony tried to talk to me, but I couldn't hold her voice in my ears long enough to respond.

I think I brushed my teeth three times one morning. Or maybe I didn't brush at all. Time was soft and slippery.

Everywhere I turned, she wasn't.

Her chair at the table. Her robe on the hook. Her slippers under the bed. All still there. All wrong.

The house was full of people, but none of them could fill the space she left.

Tia made breakfast the next morning but I decided to stay in my room. I didn't feel like eating or being bothered with the stares. After being in my room all morning, I needed another view other than this room. I was curled up on the couch, watching the walls, trying not to feel anything. The doorbell rang. A sharp, sudden sound that cut through the silence like a blade. Tia opened the door. And there he was. Juan Renaldo Morales. My father. In the flesh.

I sat up slowly, heart pounding. He looked older than the last photo I'd seen—gray strands in his black hair, eyes tired. Still handsome. I was still the spitting image of him. And I hated that.

"Divinity," he said softly, his accent curling around my name.

I didn't move.

Tia stepped in quickly. "You should've called first."

"I needed to be here," he said. "I had to come."

I stood. Not because I wanted to greet him—but because I needed to make one thing clear.

"You don't get to show up now and pretend like we're family," I said, my voice low and sharp. "She's gone. And you're late."

His face broke. "Mija, I'm so sorry."

"Don't call me that." The words came out in a harsh whisper, thick with anger. "You weren't sorry all those birthdays. Not when she needed you. Not when she was sick, or when the bills piled up. You didn't give a damn then, so don't pretend like you care now."

His face fell, but I wasn't done. "You didn't want me. You never wanted me. And now that she's gone, you think you can waltz back in and make it all okay?"

I could see the hurt in his eyes, but I didn't care. "Where were you when I needed you? You're too late, Juan. Too late for apologies. Too late for anything."

He took a slow step forward. "You get a pass for cursing at me and clearly being disrespectful because you are grieving but rather you like it or not, I am STILL your father -"

"No," I cut him off. "You're a stranger. A stranger who gave me green eyes and long hair and a last name I barely speak or use."

He looked like he wanted to cry, and for a moment, I almost felt sorry for him. Almost.

But then I remembered my mother's face, her hands, her laughter—everything he missed.

"You can come to the funeral," I said quietly. "But after that, we're done."

I walked past him, down the hall to my room.

After I left, him and Tia had a conversation. I left out of sight but I lingered so I could hear what was said. He walked over to Tia, she took a step back.

"Juan…" She said eyeing him.

"Inez… You know I deserve a chance with her."

Tia gave him a confused look. The same look I had on my face.

"Deserve? You don't deserve anything but if you love her you would sign over your rights to me. That's what her mother would have wanted."

"So you just expect me to act like I don't have a daughter?" His heavy accent said that he was upset.

"What's different now Juan? You've been doing that since the day she was born!" Tia realized that she started to raise her voice and she did not want to alarm me so she composed herself.

"I left because I thought I was poison to her. I thought she'd be better without me."

"Whatever will help you sleep at night. If that is the case, leave again and before you do give me custody of her. That is where her better life will be because it sure is not with you, a man she barely knows. Right now she needs normalcy, consistency and be surrounded with people she knows love her." He just looked at her but he knew she was right. I waited to hear his response but there was silence, no rebuttal, no smart remark… Just silence. At that point I went to my room and closed the door behind me.

That night, my phone buzzed. It was Chris. I stared at the screen, my heart like a fist in my chest. Then I turned the phone off. He left a voicemail saying, "I'm sorry for everything."

The next morning was the day I had to say goodbye to my mother and it felt heavy. The kind of heavy that lives in your bones. I moved like I was underwater—slow, weightless, detached. Tia had laid out everything for me, my mother's favorite color dress for the service, a small breakfast I couldn't bring myself to touch, tissues tucked into the sleeve of my jacket like I was a child again.

I stared at my reflection in the mirror, but I didn't see myself. I saw her. Bits of her in my eyes. My smile. The slight tilt of my nose. It was comforting and cruel all at once.

Harmony knocked softly before peeking in. She was dressed in black, her curly hair pulled back into a low ponytail. Her eyes were red.

"You look beautiful," she whispered.

I nodded, my voice caught in my throat. "I don't want to go."

"I know."

"I'm scared if I see the casket, I'll break."

"Then I'll hold your hand."

"I miss her too," Harmony said quietly. "Not like you do, but… she was like a second mom to me."

I turned and hugged her tightly. Her being there didn't fix anything, but it kept me from falling apart completely.

Downstairs, the house was already full of people. Quiet murmurs. The clink of cups. The smell of perfume and grief.

My father was there, standing in the corner like he belonged. He looked up when I came down but said nothing. I was grateful for that.

Tia walked over and gently placed a hand on my back.

"Ready, baby?"

No. But I nodded anyway.

The church smelled like flowers and furniture polish. It was overflowing. I didn't realize how many people my mother had touched. The rows were packed, and as I looked around, it hit me how much she'd meant to everyone. I never understood how many lives she'd impacted until now. And yet, all I could think about was how empty it felt without her.

I sat on the front pew with my knees pressed together and my hands balled in my lap, trying not to shake. Someone had brushed my hair too tight. My scalp still burned, but I didn't say anything.

Everything felt distant—like I was watching it all through a sheet of glass.

People kept coming up to me, saying how proud she was, how beautiful I looked, how "strong" I was being. I hated that word. Strong. It felt like another name for "silent."

The casket was closed like Tia had asked, thank God. I couldn't have handled it if it hadn't been. Still, the sight of it—the smooth wood, the shiny handles, draped in olive green and white, her favorite colors. The way it sat like a full stop at the front of the sanctuary—made my stomach twist.

Harmony sat beside me, quiet and still. I felt her hand brush mine once, but I didn't take it. I couldn't. If I held anything, I might come apart.

The pastor said things about my mother. I didn't hear most of it.

The pastor's voice faded in and out like background noise. I caught a few words—loving… vibrant… woman of faith… peace… about homecoming… about how she was with the Lord now… beautiful soul—but most of it sounded like wind. What I really heard was the silence where her voice should've been. The space she used to fill. My ears rang. My chest buzzed like something was trying to escape. I didn't cry at first. I just sat there.

Frozen.

Numb.

People shouted "Amen." Others cried out loud. I didn't move.

When the music started at the end, and they began to wheel the casket down the aisle... I stood only because Harmony tugged at my sleeve. My legs weren't mine. I folded in half, sobbing into Harmony's arms. Her arms wrapped tight around me, and she cried too. Everyone says time heals. But in that moment, time was the enemy. Because every second moved her farther away.

I don't remember the car ride home. I just remember the silence that followed us through the front door like a shadow.

Her voice wasn't there to tell me what to do next—and no one else's voice mattered.

The house was crowded. Laughter in the kitchen, foil pans clanking, someone's baby crying in the hallway.

The repast was held back at Tia's house. People talked like they hadn't just come from a funeral. Loud stories. Greasy plates. Plastic forks scraping paper. I wanted to scream just to break through it all.

I stood in the hallway watching it happen like I was behind glass. People who hadn't spoken to her in years suddenly remembered how much she meant to them. Old friends. Cousins I'd never seen before. Church ladies who hugged me too tight and told me to "be strong, now—your mama raised you right."

I nodded. Smiled like I was still human. Said thank you when my mouth worked.

Someone offered me cake. I shook my head.

The food smelled too strong. Too warm. It made my stomach turn. There was an awkwardness to it—this wasn't how my mother would have wanted to be remembered. This wasn't the celebration of her life she deserved. But life went on, and this was how people processed the impossible.

I sat in the oversized chair my mom used to occupy when she came over. No one dared sit there now. Maybe they could still feel her in the cushions, or maybe they just respected that space. But I couldn't help but feel she was still there. I could almost hear her laughter, smell her perfume, and see the way she'd softly scold me for picking at my food. Now, the chair was cold and empty, just like everything else.

I glanced around the room. Grown folks filled the kitchen, the living room, even the front steps. Kids ran up and down the hallway like it was any other Sunday. Laughter came in bursts—too loud, too fast, like if they didn't laugh, they might have to feel something. Aunt Erica was busy talking to some family friends, her face tight with frustration, her eyes avoiding mine whenever they met. She still wasn't giving me the space I needed, still acting like my grief was something that could be fixed with time and "getting over it."

Tia was moving through the room with ease, comforting people, organizing the chaos, and checking in on me when she could. Her strength was like a protective shield around me, even if I couldn't feel it all the way yet. I was trapped in a fog, and the world seemed too loud and too quiet at the same time. I didn't know if I was supposed to cry more or if I was supposed to smile through it all.

One of Tia's cousins—some woman I didn't know—rubbed my back like I was her child and said, "She's in a better place now."

Harmony came over and sat next to me. She didn't say anything at first, just sat there, her presence comforting in the silence. I looked at her—she had red eyes, but she wasn't crying. She was holding it together for me, as always.

"How are you holding up?" she finally asked, her voice soft but steady.

"I don't know," I whispered. "It feels like... like everything is wrong. And I'm just supposed to be okay. But I'm not. I'm not okay, Harm."

She nodded, her hand gently squeezing mine. "I know, girl. I know." Her eyes flickered over to Tia, who was helping some relatives in the kitchen. "Mom's been amazing, huh?"

"Yeah," I said, almost too quietly. "I don't know what I would do without her right now."

"You don't have to do it alone," Harmony said softly. "She's got you. I've got you. We all have you, Div. You're not alone in this."

I squeezed her hand back, fighting back the lump in my throat. I was tired of feeling like I was falling apart, like I couldn't keep it together for even one more second. But Harmony's words hit me like a lifeline, something to hold onto, even if I wasn't sure I could.

People came and went. They said things like,

"She was such a light."

"She loved you so much."

"Stay strong, baby. You gotta be strong now."

I nodded. I whispered thank you. I smiled when I had to. But inside, I was screaming. I didn't want to be strong. I wanted my mother.

The tension in the room grew thicker as my father stepped into the living room. His presence felt like a shadow, lingering in the doorway. He hadn't said much to me since he arrived, his expression torn between guilt and something else I couldn't quite place. I didn't want him here. I didn't need him here. But he was here, and I couldn't ignore it.

I stood up as he walked toward me. He looked older than I remembered—his hair was peppered with gray, and his eyes had the tiredness of someone who had lived a life full of regret. He was still handsome, though. Still my father, in a way.

He stopped a few feet away from me. "Divinity..." he said softly, almost hesitating.

I folded my arms across my chest. "What?"

"I know this is hard for you," he began, his voice trembling slightly. "But I need you to understand that I'm trying. I'm here now. I've been trying to reach you."

"You're here now?" I scoffed, shaking my head. "Where were you before, huh? When I needed you? When my mom needed you? You don't get to just show up now and expect things to be okay. You're too late for that."

He took a step closer, but I didn't move. "I know I've made mistakes, Divinity. I'm not perfect. But I want to make things right. I'm your father. I've missed so much of your life, but I'm here now, and I want to be there for you."

I felt a fire building inside me, but I didn't let it consume me. "You weren't there. You didn't care. Don't pretend like you're some savior, coming in to fix everything because my mom's gone. You were a ghost in my life, and now you think you can just waltz in and take it all back?"

"I'm sorry. I can't change what happened before. But I want to try now, Divinity. I want you to know I care. I do."

My jaw clenched, and I swallowed hard. "You missed out on everything that mattered. You don't get to just walk back into my life and make it all better. You weren't there when Mom cried every time she got off the phone with you. You weren't there when Mom was holding onto hope that you would come to your senses and come back in our lives. So you don't get to be there now!"

He nodded, a deep sadness in his eyes. "I know. I don't expect you to forgive me now. But I'm asking for a chance. I'm asking for your forgiveness."

"Don't. Just don't. I don't need you now. I never did." I turned away. "The only thing I need is for you to leave. You're not welcomed here."

I slid off the chair and quietly slipped into the hallway. He didn't stop me, but I could feel his eyes on me. I knew this was the end of whatever I thought we could have. There was no going back.

I crept up the stairs and into the small guest room Tia had set up for me. I sat on the edge of the bed, staring at the pink throw pillows and gold-framed mirror above the dresser. Everything here belonged to someone else. It felt wrong to grieve in a room that didn't remember her. But I sat anyway. I closed the door, locked it, and finally let the silence swallow me. I crawled onto the bed and stared at the ceiling. And for a moment, I imagined she was just in the next room, laughing, cooking, waiting for me to come find her.

The world was still spinning out there. Plates clinking. Laughter bubbling in short bursts. Life continuing. But in here? I was frozen. Alone. Everyone had someone. Even if they were grieving, they had someone to go home to, someone to cry to, someone who knew their pain firsthand. Me? I had memories, a funeral program, and a journal with a letter I already knew by heart.

Later that evening, as the repass wound down and people began to leave, I felt the weight of everything settle over me. My father was gone, and I hadn't even let him say goodbye. He didn't deserve a second chance. Not from me.

I lay in a room that didn't belong to me.

Tia had made it warm—folded blankets, a soft lamp, a pink rug with white swirls. The bed was too soft. The pillow smelled like lavender, not my mother. I was still numb, still tangled up in the grief of losing my mother and the confusion of what was next.

Her voice wasn't here.

No familiar weight on the floorboards. No quiet hum of gospel radio in the next room. No cough through the walls. Just voices I didn't want and silence I didn't trust.

I closed my eyes and reached for her hand in my mind, like I used to when I was little and scared of storms. I waited for the warmth. For the squeeze.

It didn't come.

I turned my face into the pillow and whispered, I miss you, Mommy. Over and over again. I went to sleep pretending I was still in her bed—and let the lie hold me until morning.

## 5  THE HOUSE WASN'T MINE

*"My people will live in peaceful dwelling places." – Isaiah 32:18*

**I stopped unpacking after day two.**

Tia had custody now. My father signed the papers like he was handing off a task.

The room used to be Harmony's playroom. Now it felt hollow. A twin bed. An old dresser with peeling stickers. A window that let in too much light—even with the blinds drawn.

My duffel sat in the corner like a reminder—I was still temporary. Tia said I could stay until I turned eighteen. After that, it'd be my call. But I didn't think she meant forever. And even if she did, I wasn't sure I'd make it that long.

The room wasn't mine. The air smelled too clean. The bed was too soft—like it didn't know how to hold me. Nothing creaked the way it was supposed to. No footsteps in the hallway sounded like hers.

The warmth in this house was real, but it wasn't hers. No one made fried chicken like my mom. No one played gospel on Sundays and sang along like it meant something. I tried to let it feel like home. But every time I sat down to eat, every time I walked through that door, it felt like I was stepping into someone else's life.

Six months had passed, but I was still stuck in the moment she left me. Some days I forgot what her laugh sounded like. Other days, it echoed so clearly I turned my head, expecting her to be there. Sometimes it felt like six hours. Sometimes six years. Grief didn't move in straight lines—it looped and folded in on itself.

Tia tried. She cooked. She smiled. She knocked before coming in. She never rushed me. She folded towels I didn't ask for. Left my favorite cereal out every morning, even though I never touched it.

Tia was kind. She meant well. She really did. She didn't press me to talk—just said, "Take your time, baby," and went back to folding or stirring the pot. And I was grateful. I just couldn't feel it.

Harmony tried to make things normal. She knocked before entering, told jokes I didn't laugh at, played soft music from her boombox like it might pull me back. Sometimes she just sat beside me in silence. I liked that better than the talking. She didn't get it. No one did.

Grief turned me into someone else—quieter, sharper, afraid of mirrors. I wasn't healing. I was disappearing.

Tia made dinner every night and set three plates—hers, Harmony's, and mine. I ate just enough to be polite. Said "thank you" if I remembered. Kept my eyes on the plate. The house was warm, but it wasn't mine. I didn't know how to live in it.

The silence inside me was getting louder. Some days, I forgot how to feel. I was going numb. Even to the people who still cared. Harmony's voice became a soft hum. Tia's concern faded into background static I couldn't turn off.

The anger never left. It just sank deeper, buried beneath layers of cold, quiet emptiness. I didn't know how to let it out. Didn't know where to put it. The world kept spinning in fast-forward. I was frozen in place—stuck in a life that didn't feel like mine anymore.

I started lashing out in small, quiet ways. Skipping assignments. Talking back. Sleeping too much—or not at all. I saw it in Tia's eyes, the tight worry behind her smile when I came home late or didn't speak all dinner.

But she never said anything. Just gave me space, even when I hadn't earned it.

Chris kept calling. Kept showing up. And one day, I finally answered. I don't know why. Maybe I just needed something that wasn't this house.

Being with Chris wasn't about love. It was about quiet. About leaving without leaving. I didn't care what we were—or weren't. None of it mattered anymore. After my mom died, he tried to be there. I guess that counted for something.

June came, and somehow I got promoted to tenth grade. I don't know how I passed. I just did. Summer followed—hot and slow—and I spent most of it shut inside my room. I wasn't just alone. I was unreachable.

The grief was too heavy to carry. So I didn't move at all.

And then it happened—the thing I didn't know I'd remember for the rest of my life.

It was late August, just before Labor Day, when the front door creaked open—and I froze. A chill ran down my spine. Boots on hardwood. Keys rattling. A voice I hadn't heard in years, but knew by heart.

Harmony didn't even flinch.

"That's my brother!" she called out.

But I already knew.

Darnell.

His name stirred something in me—something dark. Something I hadn't let myself feel in a long time.

As he stepped into the house, my body went stiff. The air thickened. The walls pulled closer. I didn't want to look.

But I did.

He was taller now. Older. But his face was the same—sharp, watchful. The kind of gaze that used to twist my stomach. And it still did. His eyes swept over me—slow and calculating, like nothing had changed.

But everything had.

He'd been gone for years. Military, like everyone expected. He was always wild. Stubborn. Rough around the edges. I used to hope the military would fix that.

"He came out the womb hardheaded," Tia would say.

"That boy been marching to his own beat since diapers," my mom would laugh.

Then it hit me. My mind snapped back—fast and uninvited.

I was a kid again. Just a girl, before the words for it all existed. I remembered the heaviness Darnell carried with him. His eyes—those long, heavy stares that stuck to my skin.

He was always there. Always a little too close.

When I was little, I didn't think twice about it. But as I got older, the way he touched me started to feel wrong. His hand would linger too long on my back. He'd say things he called jokes but never smiled when he said them. They weren't funny. They were tests—measuring how much I'd tolerate.

It felt like he thought I was his. To watch. To control.

He used to pull me aside at family gatherings. Start with, "How you doing?"—but the way he said it, the way his eyes moved... it wasn't right. It felt like a dare.

I didn't know how to explain it. I was just a kid. But the feeling stuck. His words, his looks—they left a mark I never erased.

And then there was that night.

56

I was ten. It was just a family dinner. I remember laughing with Harmony, not thinking about anything else—until Darnell slid into the room. His presence swallowed air. The hairs on the back of my neck stood up. He scanned the space like he was looking for something. When his eyes landed on me, I looked away fast—but it was too late.

He'd seen me.

I never told my mother. Never told anyone. I wasn't even sure it had happened—or if something inside me was just… broken.

I blinked hard. Forced myself back into the present.

Darnell stood in front of me, his gaze dragging across my face—slow, deliberate. Too long.

My body locked up as he smiled. A smile that never reached his eyes. "Divinity."

His voice was smooth. Confident. Like we were old friends. Like he was testing me—seeing if I'd flinch.

He said my name like it belonged to him.

And I hated that.

I gave a stiff nod. "Hey."

It came out more breath than word.

He didn't smile back. Just let his eyes move over me again—measuring, weighing, checking to see if I was still the same girl he used to control.

That old feeling rose up my spine—a warning. A deep, internal scream.

Harmony didn't notice. She ran straight into his arms, hugging him like nothing had ever been wrong.

I stood frozen as he dropped his duffel by the door.

"You smell like travel and trouble," she teased.

He laughed—loud, easy. Like he belonged here.

"This house still standing? That's a miracle."

Tia rushed in, arms wide.

"My baby's home," she said, hugging him tight.

I stood back, arms folded, stomach in knots. I wanted to scream. Wanted to shake them—make them see. But I couldn't. I didn't know how to explain it. Not without sounding crazy. Not without being dismissed.

So, I did what I always did, disappeared without leaving. Smiled at the wrong times. Laughed when expected. Pretended the fear was all in my head.

But Darnell's presence filled the room.

And the silence inside me got even louder.

The days after Darnell came home stretched longer and heavier. Each one harder than the last.

Every time I saw him, my body screamed—but my mouth stayed shut.

He was everywhere. In the kitchen. In the hallway. Too close. His eyes made my skin crawl. But no one else saw it. Harmony didn't notice. Tia was too busy trying to keep things feeling normal.

But nothing about it was normal. Every look, every word from him felt like a weight I couldn't lift.

I didn't say anything. Not to Tia. Not to Harmony. I couldn't. What would I even say?

Hey, your son makes me feel unsafe in your house?

Who would believe me? Not after all this time. Not with him walking around smiling, calling me kiddo like we were fine.

So I stayed quiet.

Because technically, nothing had happened.

But inside, everything in me was screaming.

I started skipping school. At first it was little things—sleeping in, saying I felt sick. Just one more day. But one day kept turning into weeks. The longer I stayed in bed, the worse it got. I'd lie there staring at the ceiling, thoughts spinning too fast to catch.

I didn't want to face anyone. Didn't want to pretend. The world outside felt like another planet. I didn't belong to it anymore. It was easier to stay in my room and disappear.

Tia noticed.

"I got a call from the school," she said one morning, voice low but steady. "They said you've missed five days."

I shrugged. "I'm tired."

"You haven't been the same, baby. I know you're hurting, but—"

"But what?" I snapped, the words sharper than I meant them to be. "You want me to fake it? Smile through it? Make sure nobody else feels awkward?"

"No." Her voice cracked. Just a little. "I want you to keep going. Because I know that's what your mother would want."

I looked away, jaw tight.

Don't bring her into this. Don't use her like that.

"Well she can't want anything now, can she?"

Before she could answer, I went to my room and shut the door. Didn't come out the rest of the day.

School didn't matter anymore. None of it did.

I used to be a good student—focused, driven. Already dreaming of college brochures. My mom used to beam when I brought home A's.

"You're going places, baby."

Like it was promised.

But now? I could barely make it through a class. The words blurred on the page. Teachers' voices melted into background noise—static behind glass.

I sat in the back, hood up, headphones in, eyes down. Pretending I didn't exist. Wishing it were true.

The only thing I could focus on was the weight in my chest. And the way Darnell's eyes tracked me every time we passed in the hallway.

Harmony noticed.

"You okay?" she asked—for the thousandth time.

"Yeah," I said—for the thousandth lie.

"You don't talk to me anymore."

"I'm just tired." That was my go-to now.

"I miss you," she whispered.

I missed her too. But I didn't know how to say that out loud. The walls I'd built were higher every day. And once you get used to the dark, the light feels too loud.

Late one night, I opened my mom's journal again. Not to read it. Just to touch the pages. Her handwriting was the only thing that still felt real—ink and loops and curves, written in her own rhythm. Proof she'd existed. That I hadn't imagined her.

I closed the book and curled up on the floor beside my bed. Pressed the journal to my chest and tried to breathe through the ache. The kind that didn't make noise, but left you shaking anyway.

She wanted me to keep going. I knew that. But what do you do when the only person who believed in you is gone?

People expected me to be okay by now.

But how?

No mother. No father. Just absence, where love used to live. And yeah, I had Harmony. I had Tia. But I missed my mom. I missed the version of me that didn't feel like this.

I stayed curled on the floor until my arm went numb. But I didn't move.

I didn't want to.

Chris became my refuge.

Not because he understood me—he didn't. But because I didn't understand myself either. And with him, I didn't have to. He gave me space to breathe. No questions. No expectations. No forced smiles or hollow comfort.

He called every day. Left voicemails I never played. Harmony said she saw him once—standing on the sidewalk outside, hands in his pockets, looking up at the house.

I didn't care.

Some days I answered. Most days I didn't.

But that day, I picked up. I didn't say anything. Just held the phone to my ear and let the silence stretch between us like thread pulled too tight.

He didn't say much either. Just breathed into the pause like he was afraid to break it.

"Hey," he said finally.

I didn't say it back.

"Divinity?" he asked again, softer this time.

I didn't know why I'd answered. Maybe I just needed someone to pull me out of the room I'd been drowning in.

"Yes," I whispered.

"Are you okay?" he asked. This time, his voice held real worry.

"I'm… okay," I said.

Then silence again.

Chris wasn't enough. Nothing was. I knew that deep down. I knew using Chris like a shield wouldn't stop the storm inside me. But I clung to him anyway—because it was easier than facing the wreckage I'd become.

We started going on drives. Windows cracked, music low, city lights sliding past like they didn't care who we were. With him—just for a few hours—I didn't have to feel anything. Not the grief. Not the shame. Not the weight of silence pressing on my chest like a second skin.

I didn't have to fake a smile. Or force a laugh. Or explain why I couldn't breathe in my own house.

Chris didn't try to fix me. Didn't ask questions. He just let me be broken.

One night, he reached across the console and placed his hand on mine. Not tight. Not needy. Just there.

I didn't pull away. And in some twisted way, that was exactly what I needed.

I started eating again—barely. Mostly fries from a paper bag. Chicken nuggets in the dark. The granola bars he kept in the glove box. Nothing real. But it was something.

He became my unofficial boyfriend again. Not because I wanted him.

Because I needed a witness. A body. A presence. Someone who saw me—and didn't flinch.

He wasn't the answer.

But he was a break from the storm.

Darnell didn't like it.

I felt it every time I walked through the door with a leftover milkshake or Chris's cologne still clinging to my clothes. His stares got longer. His comments sharper.

"You think he's really here for you?" he'd ask, low and mocking, leaning in the doorway like he owned it.

I didn't answer. What was there to say?

"You don't know boys like I do," he added, darker now.

"He's just using you."

He stepped forward—just enough to shrink the hallway. Not touching me. Just close enough to remind me he could. That I'd have to brush past him to leave.

My stomach twisted. But I didn't move. I held my ground—even as every part of me wanted to back away. He didn't care what I needed. Only what he wanted. And I didn't know what that was. Not yet.

His gaze stayed on me—too long, too hard. It made my skin crawl. And I hated that I was still scared. Still reacting. Still stuck. I tried to stay away. Slipped out of rooms when he entered. Timed showers. Moved quiet through hallways like they weren't mine.

Every time he saw me, he said something that made my stomach knot. Nothing I could repeat. Nothing anyone else would call wrong.

But it was.

Then came that night.

The one I'd been dreading without even knowing it.

Tia and Harmony were going out—shopping, a movie, a girls' day. They begged me to come. I told them I had a headache.

The truth? I just wanted to be alone.

Alone with the fear I couldn't voice. Alone in the quiet, where I didn't have to keep pretending I was fine.

But Darnell was still in the house.

I could feel it—the way you feel a shadow shift just outside the frame.

My heart was already pounding. I grabbed my phone and called Chris.

He picked me up around four.

The hours we spent together were quiet—but not heavy. Not like home. The silence in his car didn't press in. It held space for me.

His car always smelled the same, mint gum, worn leather, and too much cologne. Familiar in a way I couldn't resent.

The music played low—instrumentals, mostly. The kind of songs that didn't need words to say exactly how I felt. Outside, streetlights blinked past like soft flashes of memory. I watched them blur together until they didn't look like anything at all.

We didn't talk much. I didn't need to. My fingers brushed the edge of the rolled-down window, the night air numbing my fingertips. It felt good—not to feel so much.

For a little while, I forgot the weight in my chest. I forgot Darnell's eyes. Forgot the way I'd been holding my breath for weeks.

Chris didn't ask how I was.

And that was exactly what I needed. No pity. No pressure. Just presence. He parked at the Brooklyn Heights Promenade. The city lights spilled across the water like scattered stars. One of my favorite places.

We walked to a bench near the edge. The breeze off the river was cool, crisp—like it didn't belong to summer. We sat in silence. Just water. Wind. Cars from somewhere far below. The river was still and dark, reflecting nothing. It mirrored exactly how I felt inside.

Chris didn't try to make me smile. Didn't try to fill the silence. He let me sit in it. Let me disappear a little. But even as I stared out at the lights, I felt it—that quiet shift between us. Subtle. Slow. Like pressure building in a closed room.

He kept looking at me.

Not in a way that asked for anything. But like he was trying to solve something. Like he could feel that something in me had changed.

"You sure you're okay?" he asked, voice low, but not soft. His eyes searched mine, his brow pulled tight.

I nodded. Tried to give him a smile. But it felt fake—thin, cracked, borrowed.

"Yeah," I said. "I'm fine."

The words barely had shape. Just noise, trying to pass for truth.

Chris leaned back slowly, still watching me.

"You've been saying that a lot lately," he said. "And I can see it in your eyes, Div. Something's wrong. I just don't know what."

His words sat between us like a weight. I wanted to laugh them off, say something clever, light. But nothing came fast enough.

He must've seen it.

"You don't have to tell me," He added, quieter now. Like he could feel the wall going up. "But I'm not going anywhere. If you want to talk, I'll listen. And if you need silence... I'm good with that too."

He reached over. Took my hand. A soft squeeze. Just enough to say, I see you.

I didn't pull away. But I didn't hold on either. My hand just stayed there—awkward and still—like it didn't know what to do with gentleness.

I almost let myself feel it—like maybe the ground hadn't completely disappeared beneath me. But the moment slipped through. Like water through fingers too tired to close.

I didn't answer. We got back in the car. I turned toward the window, forcing everything back down—deep, hidden, locked.

And something hit me.

Chris could see through me. Even when I didn't want him to. Even when I tried to hold the cracks together, he saw.

By the time we pulled up to the house, it was just after seven. My stomach was knotted so tight I could barely breathe.

That familiar dread crept up my spine—slow and cold. I reached for the door handle, hesitating. Chris was already out of the car.

"You sure you're okay?" he asked, voice low, eyes searching.

I forced a smile. One that cracked before it ever reached my face.

"Yeah. I'm fine." I said it like a reflex. Not like a truth.

"Thanks for tonight."

And then I saw him.

Leaning against the front railing. Arms crossed. Casual. Too casual.

His gaze snapped toward me—sharp, focused. A cold shiver slid down my back. I knew that look. My heartbeat kicked up, frantic. I didn't move, but everything inside me screamed, Get back in the car.

Chris noticed. The shift in my posture. The way I froze.

Darnell had been waiting.

"Divinity," he said. Smooth, like always.

But the menace was there, tucked beneath the syllables.

"Welcome home."

My eyes stayed forward. Chris was behind me. That was the only thing keeping me upright.

Darnell smiled—but it wasn't warmth. It was warning.

"Who's your friend?"

His eyes moved from me to Chris—slow, deliberate. Like he was peeling something open that didn't belong to him.

Chris's posture stiffened.

"Harmony's brother, right?" His voice was careful now. Measured. He felt it, too. I saw it in his eyes when he looked at me—an unspoken *What's going on?*

"Yeah," I mumbled, eyes down.

Both of them were watching me.

Chris stepped in again, voice low but steady.

"You sure you're good?"

Then, to Darnell,

"You don't look so... friendly."

Darnell smirked. Slow. Satisfied. And stepped forward—just enough to make the space smaller.

"You think you can just come up in here and have a seat at the table?" he said, mocking. "You don't even know her. You don't know anything about her. About us."

I flinched. Took a step back without thinking. Just enough to feel the distance stretch between me and Darnell. Not enough to be safe.

Chris's eyes narrowed.

"I know enough," he said. "And I know I don't like the way you're looking at her." Then quieter, sharper tone, "There is no us."

Darnell's smirk twitched. Just for a second. Something flickered behind his eyes—something not meant to be seen.

"You don't know anything about me, son," he said, voice low, coiled.

"And you sure as hell don't know what I'm capable of."

Chris didn't flinch.

"Try me." It wasn't loud. It didn't have to be. It hit like stone. "Don't let the pretty boy look fool you. You don't want none of this. Stay away from her."

The air between them changed—two wolves with teeth showing. I stood between them. A girl made of glass.

Darnell's eyes snapped back to me.

"You really think he's here for you?" he sneered. "You think he sees you? Think he knows you like I do?"

The words sliced through me. I flinched. Chris looked at me, then back at Darnell. He saw it. He saw everything I hadn't said.

"Stop," I whispered.

"Just stop."

64

But Darnell didn't. He stepped forward, smug.

"You sleeping with her?"

"WHAT?!" I shouted. I moved so fast the world blurred. "What the hell is wrong with you?!"

Darnell didn't blink. Still staring Chris down.

Chris's jaw clenched.

His voice came out like ice cracking.

"Don't ever talk to her like that again."

It wasn't loud. But it was final.

Darnell smiled wider now. Uglier.

"You think you can protect her? From me?"

His eyes slid back to me.

"You don't even know the half of it."

I didn't meet his gaze.

"You good?" Chris asked me, too casual.

My throat tightened.

I nodded.

"I'll be okay."

"You sure?"

His voice dropped—just enough to make my skin crawl.

"Yeah." I stepped away, fast. Like moving slow might give him time to grab me.

Chris didn't speak. Just stood there—watching him. Watching me. And I knew. He saw something now. Not all of it. But enough.

"You need to stay away from me," I said.

Darnell smiled. Not with his mouth. With his eyes.

The kind of smile that said, You won't.

I went inside. Locked the door behind me. Hoped it would hold. Tried to breathe. But it didn't matter. That night—he came back.

Ten minutes later, I heard the front door. My hands started shaking. I ran to my room. Tried to lock the door.

I wasn't fast enough.

I backed into the corner and whispered,

"God, please..."

I didn't know what to say after that. I just kept repeating it.

*Please. Please let someone come home. Please let this not happen. Please—*

But no one came.

And the silence was louder than my prayers.

He didn't knock.

He didn't speak.

65

He didn't care.

He pushed the door open and stepped inside.

I screamed.

Loud. Raw. The kind of scream that rips something out of you.

I shoved him back. Hit. Clawed. Kicked.

But it didn't matter.

He was stronger. Bigger. And I was alone.

No one heard me.

No one came.

Not Tia. Not Harmony. Not God.

There was no help. No rescue. No voice louder than mine.

And after that—

I wasn't a virgin anymore.

But it wasn't about that.

It was about everything he took.

My voice. My control. My right to be untouched.

When it was over, I wasn't sure what was left.

I didn't feel broken.

I felt erased.

Like someone had wiped me clean and left only the shape of a girl behind. A quiet shape, curled in the dark, trying not to remember.

Failing anyway.

I didn't know who I was anymore. Not after that. Not after him. The shame gnawed at me. Lived under my skin. Whispered that I let it happen. And no matter how hard I tried, I couldn't escape it.

Every time I closed my eyes, I saw his face. Every time I moved, I felt his presence—lurking. Waiting. Like a shadow I couldn't outrun. I wanted to forget. Wanted to burn the memory out of me. But it clung to my chest like a second spine I couldn't break.

Every scream stayed locked behind my teeth. Every prayer evaporated before it reached heaven. I crawled into the shower. Let the water scald my skin until I couldn't feel anything.

That was the night the world stopped spinning. The night I stopped being a girl and became something else.

Not a woman.

Not yet.

Just broken.

And alone.

I didn't know what came next.

My body was bruised. My heart was in pieces. My mother was gone.

And I was left with nothing but silence. Who could I tell? Who would believe me? It felt like I was stuck in someone else's nightmare—and no one was coming to wake me up. I wanted to scream.

But the words stuck.

I wanted to run.

But where?

The person who should've protected me—was the one who shattered me. I couldn't tell Tia. Not after this. I couldn't look Harmony in the eye—not without wondering if she'd blame me.

I was alone. Completely alone. Home is supposed to be where you feel safe. But this wasn't home, was it?

The next day, I didn't move. I didn't leave my room. Harmony knocked. Left food. I didn't open the door. I cried until my body went still. Then cried again.

I hated God. What kind of God lets this happen? Takes my mother—and leaves me in a house like this? I was still sore. Still hurting. And most of all—I was scared.

So scared.

Journal, same night—

*He took everything. And I think the worst part is… I still have to see him tomorrow.*

I stared at the words until they blurred. Then I tore the page out—slowly, carefully. Like maybe it would hurt less if I was gentle. I carried it to the bathroom sink. Lit the edge with a match from the emergency kit. Watched the flame curl over every line. Each loop of ink vanishing into black.

Until there was nothing left but ash.

It wasn't time.

Not yet.

No one could know.

Not even the page.

## 6  THE SILENCE BETWEEN US

*"We stopped speaking the moment I started shrinking." – Divinity*

**I didn't sleep.**

I couldn't.

I just lay there in the dark, curled into myself—numb in some places, aching in others I didn't even know could hurt. My body didn't feel like mine anymore. It was something I was trapped inside. It had betrayed me. Or maybe I had betrayed it. I couldn't tell the difference anymore.

I wanted to scream. But I didn't. What was the point? No one would hear me. And if they did—they wouldn't believe me. I wanted my mother. Her arms. Her voice. Her prayers. I wanted her to sit on the edge of the bed and say, "It was just a bad dream, baby." I wanted her to lie to me. Tell me everything would be okay. But she was gone. And the truth was—I had no one. Not really.

How could I tell Tia that her son was a monster? How could I look Harmony in the face and say, "Your brother violated me?" I couldn't. I wouldn't. The air in the room felt heavy. Like it knew. Like even the walls were holding their breath.

My stomach turned—not from hunger, but from the weight of being awake in this body. I didn't realize I was shaking until the sheet moved. My fingers curled around the blanket, trying to hold myself still. Sweat clung to my skin, but I was cold. I hadn't moved in hours, but everything inside me was screaming.

I stayed silent. The next day, I didn't move. I stayed under the covers, letting the dark swallow me—because it was the only thing that made sense.

Harmony knocked, soft and careful. Her voice came through the door, barely a whisper:

"I brought you something to eat."

I didn't answer. I couldn't. It wasn't that I didn't want to hear her. It was that I couldn't pretend. Pretend I was okay. Pretend that food or kindness could fix what had been torn open inside me. She waited. I could feel it in the quiet. The way her feet didn't move. But eventually, she walked away—probably thinking I was still just tired. Maybe I was. But mostly, I was just... gone. Hollow.

I pulled the covers tighter, let the tears slide down into the pillow until the wet spot grew cold against my cheek. I cried myself to sleep. Woke up. Did it again. Over and over. And when the crying stopped—the questions came.

*Why me?*
*Why did God take my mother?*
*Why did He put me here?*
*Why didn't He stop him?*
*Wasn't I supposed to be loved?*
*Wasn't I worth protecting?*

I used to believe in God. I used to think He watched over me. That even when things were hard, the pain had a purpose. My mom used to say, "God don't make mistakes, baby. Even when it hurts, He's working." She'd whisper prayers over me when I was asleep—soft, steady words that felt like armor. I used to believe those prayers worked. I used to think they kept me safe.

But now? I didn't know what to believe anymore. If God was real—if He was supposed to protect me—then where was He? Where was He when my mother died? Where was He when I was violated? When Darnell's hands touched me—and I cried out in silence, begging for someone to hear?

I wasn't sure anymore. And maybe that scared me more than anything. Not the pain. Not even the memory. Just the silence where He used to be.

I used to pray. But now every word felt empty—like I was talking to a wall. I didn't feel Him anymore. Just the silence.

A silence that mirrored the one in my chest. A silence that had become my only companion.

I finally got up late that night—not because I wanted to, but because I felt like I was suffocating. The silence in the room had become too loud, pressing down on me until it felt like I couldn't breathe. I stumbled toward the mirror, clutching the edge of the dresser like it was the only thing holding me up. My legs were shaky. My head was foggy. I looked at my reflection and barely recognized the girl staring back. My eyes were red, my face puffy. I looked hollow—like someone who had disappeared inside herself and left the shell behind.

I lifted my shirt and winced at the bruises along my waist. There it was. Proof. Proof that it wasn't just a bad dream. Proof that something had been taken. My hands trembled as I reached for my journal—the one my mom gave me, the one she had written in too. I pressed it against my chest and collapsed onto the floor, my back against the bed frame.

"I miss you," I whispered. My voice cracked like a dry leaf. "I need you. Please come back."

I didn't write anything that night. I didn't open the journal. I just held it and cried until my body gave out and sleep finally took me.

The next morning, I forced myself out of bed. My movements were stiff, robotic. I brushed my teeth, combed my hair, and changed into clean clothes. From the outside, I looked like a girl trying to start a new day. But inside, I was unraveling thread by thread.

When I walked into the kitchen, Tia looked up from the stove. She didn't say anything at first, but her eyebrows lifted—surprised, maybe even relieved. She didn't smile, not really, but something in her shoulders softened, just for a second. Like she'd been holding her breath and wasn't sure whether to let it out. I couldn't tell if she saw me or just the version of me I was pretending to be. Either way, she turned back to the skillet without a word.

"Hey baby… you okay?" Tia asked, her tone laced with concern.

I nodded too quickly. "Yeah. Just tired."

Just tired. I'd said it so many times, it felt like a reflex. But at this point, how could I still be tired when all they ever saw me do was lie in bed? The excuse had worn thin, even to me.

Tia's eyes didn't blink. "Do I need to take you to the doctor?"

"No ma'am, I'll be okay," I said, forcing a steady voice. She didn't push—but I could tell she didn't believe me. I could feel it in the way her gaze lingered, longer than usual, like she was searching for something I wasn't ready to give.

Harmony hugged me tight before school. I held my breath.

She smiled and said softly, "I hope you get better?"

I didn't answer.

I tried. I really did. Every day, I forced myself to get up, get dressed, and pretend. Pretend that I was okay. Pretend that I could go back to being the girl who had dreams and plans and a future worth thinking about.

There was a time I actually liked school. I used to sit near the front, hand raised before the question was finished. I had color-coded folders, highlighted everything, and smiled when teachers said my name. I used to walk through the hallways like I belonged there—head up, headphones on, already thinking about college or what I'd wear to prom one day. But that girl felt like a ghost now. Like someone I knew from a past life.

At school, everything felt louder than usual. The hallway chatter, the teacher's voice, the slamming of lockers—it all echoed inside me like a scream. I tried to focus in class. I took notes. I even laughed at something someone said. But it was all pretend.

Harmony had already noticed I was pulling away. She'd ask if I was okay, and I'd lie. I'd tell her I was just tired. That it wasn't a big deal. But I could see the worry growing in her eyes each time. She was starting to see through the mask. She was getting closer to the truth.

But I wasn't ready to face her. I wasn't ready to face anyone.

So I pushed her out. Pushed them all out. Because if I let them in, if I let anyone close enough to see past the surface, they'd see how broken I really was.

And I couldn't let that happen.

During lunch, I sat alone under the stairs behind the gym. I picked at my sandwich until the bread crumbled in my hands. I wasn't getting better. I was just getting better at hiding. I got good at pretending—smiling when someone looked at me, nodding when teachers asked if I was okay, laughing at Harmony's jokes even though my insides felt like glass. It was easier that way. If I acted normal, they'd stop asking. If I looked fine, no one would dig deeper. I was tired of lying. But more than that, I was tired of explaining what couldn't be explained.

Weeks went by in a blur. Days melted into each other. Nothing felt solid anymore. One afternoon, out of nowhere, I called Chris. I didn't tell him why—I just asked if he could drive me somewhere. He said yes without hesitation. It wasn't until we were already in the car that I finally said it.

"My mom's grave," I told him quietly, barely louder than a whisper, like saying it too loud might make it more real.

Chris didn't ask questions. He didn't try to fill the silence. He just drove, hands steady on the wheel, the soft hum of the engine the only sound between us. I didn't expect him to understand. I didn't need him to. I just needed to feel close to her. Even if it was only by standing where she was buried.

When we got there, I walked alone to the headstone and sat down on

71

the cold ground. The wind moved through my hair, light but sharp, like it carried every word I couldn't say. I didn't cry. I couldn't. Instead, I whispered, "I don't know what to do without you, Mommy. I don't know how to be me anymore."

And somehow, for the first time in weeks, it didn't feel like I was completely alone.

Chris stayed in the car. He gave me space. I knew he was watching, but he didn't come closer, didn't ask if I was okay. I didn't cry. I couldn't. It was like the tears had dried up, leaving only this heavy, unmoving weight in my chest. And I carried that weight everywhere.

I touched the stone like it could hold me. "You were supposed to be here. You were supposed to protect me from this. I need you, Mommy. Please... I need you."

I stayed there for a long time. Just sitting. Just breathing. And for a moment, I felt close to her. Like maybe she heard me. Like maybe she knew. Like somewhere, somehow, my words found their way to her.

After that day, I tried harder. Harder to act normal. Harder to become the version of myself people wanted to see. I laughed more. Ate more. I started going back to school full-time. I even helped Tia in the kitchen again. Harmony seemed relieved.

"You're starting to be like you again," she said with a smile.

But I wasn't.

I was a stranger behind my own eyes. Smiling at the mirror just to prove I still knew how. The reflection always looked a little off, like it was mimicking me instead of being me.

And then it happened again.

It was during Thanksgiving break. The house was quiet. Harmony and Tia had gone to bed early after a long day of Black Friday shopping. I was in my room, pretending to sleep.

Then I heard it. The door creaked open.

Footsteps—slow. Careful.

The bed dipped.

A hand clamped over my mouth before I could let a scream out.

My body seized—but nothing moved. I wanted to scream, to twist away, to scratch or claw or run. But I couldn't. I was frozen.

And just like that... I was gone again. Gone from my body. Gone from my room. Gone from the version of myself I had spent the last week trying so desperately to rebuild.

When it was over, he slipped out like he had never been there. But I was still there. Frozen.

Shaking.

Destroyed.

I curled into myself and stayed that way until the sun came up. I didn't speak. I didn't cry. I just laid there... silent. Because this time? This time broke something I wasn't sure could ever be fixed. This time, I couldn't fake it. I couldn't put on a smile. Couldn't find the words. Couldn't pretend that everything was fine.

Because nothing was fine.

I was hollow. Empty. Dark. The little pieces of myself I had been trying to glue back together shattered all over again—and this time, I didn't even try to pick them up.

I stayed in bed for days. Didn't eat. Didn't shower. Didn't speak. I stared at the ceiling like maybe it held some kind of answer, but all it did was stare back.

Tia knocked every morning and every night for a week. She even stepped in a few times, and I pretended to be asleep. So did Harmony. I told them I had a stomach virus. That I needed rest.

They believed me. Or at least, I think they did. Why wouldn't they? I was a good liar. And I hated that.

I didn't want to talk to Chris. I let his calls ring out. Didn't answer the pages. Didn't even read them. He couldn't help me. Not now. No one could. What could he say? What could anyone say?

There was no fixing this.

No undoing it.

No prayer that could make it make sense.

God? I didn't want to hear His name. Where was He? Where was He when my mother died? Where was He when Darnell first touched me? Where was He when I screamed into my pillow in silence and begged for it to stop?

I hated Him.

I hated whatever version of God everyone kept preaching about— the one who "never leaves" and "always protects." Because if that God was real, He wouldn't have let this happen. He wouldn't have let me become this.

I was more alone than ever. Not because no one was around. But because no one could reach me. No one could touch the places that were broken. Because those places weren't even mine anymore.

The morning after, the world didn't stop. Birds still chirped outside the window, and the sun rose, golden and unbothered, like it had a right to wake up. I hated it for that. I hated how normal everything looked when my world had shattered into a million pieces. The world didn't care that I was falling apart.

People kept going. Moving. Breathing. While I lay there—unable to feel anything but emptiness. I wanted to scream at the sky for being so bright. For being so... alive, when all I could feel was death.

Death of my mother. Death of the person I was before all of this. I hated how normal everything looked. How the day had the nerve to be beautiful while I lay still in my bed, drowning in something no one else could see.

I didn't move. Not for hours.

I just laid there, staring at the wall, the blankets pulled to my chin like they could protect me from what had already happened. My body was stiff. My thoughts were blank. And my soul felt... vacant. There weren't any tears left. Only silence. And that silence was so loud it made my head throb.

Harmony knocked softly around noon.

"You okay?" she asked through the door. "I brought you some tea and toast."

I didn't answer.

A moment later, she opened the door slowly to see if I was asleep. She stood there for a moment, and I knew she was looking around my dark room. I heard her sigh and set the plate down on my dresser. My eyes were closed, pretending I wasn't even here.

Tia came later that evening. She opened the door just enough to peek inside.

"You've been in bed all day," she said, her voice cautious. "You barely touched your food yesterday or today."

I turned my face to the wall.

"I don't feel good," I whispered.

There was a pause.

Then she walked in and sat on the edge of my bed. Her hand touched my back—warm, gentle.

"I know you're hurting, baby," Tia said. Her voice was soft but steady. "I know it's been hard since your mom passed. But I think it might be time to talk to someone—someone who can help. A real therapist. Someone who can help you cope with the grief."

I wanted to scream. I wanted to tell her it wasn't just grief. It wasn't just my mom. But how could I say that? How do you look at someone who took you in and tell her the truth?

The truth was that I wasn't just grieving my mother. The truth was that something else had broken me. That I was shattered in ways I didn't know how to explain.

But the words wouldn't come.

All I could do was lie there and let her think I was just sad. Just grieving. Just... normal.

How do you look into the eyes of someone who took you in and say, your son ruined me? He came into my room. He put his hand over my mouth. He took everything from me and then walked away like nothing happened. And now I have to sit here and pretend I'm just tired. Just sick. Just grieving. But I'm not. I'm broken, and I'm scared, and I'm sick of hiding it. I need help. But I don't know how to say it. I don't know how to live with it. I don't even know how to look you in the face, Tia, without thinking of him. Without hating myself.

She ran her hands through my hair, looking at me with saddened eyes while my insides was screaming wanting to tell her the truth.

"Div, I'm here, and I'm not going anywhere. When you're ready to open up, I'll be here to listen."

I didn't respond.

So she got up, looked at me one last time, and walked out the door.

That night, the nightmares returned. But they were different now. Worse. Before, they were just flashes—images of my mother, fading in and out. But now, they were darker. More vivid. I could hear my own screams in my ears, muffled and distant, as shadows loomed over me, creeping through the cracks in the door. I could feel hands where they shouldn't be—on my skin, in places that made my body freeze with terror.

I woke up drenched in sweat, my heart pounding like it wanted to burst from my chest. But the fear didn't go away. It lingered in the corners of the room, in the tightness of my throat, in the ache of my bones. I sat in the dark, heart racing, afraid to close my eyes again. Afraid the nightmare would swallow me whole.

I didn't sleep again for three days.

I stopped looking in the mirror. Every time I tried, I saw her. The girl who was too weak to fight back. The girl who let it happen again. The girl who would never be clean.

I couldn't eat. Couldn't laugh. Couldn't pray. Everything felt numb. Even the simple act of breathing seemed too much.

I shut everyone out. Even Chris, who had always known how to make me smile. He stopped reaching out, stopped calling, and I didn't even feel the guilt I knew I should. His messages were short now, like he was afraid of pushing me too hard.

Honestly? I was relieved. I didn't want to talk. I didn't want to be comforted. I just wanted to disappear. I wanted the silence to swallow me whole, to drown out the screaming in my head. Because if I stayed quiet enough... if I just shut everything out...

Maybe I could make it stop.

Some days, I almost told someone. I'd open my mouth to say something to Harmony or Tia—but the words wouldn't come. Shame is a heavy thing. It wraps itself around your throat and convinces you that silence is safer. That speaking makes it more real. That if you just stay quiet, maybe... maybe it'll all fade.

But it didn't. And it wasn't.

Later that week, I walked past the kitchen on my way to the laundry room and heard Tia's voice. She was on the phone. I froze in place when I heard my name.

"She barely speaks. She doesn't eat. And the way she flinches when people touch her..." Her voice cracked. "I don't know what else to do."

Silence.

Then, softly, "I'm trying, Juan. I really am. But I feel like I'm failing her."

Juan?

I blinked.

That was my father's name.

I stepped back, heart pounding, and leaned quietly against the wall just out of sight.

"She won't open up. Not to me. Not to Harmony. And this girl has been through so much already. I just... I don't know if I'm enough."

There was a pause. I imagined the person on the other end saying something comforting, but Tia's voice only trembled more.

"I'm praying this therapist can help. Because I can't lose her too. I promised her mother I'd take care of her. And I will. But she's slipping through my fingers."

I held my breath. My chest felt tight.

Was she talking to him? My father? The man I never knew? A thousand questions flashed through my mind, but I couldn't ask any of them. I backed away, the sound of her voice chasing me like a shadow.

The next morning, Tia drove me to therapy. The car ride was silent. She didn't press. Just rested her hand on mine for a moment before we got out.

The office was small and warm—painted soft yellows and muted blues. The woman I met had kind eyes and curly salt-and-pepper hair. Her name was Dr. Shaw.

"Hi, Divinity," she said, offering a gentle smile. "You can call me Dr. S. This space is yours, okay? No pressure. No judgment."

I nodded and sat on the edge of the couch, arms crossed so tightly they started to ache. She talked. A lot. About how grief and trauma can live in the body. About safe places. About breathing, journaling, and emotional grounding.

I nodded when I thought I was supposed to. Said "I'm fine" when she asked how I was doing. She said something about how trauma lives in the body—and I felt my throat tighten, like my body already knew that. I almost said it. I almost told her. But then I didn't.

Because if I told her what really happened, she'd have to tell someone. She'd call the police. Then Tia would find out. Harmony. Everyone. And then what? A home ruined. A family shattered. Because of me. Because I didn't fight hard enough. Because I let it happen.

So I stayed quiet.

And when the session was over, Dr. S smiled again.

"I hope you'll come back," she said softly, her voice full of warmth, like she truly believed I would find a way to open up. I nodded. I knew that was what she wanted to hear.

But inside, I was already gone. My mind was locked in a cage, and the key was something I didn't know how to find. I wasn't ready to talk. I wasn't ready to admit what had happened.

How could I? How could I trust someone when I couldn't even trust myself? So I nodded, and I lied. "I'll come back." But the truth was, I didn't know if I could.

That night, I lay in bed staring at the ceiling again. Therapy was supposed to help. That's what they said. But all it did was remind me how broken I was. How far gone I felt.

Dr. S had asked me to keep a journal. Said it didn't have to be deep— just honest.

I opened it once, pen in hand, and wrote one line before slamming it shut,

*I can't tell the truth because the truth ruins people.*

That was it. That was all I had in me. I buried the journal under my pillow and turned off the lamp. In the dark, my mind never rested. I kept hearing her voice—Tia's—whispering into the phone, "I feel like I'm failing her."

She wasn't failing.

I was.

She didn't know what lived in this house. What visited my room in the dead of night.

I thought about Harmony, asleep across the hall. She didn't know either. If she ever found out... she would never look at me the same. No one would. So I told myself again,

Just keep quiet.

Keep pretending.

Keep surviving.

But surviving was getting harder. I was losing pieces of myself by the day. Pieces I wasn't sure I'd ever get back.

The nights stretched longer. My appetite disappeared again. I avoided the mirrors. I wore long sleeves even when it was warm. I flinched when someone spoke too loudly. Even breathing felt like a task.

I didn't feel like a person anymore. I felt like a memory trapped inside a body.

And the silence?

It was swallowing me whole.

## 7 TRAPPED BETWEEN THE WALLS

*"Some prisons have pillows. That doesn't make them soft." - Divinity*

**Weeks passed, and finally—**

I became a master of pretending. Again. I smiled when someone waved. Laughed at the right moments. Answered questions just enough to seem present. But I wasn't really there. Not at school. Not at home. Not anywhere. I was floating above my life, watching a version of me perform the role of "normal girl," while inside I was trapped between silence and the truth. And both hurt.

Harmony started watching me more closely. "You okay?" she asked one afternoon at lunch, her eyes squinting like she already knew the answer.

"Yeah, just tired," I said, taking a sip of my juice and avoiding her stare. But she didn't let it go.

"How can you still be tired when all you do is sleep?" she asked. "Every time I come to your room, you're asleep. Div, you're my sister. Please let me be there for you. Let me help you." Her voice cracked.

I wanted to let her in. I did. But the weight I was carrying didn't have space for anyone else—not even Harmony. I couldn't give her what she wanted, because I didn't even know who I was anymore. What would I say?

*Your brother ruined me. I can't sleep without seeing it happen again. I don't feel like a person anymore.*

She didn't deserve to carry that. So I looked away. I used to think I'd tell my mom one day. Back when I was younger—maybe ten, maybe eleven—I almost did.

*It was a Wednesday. I remember because it was the day she always did laundry and let me eat dinner on the couch. We were watching some old movie with too much talking and not enough action. She had her legs curled under her, folding towels while*

79

*I picked at a bowl of mac and cheese that didn't taste like anything.*

*I kept glancing at her. At the way her mouth moved when she counted towels. At her hands, always doing something—folding, fixing, holding the world together. I kept trying to find the right second. The right words. But I didn't even know what I was trying to say.*

*"Ma?" I asked. She looked over, gentle like always. "Yeah, baby?" My stomach twisted.*

*"How do you know if something bad happened to you, but you don't really... know?"*

*She frowned a little, her hands pausing mid-fold. "What do you mean?"*

*I stared down at my bowl.*

*"Like... if you think something maybe wasn't okay, but nobody else saw it, and it didn't hurt... not really, but it still makes you feel weird inside after."*

*She was quiet for a second. Then she scooted closer and brushed my hair out of my face.*

*"Did something happen?"*

*I shook my head too quickly. "I was just wondering."*

*She searched my eyes, like she could read between the blinking. Then she nodded slowly. "Well, if something ever does happen... anything... you come tell me. Doesn't matter what it is. You don't have to figure it out by yourself, okay?"*

*I nodded. She kissed my forehead. "Okay?"*

*"Okay."*

But I never did tell her. Because back then, I didn't even know what I was carrying. I just knew it made my chest feel tight and my body feel wrong.

And now she was gone.

"There's nothing you can do, Harmony. So there's nothing else for me to tell you." She stepped back and looked at me. I could see the tears welling in her eyes, but she didn't respond. She just hugged me—and walked away.

Later that week, she caught me zoning out in the hallway between classes. "Div... where'd you just go?" I blinked. "What?" "You were just standing there. Like... gone." I forced a laugh. "I was thinking about a test. Nothing serious." She tilted her head, her concern soft but steady. "You sure?" I nodded. I lied.

Chris was harder to dodge. He gave up on waiting for me to contact him, so he paged me. Called. Left voicemails I listened to but never answered.

One day, he caught me outside school. "Yo, what's going on with you?" he asked, stepping between me and the bus. "You haven't been the same since that night—me and that dude Darnell got into it." I froze for a second, wondering if he knew something had happened. There was no way he could.

"I've been busy," I mumbled, trying to move past him. He stepped aside, but not before he said, "If something's wrong, you can tell me, D. I'll listen." I kept walking. Because if I stopped... if I opened my mouth... I might tell him everything. And then what?

He'd call the police. He'd tell someone. He'd try to fix it. But some things weren't fixable. And I wasn't ready to be someone's burden.

When I got home, I went straight to my room. The lights stayed off. I didn't even take off my jacket. I just sat on the edge of the bed, staring at the blank wall across from me like it might give me an answer. My backpack slid to the floor. I didn't care. I couldn't even remember what class I'd had last.

I reached under my pillow and pulled out the journal. I opened it to the page where I'd written that one sentence. *I can't tell the truth because the truth ruins people.* I stared at the words. Not reading them. Just... watching them. Like they might rewrite themselves if I waited long enough. I thought about adding more. Something honest. Something ugly. But my hand wouldn't move. So I closed the book. Shoved it back under the pillow. And lay down fully clothed. I stared at the ceiling and listened for the silence.

Not again. At this point, telling what happened will only do harm, not good. Telling what happened won't make me feel whole again. How could it?

That night, Tia made spaghetti for dinner. She thought it was my favorite. Truth was, my favorite had always been my mother's pork chop Thursdays—something I'd never taste again.

She set a plate in front of me and sat across the table, watching me with eyes that held more questions than words. I picked at the noodles.

"Baby," she said gently, "I've been thinking about our next therapy session." I didn't look up. But I could feel Darnell's eyes on me. Being at the same table with him made my stomach turn. I never made eye contact.

She continued anyway. "I know you didn't say much last time. But sometimes it takes a few tries. I just... I want you to know I'm proud of you for even going."

My throat tightened. She was proud of me for showing up? If she only knew what I was really carrying.

I nodded, swallowing the lump in my throat along with a small bite of food. She reached across the table and touched my hand. "I'm not gonna push. I just want you to know—whatever it is, whatever you're holding— I'm here."

Her voice cracked on the word here, and it almost undid me.

I opened my mouth to speak. To say something. Anything. But shame slammed the door shut before the words could make it out.

And then I heard his voice again—his voice—replaying like a curse, *No one would believe you, so it's best you not open your mouth.* The tone was terrifying.

I forced a small smile instead. "Thanks," I whispered. She squeezed my hand once, then let go.

Later that night, I stood in the bathroom and stared at myself in the mirror. I looked fine. That's the problem.

Bruises fade. Pain hides. And silence? Silence looks like strength to people who don't know better.

I pressed my palms to the edge of the sink, willing myself to breathe. Just say it. Tell her. Tell someone. But the voice inside me screamed louder, *You'll ruin everything. They'll hate you. They'll hate him—and it'll be your fault.*

So I walked out of the bathroom and said nothing. Again.

That night, before the shadows came, I dreamt of her. My mother.

She was standing in the kitchen with sunlight behind her like some kind of halo, hands deep in a sink of soapy water, humming a song I didn't recognize. The table was set for dinner—real dinner, not spaghetti from a box. Cornbread, pork chops, something green I would've pushed around the plate.

She looked over her shoulder and smiled. "There's my girl." It felt so normal I forgot it wasn't real.

I moved toward her, but the kitchen stretched the more I walked. Like it was trying to keep her far away. Still, her voice reached me.

"You look tired, baby. Come sit."

I opened my mouth to speak—to finally say something—but no sound came out. I pressed a hand to my throat, panicked.

She dried her hands and turned to face me. Up close now. Her eyes soft. Familiar. Unbelievingly near.

She touched my cheek. *"You don't have to carry it all,"* she whispered. *"You were never meant to."*

I blinked, and suddenly the room darkened. The sink was empty. The table bare. She was gone.

I woke up with my hand still on my cheek.

I couldn't sleep. Again.

I stared at the ceiling. Then at the wall. Then at the shadows moving through my room like ghosts I couldn't shake. I tossed the blankets off and reached under my pillow for my journal—the one I'd stopped writing in because words felt too dangerous. I opened it and stared at the blank page. Then I started to write.

Not carefully. Not poetically. Just honestly.

*I wish I could disappear. Not die. Just… stop existing. Stop waking up. I hate what happened to me. I hate that I let it happen again. I hate that I can't say his name or see his face without wanting to disappear… I hate that I feel like it's my fault. I hate God for not stopping it. And I hate myself for still believing he might someday help me.*

I stopped and let the pen fall from my hand. The tears came quietly this time. No sobs. No shaking. Just soft drops sliding down my face and soaking into my pillow.

I cried until my body gave out, and I drifted into sleep with the journal open beside me. I didn't know what would happen tomorrow. Didn't know how long I could keep walking this tightrope—between holding on and completely letting go.

But I knew this, the silence was getting heavier. And sooner or later, something had to give.

The next few days blurred together. I went to school. I came home. I avoided mirrors.

I nodded when people spoke to me, laughed when I was supposed to, and said "I'm fine" so many times I almost believed it. Almost. But it was getting harder to keep up the act.

On Thursday, a girl bumped into me in the hallway. It wasn't hard. Just clumsy. A typical school moment. But I froze. The contact sent a jolt through my spine and I dropped my binder like it had burned me.

"Sorry!" she said, bending to help me pick up the papers.

I couldn't speak. My hands shook as I reached for my things. My heart was racing. Loud. Violent. Like I was being chased from the inside.

"Are you okay?" she asked. I nodded quickly and turned down the hall, ignoring the sting in my eyes.

I ducked into the nearest bathroom and locked myself in a stall. My knees gave out. I sank to the floor and held my chest, trying to breathe.

This wasn't normal. None of this was normal.

That night, Tia mentioned therapy again. She did it gently, like she was walking barefoot across broken glass. "Dr. S said she's available Saturday morning. I can take you if you want."

I didn't say anything. "I know it's hard," she added. "But talking helps. Eventually." I nodded. Because that was easier than explaining how every word I wanted to say got strangled by guilt before it left my throat.

Saturday came. The therapy room smelled like peppermint and old books. It was quiet. Too quiet.

Dr. S sat across from me, her legs crossed, a notepad resting in her lap. She gave me space. Tried to draw me out with small questions and soft affirmations. But I sat stiffly on the couch, hands clenched, eyes on the floor.

"I want you to know you're safe here," she said gently. "Whatever you say, I will take seriously. And I will hold it carefully."

I wanted to believe her. I really did. But all I could think was, *If I say it… everything falls apart.*

I saw it play out in my head. Police reports. Investigations. Harmony crying. Tia's face collapsing. Darnell denying it. The house turning cold. And me—somewhere in the middle—hated by everyone and homeless.

So I sat there and said nothing.

Dr. S talked about emotional triggers. Deep breathing. Safe spaces. I nodded occasionally. But I didn't speak. I couldn't.

Before the session ended, she offered me a journal with a soft purple cover and said, "You know, Divinity, this can only help if you participate." I was silent. "If you can't talk yet, maybe try writing," she added. "Sometimes our hands speak before our mouths do."

"I already have a journal," I managed to say. "It doesn't make anything better."

Dr. S looked at me strangely, realizing I had said that while tears streamed down my face—tears I hadn't even known were falling.

"Is this still about your mother, Divinity?" she asked, reading my body language.

I stood. And walked out the door, ignoring the question—because the answer led to too many places. And she'd already picked up on one.

Back at home, I placed the journal in the drawer next to my bed. Untouched.

That night, I stayed up staring at the ceiling and letting the radio play low beside me—blank-faced and detached—until the DJ's voice melted into static and my thoughts blurred into noise.

Everything around me felt distant. Muted. Like I was living inside a bubble no one else could see.

Harmony came into my room without knocking. She flopped down on my bed and held up a photo from her phone—something someone sent her from AOL. Some boy had emailed her a picture. He wasn't cute at all, and she couldn't stop laughing.

I forced a laugh. It sounded thin. She smiled anyway. "There you are."

She didn't know I wasn't. Not really.

The following week, I stood outside Dr. S's office again. It was a warm morning, unusually still. The trees swayed gently. The sidewalk glistened from a light rain. The waiting room inside glowed through the glass like something out of another life.

I was early. Too early. Tia had offered to walk in with me, but I told her I needed a moment. She respected that.

Now I just stood there, frozen on the curb. Therapy wasn't scary because of the room. Or the therapist. Or the questions. It was scary because it made me feel. And feeling meant facing things I'd buried so deep I was scared they'd kill me if I brought them to the surface.

I stared at the door. People walked in and out. I stayed where I was.

I thought about telling the truth. I thought about my mother. I thought about what it would feel like to be free.

But shame still had its hands wrapped tight around my voice.

And once again, I turned around. I walked away from healing. And back toward silence.

That night, I lay in bed with the purple journal in my lap. I traced the embossed flowers on the cover with my fingertip. I opened it once. Wrote two words,

*Help me.*

Then I slammed it shut and shoved it under the bed.

The next Sunday, Tia gently knocked on my door before church. She cracked it open, peeking in with her usual softness. "Hey baby, we're getting ready for service. Wanna come with us today?"

I didn't even lift my head from the pillow. "I'm okay," I mumbled.

She stepped inside, sitting on the edge of the bed like she always did when she was trying not to push too hard. "I know your faith's been shaken. I get that. But sometimes being in God's house—around people who pray for you—it can bring a little peace."

I didn't respond.

She sat there quietly for a moment, then sighed and rubbed my shoulder. "Alright. We'll be back later this afternoon. Harmony and I both want to see you downstairs later, okay?"

I nodded, just to make her leave.

As soon as I heard the front door close, I sat up. There was no way I was staying in the house with him. Not today.

I didn't know where I was going, but I grabbed a black hoodie, laced up my sneakers, and slipped out the back before my fear could catch up with me.

I walked for what felt like hours. No music in my ears. No destination. Just silence. And cracked pavement. And the kind of wind that makes you feel like maybe the world is trying to push you forward—even when you don't want to move.

I ended up downtown, somewhere near the old overpass. I hadn't been here in years.

The sidewalks were lined with sleeping bags, cardboard shelters, old tents sagging with the weight of hopelessness. People were everywhere. Some looked through trash bins. Some sat quietly against the wall with blank eyes. A few were passed out on benches, their lives reduced to shadows most people tried not to see.

I even saw a group of teens—maybe not much older than me—huddled on a corner. One of them held a cardboard sign that read, *Anything helps. Please.*

I stopped. Watched them. Felt something rise in my chest I couldn't name.

This could be me. If I walked out and never came back. If I broke just a little more. If I didn't tell someone.

I didn't realize my feet had led me to Chris's street until I was sitting on the steps of his brownstone, hoodie pulled up, hands trembling in my lap.

It was early evening now. The sky was starting to bleed orange and lavender. I didn't knock. I just sat. Frozen. Waiting.

A few people walked by. A kid on a bike. Someone walking a dog. But I stayed.

Because today, I had almost disappeared. And if I didn't speak soon… I knew I would.

When Chris finally opened the door, he blinked, surprised. "Div?"

I didn't say anything. I just looked up at him with tired, swollen eyes and whispered:

"I have to tell you something."

## 8  NOT ANYMORE

*"He brought me out into a spacious place." – Psalm 18:19*

**Chris sat beside me on the steps, his body tense but still.**

His presence was quiet but solid, like an anchor dropped beside me in the middle of a storm. He didn't touch me. Didn't rush me. Just breathed beside me. And I hated how that made me want to cry.

For a second, I was back to a night two years ago. A different set of steps. A different storm. My mother had just died, and I had sat outside the hospital while it rained, thinking if I stared hard enough at the pavement, maybe the world would reverse itself. Back then, I didn't have anyone sitting next to me. Just the sound of my own breath and the way grief hollowed out every corner of my chest.

Now, I had someone beside me. And even though I couldn't tell him everything—couldn't bring the words out—I wasn't alone.

And that... that terrified me just as much as it comforted me. He didn't touch me. Didn't rush me. He just waited. And I hated how that made me want to cry.

"I didn't know where else to go," I said finally, my voice barely above a whisper.

He nodded slowly. "You don't have to explain. I'm glad you're here."

We sat in silence for a moment—the kind that feels both comforting and heavy. Then he looked at me. Really looked at me.

"Div... did something happen?"

I looked away.

"Something bad?"

His voice cracked on the word bad, and that nearly broke me.

I opened my mouth. Closed it. Opened it again.

"I—" My throat tightened.

He turned towards me. "You're scaring me. I've seen you break before, but this… this is different."

I could feel it bubbling up. The words. The truth. The scream behind my ribs.

I wiped at my face and whispered, "I just feel like I'm drowning, Chris."

He didn't interrupt.

"I feel like I'm falling apart, and no one sees it."

Still, he waited.

I glanced up at him, eyes full of everything I couldn't say.

He asked one more time. "Did something happen at home? Did something happen that night?"

My stomach dropped.

*Yes.* The word echoed in my mind. *Yes. Yes, yes, yes.*

But instead, I said, "I don't want to talk about it."

He nodded, but his jaw clenched. I knew he saw my change after that night.

"Okay," he said softly. "But when you're ready… I'm not going anywhere. I'm here for you."

I leaned into his shoulder. Just for a second.

Because even though I couldn't tell him… I needed to feel like someone was still there.

Maybe if Chris had pushed harder, I would've said something. Maybe if he looked me in the eyes and demanded to know what was wrong, it would've ripped the words right out of me.

But he didn't. He just let it be.

And I couldn't blame him. But a part of me wished someone— anyone—would just see it without me having to explain. Because explaining felt impossible. I sat there with Chris a little longer and my phone chimed. It was Tia.

I almost didn't answer. I clicked the green button.

"Yes ma'am?" I answered.

"Where are you? It's getting late." She sounded worried and a little angry at the same time.

"On my way home." It felt weird to even call that place home.

"Okay, do you need me to meet you?"

"No, I should be there in no more than ten minutes." I said and hung up.

I turned to Chris and thanked him for listening to me—even though I didn't say much that would help him understand what I was going through.

When I got back to the house, I crept in through the back door and tiptoed upstairs. I didn't want Harmony's questions. I didn't want Tia's soft concern. I didn't want anyone. I just wanted to disappear into my room and pretend none of it had happened.

But as I passed the cracked door to Tia's bedroom, I heard her voice—low, weary, and trembling.

She was praying.

I paused outside her door and listened, heart thudding in my chest.

"Lord, I don't know what's going on with that child," she whispered. "She's not the same. I see her slipping away, and I don't know how to catch her."

Silence.

A shaky breath.

"She doesn't trust me. And maybe I haven't done enough, maybe I missed something… but God, I love that girl like my own. You know that."

Another pause. The bed creaked.

"I don't need all the answers. I just need her to open up. Please—whatever it is, give her the strength to speak. And give me the strength to listen."

I backed away from the door, eyes stinging, throat tight. She had no idea. And that made it worse. Because she cared. And still—I couldn't say it.

I shut my door quietly and sank onto the floor. My journal sat in the corner where I'd kicked it earlier that week. The purple one. The "safe space."

I didn't touch it. I didn't move. I just sat there, numb, staring at the space beneath my bed like it held answers.

Tia's voice still echoed in my head: *"Give her the strength to speak…"*

I wanted to scream. To rip the silence from my throat and hand it to someone—anyone—just so they could carry it for a while.

But instead, I closed my eyes.

And a memory came.

*It was summer. I was maybe nine or ten.*

*I was sitting at the kitchen table, legs swinging, eating watermelon while my mother wiped down the counter. The news was on in the background—some story about a girl who had been hurt by someone close to her.*

*I remember asking, "Why didn't she tell?"*

*My mother paused.*

*She turned around, leaned on the counter, and said, "Sometimes when people are hurt, especially by someone they know, they're scared to tell. They think it's their fault. Or they think no one will believe them."*

*I scrunched my nose. "But that's not fair."*

*"No, it's not," she said. "But it happens. That's why you have to speak up, Divinity. Always. I don't care if it's a stranger or someone we know. If anyone ever hurts you— or makes you feel uncomfortable—you tell me. You hear me?"*

*I nodded slowly.*

*She knelt in front of me, her hands warm on my shoulders.*

*"I will believe you. I will protect you. Always."*

The memory faded. I was back in my room. But the echo of her voice lingered.

*"You tell me…"*

I wanted to believe someone else could be that safe place. But she was gone. And the world had changed since she left.

Later that night, I sat on my bed with a pen in hand and my mother's journal in my lap. My legs were crossed under me, the blanket tucked around my waist like armor. I stared at the page for a long time, the blank lines blurring with the weight of everything I couldn't say out loud. My hand trembled, the pen hovering above the paper like it was afraid too.

I could almost hear her voice—gentle, low, humming something soft in the kitchen while she cooked. If I listened hard enough, I could see her handwriting curl across the page before mine did.

*"It's okay, baby,"* I imagined her whispering. *"Say what you need to. I'm listening."*

I closed my eyes, swallowed hard, and started to write. The first word felt like tearing open a wound. The second, like letting it breathe.

My tears fell silently onto the page, and I didn't wipe them away. I just kept going. Because for once, I wasn't writing to survive—I was writing to be heard.

Then I went to the same journal she had written in before she died.

There were still blank pages at the end—pages I hadn't dared touch. Until now.

My hands trembled as I turned to a fresh page. And then, without thinking too hard, I started writing.

*Dear Mommy,*

*I don't even know where to start. Everything hurts. Not just my body—my heart, my mind, my spirit. I feel like I'm walking through the world covered in bruises no one can see.*

*There's something I haven't told anyone. Something bad happened. Someone hurt me. Someone who was supposed to be safe.*

*I can't write the details. I can't say it out loud. But I need you to know that I didn't let it happen. I didn't ask for it.*

*I froze. I fought. I thought about you. I thought about what you said when I was little... about always telling you if someone made me uncomfortable.*

*I wish you were here so I could tell you. But all I have is this page. And my silence. I'm trying. I promise. I just don't know how to say it.*

*Love,*

*Your baby girl*

I closed the journal and held it to my chest, rocking slightly like I used to when I was small and scared. But tonight, I wasn't just scared. I was tired. And something else started to grow inside me—quiet but fierce.

Before I went to bed, I got up and propped the old chair in front of my door. It was something I'd started doing again—wedging it at an angle so it would screech and tip over if someone tried to open it. Just in case.

And that night...

It saved me.

Around 3 a.m., I heard the doorknob turn softly. Then a slow push.

The chair scraped loudly across the hardwood floor and clattered to the ground.

My heart stopped.

Footsteps backed away.

Silence.

I sat frozen in bed, tears pooling in my eyes—but not from fear this time. From fury.

I was done playing the victim in my own house. I was done feeling helpless.

My chest rose and fell like waves crashing into something solid. He was still trying. Still pushing. Still believing he could take whatever he wanted from me.

My silence had made him feel protected—had made me a prisoner. And I hated him for it. I hated that he thought I would stay quiet forever.

The next morning, I didn't hide.

I got up early. Showered for the first time in days. I stood under the water until my skin flushed pink and the mirror fogged over. I moved slowly, deliberately—like I was peeling him off me, layer by layer.

I opened my dresser and stood there for a long time, staring at the clothes I'd been avoiding. I didn't reach for the hoodie. Or the baggy sweats. Not today.

Instead, I pulled on the fitted jeans my mom bought me the summer before she died. They hugged my legs. And I didn't care. I slipped on a white ribbed tank. Layered it with a cropped black jacket. Sleek ponytail. Silver hoops. Lip gloss with just enough shine.

Not for them. Not for him. For me.

Let him see me. Let him know he didn't kill me.

At breakfast, Harmony blinked when I walked in.

"You look... different," she said slowly.

"I feel different," I said, pouring juice.

Darnell looked up like he'd seen a ghost. Good. Let him feel unsafe for once.

Tia turned from the stove and paused. "Well, good morning, beautiful."

"Good morning," I said, sitting down.

She watched me for a long second, like she wanted to ask something. But instead, she smiled.

I ate. Not much. But enough.

After breakfast, I followed Tia into the laundry room, where she was sorting towels.

"Can I talk to you?" I asked quietly.

She looked up. "Of course, baby. What's on your mind?"

I hesitated, brushing the edge of the dryer.

"I just... need you to know I'm grateful."

Her brow knit, confused.

"I know I've been hard to be around. Distant. And maybe it's felt like you've been doing something wrong. Like you're failing me. But you're not."

"Div—"

"No. Let me say this."

I steadied myself.

"You stepped in when my world broke. You gave me a home. You loved me when I didn't know how to love myself. That's not failing.

93

That's everything. I just… wish I could give you the same."

Her eyes brimmed.

"Whatever you're going through, I'm here. When you're ready."

I nodded.

"I'm getting there."

That afternoon at school, people noticed. They didn't say it, but they looked. Whispers. Double takes. Chris stared across the courtyard like he didn't recognize me. I didn't smile. Didn't wave. But I didn't look away either. They didn't know who they were looking at. That made two of us.

Between classes, I walked differently. Head high. Back straight. No headphones. No distractions. I didn't avoid eye contact. I welcomed it. Because silence had taught me something: They didn't get to define me. He didn't get to decide how I moved through the world.

Chris caught up with me in the hallway. He looked unsure—like he didn't know whether to hug me or back off.

"Hey," he said. "You okay today?"

I looked at him. Something in my face made him pause.

"I'm better than I was," I said.

He searched my eyes. But I didn't give him softness. Not today.

"Alright," he said. "Well… I'm here."

"I know."

And I kept walking.

I didn't mean to be cold. But I couldn't afford to be vulnerable.

Not yet.

When I got home, I didn't go to bed. I stood just inside the door for a long moment, staring at the shadows cast across the living room floor. My hand still clutched the strap of my backpack like it was holding me together. I could hear faint music from Harmony's room, the clink of dishes in the kitchen, and my own pulse throbbing in my ears.

I wanted to go upstairs, shut my door, and forget the house existed. But something inside me—something new, raw, and rising—kept me rooted.

I was tired of feeling like a ghost in this space.

I walked to the kitchen slowly, each footstep measured. The overhead light hummed. I turned on the faucet and rinsed my glass, watching the water swirl away. The sound should've been nothing. But tonight, it felt like a warning. A countdown.

I sensed him before I saw him.

Darnell walked in like he always did—soft steps, lazy expression, that same false calm. But this time, I didn't shrink.

I turned. I looked right at him.

And I didn't blink.

His eyes met mine for a split second, and I saw it. The flicker. The shift. He didn't expect me to meet his gaze. He didn't expect... defiance.

He cleared his throat. "You, uh... need help with that?"

"No," I said simply. My voice didn't shake.

He nodded like that settled something, then backed out.

Tia's voice floated from the hallway. "Everything alright in there?"

"Yeah," I said, still watching the doorway.

I wiped my hands on a towel slowly, folded it with care, and walked away like I owned the space. Heart still throbbing.

Because tonight, I did.


Later, I lit a candle—jasmine and lavender. It smelled like calm. Like safety. I sat on my bed, journal in my lap—not the purple one. My mother's. I flipped to the page I wrote last night. The words stared back at me: *Someone hurt me. Someone who was supposed to be safe.*

I didn't cry.

This time, I wrote two more,

*Not anymore.*


That night, I dreamed I was sitting on the stoop of our old apartment building. The sun was low, painting the sky orange like fire behind smoke. The chipped concrete step felt warm under my legs, and the scent of jasmine mixed with fried onions drifted up from the bodega downstairs. A box fan buzzed from a window above. I was swinging my legs over the edge of the stoop like I used to when I was little, the rhythm calming in a way only dreams allow.

The door creaked behind me, and I turned.

She was there.

My mother.

Wearing that soft green house dress she always wore when she didn't plan on going anywhere. Her hair was wrapped. She held a yellow mug in both hands—her favorite chipped one that said *"Don't Talk to Me 'Til Coffee."* Her eyes were kind but serious, just like always.

She sat beside me, sipping from the mug, steam curling in the orange light. She didn't say anything at first. Just looked out at the street like she was waiting for something.

"Feels quiet," I whispered.

"It always gets quiet right before something shifts," she said softly.

A breeze tugged gently at the hem of her dress. Her hand found mine and squeezed.

"You've been holding too much, baby girl."

I looked down. My hands were small again. Child-sized. One knuckle still scraped from a bike fall I couldn't quite place.

"It's not your job to carry the blame for other people's sins," she said. "You don't have to stay quiet to keep others comfortable."

I bit my lip. "But if I say it... won't that make it real?"

"It's already real," she said. "Speaking it won't make it worse. It just frees you from holding it alone."

I turned to her, tears stinging. "I'm scared."

"I know," she said, brushing my hair behind my ear. "But fear can't live where truth breathes."

I rested my head on her shoulder, the fabric of her dress soft and warm.

"I don't know how to speak it."

"You will," she said. "When you're ready, the words will find you. Just don't bury yourself waiting for the perfect moment."

She turned to kiss the top of my head, her lips feather-light. She stood, the mug still in her hand, and walked back toward the doorway, light spilling around her like a frame.

I opened my mouth to call out to her—to beg her to stay—but before I could speak, she was gone.

I woke with tears already falling, soaked into my pillow. The dream clung to me like perfume. I couldn't shake it. I didn't want to. But it stayed with me, warm and present.

Later that night, I found Harmony sitting on the couch in a blanket, flipping through TV channels.

"Hey," I said, surprising even myself.
She turned, startled, then softened when she saw me. "Hey."

I sat beside her. We didn't say much. Just watched some rerun neither of us cared about.

After a few minutes, she leaned over and started braiding my hair, like she used to when we were little. No questions. No tension. Just the quiet rustle of her fingers through my curls.

I closed my eyes and let her. For once, I didn't pull away. I didn't tell her about the dream. I didn't tell her about the journal or what almost happened last night. But I let her braid my hair.

And for once, I let her care for me—not as the girl I used to be, but the one I was becoming.

# 9  THE COST OF QUIET

*"Silence gave me bruises too. Just not the kind you could see." – Divinity*

It had been about a week now, and I didn't wake up angry. Not exactly. But something inside me was tight—coiled, waiting. Like my body was holding a scream I didn't remember swallowing.

I got dressed the same way I had for the past few days—sharp, clean, put together. Tight black jeans. Fitted burgundy long-sleeve. Black boots. Hair slicked back into a low ponytail. I lined my lips. Glossed them with a calm I didn't feel. Looked in the mirror. Nodded once.

This was the new me.

And I was tired of playing nice.

At school, the air felt different. Every sound hit too hard. Every hallway was a minefield. Every face looked like it was hiding something. In homeroom, I sat dead center, tapping my pen against the desk like a clock about to detonate. My leg wouldn't stop bouncing.

That's when it happened.

Some girl, two rows over. Loud enough for her friends, soft enough to pretend it wasn't for me.

"I don't know why she walks around like she's better than everyone now. Like dressing up erases whatever's wrong with her."

Snap.

The pen cracked in my hand, ink spilling like blood across the worksheet. Thick. Sudden. Ugly. I stared at it.

Breathed in.

Out.

My chest burned.

Another girl giggled. "I heard she's been passed around. She probably thinks if she looks expensive, people will forget."

I don't remember standing.

I don't remember walking. All I remember is her face when I slammed my hands on her desk.

"You wanna say something?" I said, voice low and trembling like a lit fuse.

She blinked. "Excuse me?"

"Don't act confused now." My eyes didn't move. "You wanna talk? Talk to me. Say it to my face."

The whole room went still. The teacher started moving fast. "Divinity—sit down. Right now." But I couldn't. Because it wasn't just about her. It was about all of it.

About my mother being gone.

About the nights I cried so hard I stopped making sound.

About Darnell.

About silence.

About God.

I didn't hit her. But I wanted to. And that scared me more than anything. So I backed away—hands shaking, chest rising too fast, vision going grey at the edges.

"I need to go," I muttered, pushing past the teacher.

"Divinity!" she shouted. "Office. Now."

I didn't go to the office. I went outside. I sat on the curb near the gym, elbows on knees, trying to breathe without falling apart. Eventually, I heard the double doors hiss open. I didn't look.

"Hey."

It was Harmony.

I hadn't seen her all day—not in homeroom, not in the hall. But here she was. Hoodie zipped halfway, phone clutched like a shield.

"I heard what happened," she said, voice quieter than usual. "They said you blacked out and tried to fight somebody."

I didn't answer.

She kicked a pebble with her shoe. "You okay?"

I wiped my hand on my jeans, stared at the parking lot. "I didn't touch her."

"I know."

"They don't believe that, though."

"I do."

Something in her voice made me look up. Harmony didn't smile. Didn't joke. She just stood there, not moving closer, not backing away either. Like she knew I needed space but wasn't going to pretend this was normal.

"You want me to get someone?" she asked. "My mother?"

I shook my head.

"You want me to sit?"

Another shake.

"Okay," she said softly. "I'll be right inside. If you need me."

And she was gone.

But not really.

Security found me fifteen minutes later, crouched by the gym doors like a kid lost at a bus stop. They didn't yell. Just stood near, arms folded, walkie-talkies buzzing low. One of them said my name like it was fragile. "Divinity? Come on, now."

I didn't argue.

Didn't speak.

Just followed.

They put me in a small room with no windows and beige walls that looked like they'd been painted over too many times. The kind of place meant to be quiet. Empty. A staffer brought a paper towel for my ink-stained hand. I didn't use it.

Through the door, I heard murmured voices—tight and clinical

"She's been withdrawn, but this is the first outburst..."

"She's not violent—just overwhelmed."

"Maybe she needs time off."

Words like case file, wellness referral, home instability floated through the cracks in the wood. They didn't call my father. They called Tia.

Thirty minutes passed. Then the door opened, and there she was—purse still on her shoulder, keys dangling from one hand, worry carved into every line of her face. She sat beside me, quiet at first.

Then, "Want to tell me what happened?"

I shrugged. "Nothing."

Her jaw worked. "Baby, the school says you almost fought another student."

I didn't deny it. Didn't explain. Because what I really wanted to say was, I almost did. And not because of her. Not really. But because I'm not okay. Because I'm breaking.

Tia leaned back, arms crossed. "I know something's wrong, Divinity. I've known for weeks. I know you don't want to talk about it. But this isn't you."

"How would you know?" I said, too fast, too loud.

Her face dropped, just a little.

"You didn't know me before my mom died," I said, pushing the

100

words like they might cut deep enough to end the conversation. "You didn't know who I was supposed to be. So maybe this is me now. Maybe this is just who I am."

She didn't snap back. She didn't argue. She just looked away and said, barely above a whisper, "I didn't say that to hurt you."

The silence that followed wasn't empty. It was loaded. Like something unsaid had just shifted the room. She didn't speak again until we got in the car. She didn't yell. She didn't ask questions. But she didn't soften either.

The engine hummed low as we pulled out of the school parking lot. I stared out the window, bracing for silence.

But her voice came—low. Firm.

"You're not the only one grieving, Divinity."

I blinked.

"Losing your mama broke me too," she said, hands on the wheel, eyes forward. "I've been giving you space because I thought that's what you needed. But I see now I've been doing you a disservice."

I stayed quiet.

"I wouldn't let Harmony skip school or lock herself in her room for days. I wouldn't let her talk to me sideways or lie to my face."

The air in the car thickened.

"But I've been letting you. And that's on me."

My throat tightened. I stared harder at the window like it could open into some other version of my life.

"When your daddy let me to take you in, I was happy because I love you. Because your mama was my sister. But I'm not your roommate, baby. I'm not just the woman keeping the lights on."

Her voice trembled—but she didn't stop.

"I'm the parent in this house. And it's time I start acting like it."

I didn't know how to respond. Part of me felt angry. Another part... relieved. Like maybe someone was finally strong enough to see the mess I'd been trying to hide.

When we got home, she didn't send me to my room. She didn't storm off. She just said, calm and steady, "No phone. No TV. No leaving the house this week."

I opened my mouth. She cut me off.

"You'll be writing a letter to the school. You don't want to talk to me? Fine. But you will be talking to Dr. S."

I expected to feel punished. But I didn't.

I felt... seen.

That night, after the dishes were done and the house fell into its usual hush, I sat on my bed cross-legged, picking at the hem of my sleeve like it might come undone in my hands.

The silence wasn't hostile.

It just... was.

Then a knock. Soft. Followed by the door creaking open before I could answer. Harmony stepped inside wearing a hoodie big enough to drown her and plaid pajama pants that dragged the floor. Her bonnet was lopsided, like she'd put it on in a hurry. Or didn't care.

"You okay?" she asked, leaning against the doorframe.

I nodded. "Yeah."

She didn't buy it.

But she didn't say so.

Instead, she stepped in further, arms crossed. "You got in trouble today."

"Guess so."

She didn't laugh. Didn't tease. Just watched me.

Then, "She gave you the speech, huh?"

I shrugged.

"She used to give it to me, too. Mostly when I did stupid stuff. Talking back. Cutting class. Being smart in the wrong tone."

I smirked, just a little. "You?"

"Please." She rolled her eyes. "I practically had a seat saved in detention my freshman year."

I looked up, surprised. "You?"

She smiled faintly. "I wasn't always the well-behaved sister with matching socks and perfect hair, okay?"

I didn't say anything.

Harmony sighed and dropped onto the floor beside my bed, legs stretched, head resting against the wall.

"She was strict with me," she said after a moment. "Always has been. That's how I knew she was scared when it came to you."

I glanced over.

"She tiptoed around you, Div. For months. We all saw it."

Her voice wasn't judgmental. Just honest.

"And I get it," she said. "You were going through it. Still are. But..."

She trailed off, fingers fidgeting with a loose string on her sleeve.

"You're not the only one hurting."

That part hit harder than I expected.

"I know," I whispered.

Harmony tilted her head back, staring at the ceiling. "You ain't gotta be perfect. But you don't gotta disappear either. You scared the crap outta me, the way you checked out after the funeral. Then Darnell came home and..."

She didn't finish that sentence.

But I knew.

The air in the room felt thinner.

She picked at the string again. "You started changing. And I didn't know how to reach you without breaking something."

"You didn't make it worse," I said, voice barely audible.

She gave a sad smile. "I didn't make it better either."

A long silence passed between us.

But this time, it didn't feel awkward. It felt earned.

"I'm not mad at you," I said, quieter now. "I never was."

Harmony nodded slowly. "I just want you back. Even if it's a different version."

That line cracked something in me.

Because I didn't know who that version was yet.

But maybe I didn't have to figure it out alone.

She stood, brushing off her sweatpants. "You still mad I came in here?"

I shook my head.

"Good," she said, walking to the door. "Because I'm not gonna stop. Not this time."

She left it open behind her.

And somehow, that felt like an invitation instead of an oversight.


Later that night, thirst pulled me out of bed.

Normally, I kept water in the room, but I was out. I didn't want to go downstairs—it was late, and something about the dark kitchen made my stomach twist.

But I went anyway.

The hallway creaked beneath me. A draft licked my ankles. Every sound felt louder than it should. I stepped into the kitchen and froze.

He was there.

Darnell.

Coming in from the back, chewing something with the wrapper still in hand. Tossed it into the trash like this was just any night.

Like nothing had ever happened.

Our eyes met.

He smiled. That same practiced, polished smile that used to fool me.

"Rough day?" he asked, like he was trying to sound concerned. Like he had the right.

I didn't answer.

He took a step closer. His voice lowered. "You know... you can talk to me."

That was it. That was the line. My skin crawled. My throat tightened. My blood burned. The chair behind me scraped loud across the tile as I stood.

"Don't talk to me!" I said. My voice didn't shake.

It cut.

His eyes narrowed. "What's your problem?"

"You."

The word landed like a slap. Cold. Final.

I stepped forward.

"Don't come near me. Don't speak to me. Don't even look at me."

He didn't move.

But something in his face changed. Just for a second. Like the mask slipped. I didn't flinch. Not this time.

I turned and stormed upstairs, slamming my door hard enough to rattle the frame.

My whole body shook. He had tried to comfort me. Like he hadn't stolen something from me in the dark. Like he hadn't broken me. I didn't scream. I packed. Grabbed my backpack, stuffed in a hoodie, a pair of jeans, a few bills I'd been hiding in a sock drawer. Lip balm. Charger. My journal.

Then I opened the window, climbed down the fire escape, and ran.

No plan.

Only an exit.


The train station on Jefferson was mostly empty that time of night. The vending machines buzzed like dying insects. Fluorescent lights flickered overhead, casting shadows that didn't always match the shapes that made them. I sat on a bench near the end. An old woman with plastic shopping bags dozed beside me. A man two benches down snored under his coat.

I folded my arms. Pulled my hood up. Sat in silence. Cold crept into my sleeves. My fingers stiffened. My jaw ached from clenching.

The silence wasn't peaceful.

It was punishing.

My stomach growled. My thighs itched from sitting too long. A part of me kept flinching at every cough, every scuffed footstep.

I didn't feel free.

I felt hunted.

An hour passed.

Maybe more.

No voice from heaven. No rescue. No big flashing sign telling me You Did the Right Thing. Just the slow, heavy realization No one was coming to save me. If I wanted peace, I'd have to make it myself.

I stood—legs aching, back sore—and walked.

Not far. Not brave.

Just away.

Back the way I came.

When I got home, it was after midnight. The stoop was dark, slick with dew. The house looked asleep—like nothing inside had shifted. But the stove light in the kitchen still glowed faint and warm. Tia was at the table, phone clenched in both hands. Her eyes were red, swollen. Her face looked like it had been held together by prayer and panic.

When she saw me, she shot to her feet.

"Jesus... baby, where were you?" she whispered, voice raw. "I've been calling—I didn't know what to think. Are you okay?"

I nodded. "Just needed air."

She stepped forward like she wanted to hug me—but stopped short. Her eyes searched mine.

"I'm sorry I scared you," I said softly.

Tia nodded slowly, a tear slipping down her cheek. "I was terrified you were gone for good."

I managed a small smile. Honest. Apologetic.

"Not yet."

She exhaled.

Long. Heavy.

Then wiped her face, squared her shoulders, and said, voice steady again.

"I'm glad you're safe."

A pause.

"But just so we're clear—your punishment still stands."

I blinked, surprised.

She raised an eyebrow. "Don't mistake relief for forgetting."

There it was. Not just the aunt.

The parent.

"Yes ma'am," I said.

She nodded once. "We'll talk tomorrow."

And with that, she turned and went upstairs, her steps slow, but certain.

That night, I didn't even bother changing clothes. I sat on my bed in the dark, hoodie still on, shoes kicked off but unlaced, arms wrapped tight around my knees like they might hold everything in.

My backpack leaned against the wall. Still packed. Still waiting. I didn't unpack. Didn't move.

The silence wasn't heavy tonight. It was... honest. And in it, I whispered to myself, "I can't stay here forever." Because even if I told the truth... Even if Tia believed me... Even if Harmony didn't hate me... The damage would still be done. This house would never be a home again. That friendship would never be simple again.

And me?

I'd never be the same.

I thought about the teens I'd seen under the Jefferson overpass last year. Blankets bundled around their ankles. Cardboard signs scrawled in Sharpie. Blank stares. Hollow laughs. That could've been me. In some ways, it already was. I didn't have a sign or a corner. But I had the same hunger—for peace, for safety, for silence that didn't cost me everything.

I laid back on the bed, staring at the ceiling. Sleep came eventually. But not gently.

In the dream, I was in my old bedroom. The one from when Mom was still alive.

The window was open. Morning light poured in like honey. Gospel music hummed down the hallway.

"Blessed assurance... Jesus is mine..."

I stepped into the doorway. "Mama?"

No answer.

I walked through the house.

Room to room.

Empty.

The humming changed. Slowed. Shifted into something colder. Deeper.

I turned a corner and saw him.

Darnell.

Standing in the kitchen.

Hands behind his back. Smile sharp and wrong.

"No one's coming, Divinity," he said. His voice was too loud, like it belonged to the walls. "You never told. You never will."

I turned to run.

Tried to scream.

But the door wouldn't open.

And my voice—gone.

Then—

A hand on my shoulder.

Soft.

Familiar.

I turned.

And there she was.

My mother.

Her eyes glowed. Her face was soft. Sad.

She leaned in close, brushed my cheek with her fingers, and whispered, "You can speak now, baby."

Everything went black.

I sat up in bed, breath caught in my throat, chest rising too fast. I wasn't crying. Not this time. I wiped my face anyway. And then I whispered back,

"I will."

I didn't know who I was talking to.

Her.

God.

Myself.

Maybe all three.

But I knew one thing for sure, the silence was ending. Not tonight. But soon. And when it did, I'd need more than courage. I'd need a way out.

I got out of bed and pulled my journal from under the mattress.

Flipped past the poems, the prayers, the pages blacked out in ink.

And opened to a blank spread.

I drew two columns,

**IF I STAY**

- Everyone will know
- Harmony might hate me
- Tia will be devastated

- Darnell will lie
- I'll never feel safe here again

**IF I LEAVE**
- Where will I go?
- No money
- Alone
- But free

I stared at the words like they were coordinates on a burning map.
Silence had a price.
So did freedom.
But only one could save me.
I turned to a clean page and wrote,

**MY WAY OUT**
- Ask Chris if he knows anyone who rents rooms
- Look into youth housing programs
- Check the library for job boards
- Keep a go-bag ready
- Save what little I can

Every line was a seed.
Every step, a thread pulling me toward something brighter.
I didn't know when.
I didn't know how.
But I knew this, I would tell.
And when I did.
I wouldn't just break the silence—
I'd walk out of it.
On my own two feet.

## 10  THE FIRST SPARK

*"Your word is a lamp to my feet, a light on my path." – Psalm 119:105*

**Seven months had passed.**
And things were no better.
They couldn't be.
Darnell still hovered—too close, too often, with that same casual threat behind his every gesture. He didn't need to say anything anymore. A brush of his hand, a glance that lingered too long—it was enough to remind me, *Say something, and I'll twist it. I'll make you wish you hadn't.*
So I stayed quiet. But I didn't stay still. Because my escape plan didn't start today. It started seven months ago, the night I packed my bag, the night I wrote the words I couldn't say aloud. Since then, I'd learned how to live two lives.
The one they saw.
And the one I planned, in silence.

That morning, I got up like I always did. The alarm buzzed once. I didn't hit snooze. I moved automatically—shower, teeth, lotion, bun slicked so tight it might've been carved from glass. I didn't look at my face until the very end.
The mirror fogged slightly from the steam. I wiped it with the edge of a towel and stared at myself—really stared. Dark eyes, sharper than they used to be. Mouth lined with steady precision. I pressed my lips together like punctuation.
One breath in.
One out.
Then I said it, like I did every morning,
*"Be invisible. Be prepared."*
Sometimes I added, *"Make him think you're okay. Make them believe you're free."*

Today, I didn't need to. I knew the script by heart. I dressed with the same math I'd been using since March—layers, long sleeves, nothing clingy. Everything chosen to hide the body I was slowly reclaiming inch by inch.

My backpack was already packed. Not the go-bag—that stayed hidden. Just books, a sandwich, backup deodorant, and lip gloss with no shine.

I left my room quietly, slipping past Harmony's closed door. She still snored lightly in the mornings. One time, months ago, she asked if I ever slept anymore. I told her I had insomnia.

That wasn't a lie.

I just didn't tell her why.

Outside, the June heat clung to the streets like memory. By 7:20 a.m., Boys and Girls High was already sweating. The air smelled like burned asphalt, overripe fruit from the corner bodega, and the desperate sweetness of cheap perfume.

Inside, it was no better.

The hallways buzzed with end-of-year chaos. Final tests. Loose rules. Countdowns. Graduation banners curled off the walls in waves, corners barely taped down. Students posed with filtered grins and matching T-shirts. They talked about dorm rooms and summer trips and what freedom was supposed to taste like.

I moved through them like fog.

Seen.

But never held.

My locker was pristine. Not because I was neat, but because I had nothing worth leaving behind. No decorations. No mirror. No photos. Just books. A backup sweatshirt. A pack of gum no one else had touched.

Once, a girl asked me what I was doing after graduation. I said, "Taking a breath. Wasn't my graduation."

She laughed.

I didn't.

The building didn't feel like school anymore. It felt like a place I passed through on my way to elsewhere. Like a layover between survival and something else I hadn't named yet.

People whispered less now. They'd stopped caring. The outburst in November? Old news. The fire that followed me for weeks had burned out. Now I was just quiet.

And people didn't mind quiet, as long as you didn't make noise with it. I had become an expert in quiet. An artist. I didn't disappear. I just stayed out of the way.

I stopped laughing loudly. I changed how I walked—no bounce, no swing in my arms. I watched how my classmates moved and copied the parts that looked normal. Normal was protection. Normal kept people from asking questions they didn't want real answers to.

My go-bag waited in the back of my closet, folded behind old jackets and boxes marked "summer." Four clean outfits, rolled tight. Travel-size toiletries. Socks wrapped around a wad of bills—$225, scraped together from returned birthday gifts, skipped cafeteria meals, and Harmony's forgotten Visa gift card.

And the journals. Both of them.

They held everything I never said. Memories. Lists. Letters to God. Letters to ghosts. Letters to myself. Sometimes I dreamed about throwing it into the East River, the purple one. But I never would. It was the only thing that knew the full story.

Between second and third period, someone brushed against me in the hallway. Too close. Too fast. A hand grazed the small of my back—right above the waistband of my jeans. I froze. Everything went silent, like my brain hit mute. My hands tightened around my books. My breath caught.

I blinked. Once. Twice. Kept walking. That's what survival looked like.

Pause.

Pretend.

Repeat.

But someone saw.

Ms. Eden. My history teacher. The quiet one. The one who wore soft sweaters in muted colors and let you retake quizzes without making it feel like failure. She didn't lecture. She didn't push. She just... noticed things.

And that day? She noticed me. She didn't say anything in the moment. But the next day, after class, when the bell had rung and the noise had cleared, she said, "Divinity? Can I talk to you for a second?"

I paused at the door.

"It's not about grades," Ms. Eden said, as if reading my hesitation. "Just a minute."

She didn't say it like a command. She said it like an offer.

I stepped inside.

Her office was small, tucked behind the classroom like a forgotten room in a big old house. The blinds were half-drawn. Dust danced in the beam of sunlight cutting across the floor. A tall plant slouched in the corner, its leaves begging for water. On the shelf, books with cracked spines, a lava lamp that hadn't been turned on since the '80s, a snow globe that said "Cleveland."

She didn't sit behind her desk.

She leaned on the edge of it, arms folded loosely across a soft olive sweater.

"I've been teaching a long time," she said, voice low but sure. "And I've learned to tell the difference between kids who are just tired… and kids who are surviving something."

My pulse picked up.

She didn't accuse. She observed.

"You don't have to explain," she said. "But I see you."

She paused, just long enough for the words to sink in.

"You flinch when people get too close. You walk like you're bracing for something. You haven't raised your hand in class in months, and when you smile, it doesn't touch your eyes anymore."

I stared at the floor.

A scuff mark near the baseboard looked like a crooked smile.

"I've read essays where your voice used to shine," she continued. "Now it sounds like you're hiding inside your own sentences."

My throat tightened.

"You've gotten in trouble a few times this year," she added. "But I don't think it's because you're a problem. I think it's because you're in pain."

That was the first sentence that felt like it came with a door.

A way out.

I didn't open it.

But I stepped closer.

"I just want you to know," she said, "you don't have to carry it alone. Whatever it is."

I didn't speak. I stood there just listening.

She waited.

Not with pressure—but with patience.

"My sister didn't tell anyone for three years," she said. "Not her friends. Not my parents. Not even me."

I looked up, startled.

Ms. Eden smiled gently. "She got really good at hiding. Straight-A's. Clean room. Always polite. People thought she had it all together. But she didn't."

She sat down across from me—not behind the desk, not across a table. Just beside me. Eye level. Still.

"She told me the truth on a Tuesday," she said, voice thinning around the memory. "I was home from college. She just blurted it out. And for five whole seconds, I didn't believe her." She looked away.

"I hate those five seconds."

Silence.

She let it breathe.

"After that," she said, "I believed her with everything I had. I haven't stopped."

Her gaze returned to mine.

"I just want you to know that if you ever say something—if you ever need to say something—I will not waste those five seconds."

She looked down. Her voice gentled even more.

"I'll believe you."

My stomach twisted. My tongue felt heavy. I opened my mouth. Closed it. I wanted to say something. Anything. But there were no words that wouldn't collapse if I touched them.

Ms. Eden didn't ask again. Didn't push. She just sat there. Present. Still. Waiting, but not expecting. Like she knew the hardest part wasn't telling. It was deciding if you were worth being heard.

"Was she okay?" I asked, finally. "Your sister."

A small smile tugged at her mouth. "She's alive. She has her own bakery now. Makes a terrible red velvet but the best apple pie I've ever had."

My lips twitched, almost a smile.

"She's okay now," Ms. Eden said. "But it took time. And help. And people who didn't flinch."

The bell rang faintly in the hall—another class change.

Ms. Eden glanced at the door, then back at me.

"Whenever you're ready," she said. "Or even if you're not. I'm here."

She paused.

"I'll believe you."

That hit harder than anything else.

Not I'm here for you. Not you're not alone.

I'll believe you.

No one had said that to me since my mom.

And even then, not in those words.

She stood. Walked past me. Didn't touch me. Just opened the door and left it wide behind her.

I sat there for a moment longer, knees tight together, hands folded so tight my knuckles hurt.

Then I stood.

And followed the light back into the hallway.

That evening, I sat on my bed with the purple journal in my lap. Not the one my mother got me. The one from Dr. S. The corners were soft from being opened and closed too often. The elastic band was stretched thin. Some pages curled with the memory of sweat, or tears, or both.

I hadn't written in days. Maybe weeks. Planning my escape had taken up too much space in my head. Mapping out logistics, hiding cash, double-checking the fire escape. Memorizing the exits in every building I entered. Counting how many paces from the front door to the closest bus stop.

The journal had become less a place to feel, and more a place to store blueprints.

But tonight felt different.

Not safe.

Just... quieter.

Ms. Eden's voice was still in my ears like a background hum I couldn't shut off.

*I'll believe you.*

It wasn't a dramatic promise. It wasn't said like a vow. But it landed deeper than anything loud could have. No one had told me that—not in those exact words. People always said I'm here for you. Talk to me. You're not alone. But "*I'll believe you*"? That was something else. That was trust before proof.

Love without conditions.

It reminded me of how my mom used to say I know what you're not saying when I came home quiet. How she'd make hot cocoa without asking and sit beside me until I cracked.

I turned to a blank page and pressed the pen down fast—before I could stop myself.

No date. No title. Just this,

*I'm not ready to say it. But I think I'm getting close.*
*Someone saw me today.*
*Not just the clothes or the silence or the fake smile.*
*They saw underneath.*
*And they didn't look away.*

*That scared me.*
*But it also made me feel like maybe I could keep going.*

I paused.
My hand trembled slightly.
I added,

*I've gotten so good at pretending I'm fine that sometimes I forget I'm not. Today*
*reminded me. I don't have to disappear to survive.*
*Maybe I just need the right witness.*
The ink pooled slightly at the bottom of that last word.
*Witness.*

I set the pen down and leaned back, the journal still open across my
lap. The room was dim except for the streetlight leaking through the
blinds, casting slatted shadows across the wall.

Outside, someone argued half a block away. A car rolled by with the
bass too loud. Somewhere, a baby cried. Life, as always, kept happening
without permission. But inside this room? For the first time in weeks, I
didn't feel like I was sprinting.

I was just sitting.
Breathing.

I closed the journal and slid it beneath the bed, tucking it next to my
shoes like a secret I might still need to carry a little longer.

My eyes moved to the closet—where the duffel bag waited. I thought
about unzipping it. Thought about packing one more pair of socks.
Instead, I lay back on the bed, arms crossed under my head.

I didn't fall asleep right away, I stayed up. But I didn't cry. Didn't
count the hours until morning. Didn't imagine the floor caving in
beneath me.

I just breathed. And for the first time in a long time…
That felt like enough.

A soft knock took me out of my thoughts. Then the door creaked
open before I could answer.

Harmony stepped in with a sleeve of peanut butter crackers and a cold
can of Sprite. She wore her bonnet and an oversized hoodie that fell past
her thighs—probably one she'd stolen from me years ago and claimed as
her own.

"Peace offering," she said, holding up the snacks like a truce flag. Her
tone was light, but her eyes scanned me the way they had been lately—

careful, like I might vanish if she looked too hard.

I nodded toward the edge of the bed. She sat without asking again. For a few minutes, we ate in silence. The crackers crunched softly between us. The can hissed open. We watched the ceiling fan rotate in slow, lazy loops.

Then Harmony stood and stretched, arms above her head. "You still got my hoodie, huh?" she said, walking to the closet.

"It's mine now," I murmured, mouth full of cracker.

She smirked. "You keep saying that like it's legally binding."

She opened the closet, rummaging with one hand. But then—she paused. Her hand fell on the duffel bag. Small. Gray. Meant to be invisible. But not anymore.

"What's this?" she asked, already crouching.

"Wait—" I sat up, too fast.

But she was already unzipping it.

And then she saw it.

The clothes, rolled and stacked with quiet precision. The toiletries bag. The wrapped cash. And finally—the purple journal. Her fingers brushed over the worn cover.

She didn't speak.

She opened it.

Just a few pages.

A few lines.

Her eyes moved fast. Too fast. Like she already knew what she would find but was hoping to be wrong. Then her breath caught. She stepped back.

"Oh my God," she whispered. "Oh my God…"

She hugged the journal to her chest like it might shatter if she let it go.

I stood, but I didn't move closer.

"Harmony…"

She didn't answer. She wasn't looking at me. She was looking through me. Like she was watching every moment she'd ignored flicker back into view.

A memory flicked on inside her.

*A Saturday in April. Darnell had walked past Divinity in the living room. His hand brushed her shoulder—too slow. Too casual.*

*Divinity flinched, barely. But Harmony saw it.*

*She had told herself it was stress. That Divinity was still adjusting.*

116

*She remembered another night—Divinity didn't come downstairs for dinner. Harmony left a plate outside the door and whispered, "You okay?"*

*No answer.*

*She thought, bad day. Leave her alone.*

But now?

Now, standing in this room with this bag, with this journal in her hands?

It was like watching a magic trick in reverse.

Every small moment she had buried came flooding back.

"You've been holding this in... alone?" she asked.

My voice cracked. "I didn't know how."

Harmony's hands shook. She placed the journal down on the bed like it was made of glass.

"You could've told me, "She said. Her voice was soft but broken. "I wouldn't have fixed it. I know that. But I would've been here."

"I was scared," I whispered. "Scared you'd look at me different."

She crossed the room and sat beside me.

"I do look at you different," she said.

My chest tightened.

"I look at you like you're stronger than anyone I know."

And just like that, I broke.

The tears came before I could stop them.

She pulled me into a hug. Tight. Real. Unflinching.

"I'm sorry," I said. "I didn't mean to keep it from you. I just... I didn't want to destroy everything."

"You didn't destroy anything," she whispered into my shoulder. "He did."

We stayed there, tangled in silence.

For the first time in months, I let myself be held. Harmony didn't let go. Not when I cried so hard I couldn't breathe. Not when I buried my face in her hoodie and soaked it through with guilt and grief.

She held on like she'd been waiting months to do it.

And maybe she had.

"I kept telling myself you'd be okay," she whispered. "That you just needed time."

I didn't answer. I couldn't. My throat was tight, my chest hollow.

"I saw the changes," she said. "I saw how you flinched when people touched you. How you stopped coming out of your room. How you started sleeping in hoodies again—even when it was hot."

She pulled back just enough to look at me.

"I saw it, Div. I just didn't want to know."

That line cracked something deeper.

Not because it was cruel.

But because it was true.

"I didn't want to believe someone could hurt you like that," Harmony continued.

Her jaw clenched, and for a moment she looked like she wanted to scream.

But she didn't.

She stayed still, focused on me.

"I didn't want to lose the version of our life I thought was still real."

I nodded slowly, tears running unchecked. "Me too."

She pulled me back into the hug.

"I would've helped you pack," she said, barely audible. "I would've stood at the front door with you and waited if that's what you needed."

I closed my eyes.

"I was going to leave without telling anyone," I admitted. "Just... disappear."

"I know," she said.

"I thought it would be easier."

"It's not."

"No," I said. "It's not."

We sat like that until my tears ran dry. Until my breathing slowed. Until the panic faded into something quieter. Something I could survive.

She eventually let go—but gently. Like putting down something sacred. "I want you to tell," she said, voice low.

"I know."

"Not just to me. To someone who can actually stop him."

My stomach turned because she didn't realize she was talking about her brother.

Harmony saw it.

"You don't have to do it alone," she said quickly. "I'll go with you. Or... I'll wait outside. Whatever you need."

I nodded, but the fear was still there. So was the shame. And the ache. But also... her. And for the first time, that felt like enough. She stayed in my room for hours. She didn't ask more questions. Didn't press for details.

She just made space.

Every time I looked at her, she was still there. And that, more than anything, helped me breathe.

Chris had been showing up early for weeks now.

Leaning against the chain-link fence just outside the school gate, hoodie sleeves tugged down over his hands, backpack slung low on one shoulder, eyes sweeping the crowd like he was waiting on trouble.

Or for me.

But the truth was—he was watching everything.

Especially Darnell.

He didn't know why at first.

Didn't know why he couldn't look away when Darnell pulled up at the curb, always with the same casual lean, the same too-wide grin, window rolled halfway down like he was somebody's cool uncle.

Except he wasn't.

Not to Chris. And definitely not to me. It was the way I moved around him. That's what made it click. I didn't walk the same near Darnell. Didn't stand the same. I folded in. Tensed up. Looked smaller. Chris had seen that body language before.

Different girls.

Different stories.

But the same shape.

A kind of quiet that sat under the skin like static. A kind of silence that meant danger was too close to speak about.

He remembered the day I showed up on his stoop in March. Hollow-eyed. Shaking. He hadn't pushed. Hadn't asked. He thought he was being respectful.

But now?

He wasn't sure if that silence had protected me or kept me locked in something I didn't know how to escape.

That afternoon, Darnell pulled up just like always.

Same car.

Same song bumping low through the speakers.

Same voice calling out like we were all in some feel-good sitcom.

"You all ready?" he asked, grinning.

Harmony waved. "We'll be right there!"

Chris watched me freeze. Just for a second. It was subtle. Most people wouldn't have caught it.

But he did.

I didn't walk forward. Didn't answer. I just stood there—arms crossed, back too straight.

"I'm not getting in his car," I muttered.

Harmony blinked. "What?"

"I'll walk."

"But it's hot—"

"I said I'll walk."

My voice didn't rise.

But it cut.

Chris crossed the street quickly and fell in beside me.

"You good?" he asked.

"I'm fine," I said, eyes forward.

"You sure?"

I nodded. "You offering a ride?"

"Yeah."

And that silence—that easy, shared silence—told him more than words could've.


Later that night, Chris sat in his room.

Photos spread out across his bed. His phone on silent. Lights dimmed. There was one photo of us at the park—my head tilted back, laughing. Except now, when he looked at it, he didn't see laughter.

He saw the tightness in my shoulders.

The way my arms folded inward.

The way my eyes never quite met the camera.

Another picture showed me on the train, smiling with a soda in my hand. But even there, something looked off. He hadn't noticed it at the time.

But now?

Now it was all he could see. Chris rubbed his temples. Searched his memory for more clues. For the last few months, I had been pulling away. Slowly. Subtly. Like I was shrinking into myself to survive.

He had thought maybe I was just grieving.

But this was something else.

He opened his laptop and typed,

*"How to tell if someone's being hurt at home."*

Then,

*"Signs of trauma in teens."*

He read in silence. Shoulders hunched. Jaw tight. He clicked away quickly when the results felt too invasive. But his gut was already screaming. And it wouldn't shut up.

He leaned back against the wall and whispered, *"If it's him…"*

He didn't finish the sentence.

Because finishing it would mean believing something he wasn't ready to believe.

Not yet.

But deep down?

He already knew.

The journal sat in my lap like it had a pulse.

My purple one—not Mama's.

The pages were warped at the corners, some crinkled where tears had dried. My pen hovered above a fresh page, the ink heavy at the tip, like it was already bearing the weight of what I hadn't written yet.

I couldn't breathe.

Not the way people do when they're relaxed, sitting in bed, listening to music. I was breathing like I'd run a mile in bare feet on broken pavement. Like every breath came with its own fight.

The lamp glowed soft beside me, casting long shadows on the floor.

I touched the pen to paper. Paused. Tried again.

My fingers trembled.

My jaw locked.

The sentence had been inside me for so long it felt like part of my bones. But now I had to write it. Had to say it. And that scared me more than anything. Because once it was written—once it was real—I couldn't take it back.

I stood and walked to the mirror, barefoot, the carpet cool under my toes. The girl looking back at me wasn't a stranger—but she wasn't familiar either. Her hair was neat, her posture tense, her eyes older than they should've been.

I reached for the light. Clicked it on. I flinched at my own reflection. But I didn't look away.

"You're still here," I whispered.

The words barely made a sound. But they were true. I looked at my arms. My collarbone. My mouth. Nothing was broken. But everything had been. I placed a hand flat on the mirror.

And said the second sentence.

*"It wasn't my fault."*

This time, it landed. Not soft. Not loud. Just there. Like a stone on sacred ground.

I went back to the bed. Picked up the pen. Held my breath. And wrote it,

*He raped me.*
Three words.
Twelve letters.
An entire world cracked open. The pen slipped from my fingers. I stared at the sentence. The air in the room changed.
Still. Heavy. Final. I didn't cry.
Not this time.
I just stared.
Because it was real now.
Not buried.
Not implied.
Not hidden between lines.
Written.
Said.
Alive.
I whispered it.
"He raped me."
I didn't know who I was saying it to.
Myself.
God.
The walls.
Maybe all three.
The sentence echoed back like a voice in a canyon. It didn't echo because it was loud. It echoed because it had waited too long to be heard.

Outside my bedroom door, Harmony stood frozen. She had a bowl of ice cream in one hand, spoon already melting down the side. She'd come upstairs to ask if I wanted to watch Love Jones for the thousandth time.

She was ready to forgive the journal. To breathe through the silence with me. But she hadn't expected this. Those three words hit the hallway like a body through glass.

*He raped me.*

The bowl slipped from her hand and hit the carpet with a muted thud. The spoon clinked softly against the ceramic, then rolled once. Her back pressed to the wall.

Her hand covered her mouth. Tears flooded her eyes. She didn't move. Didn't speak. She just stood there, heart breaking in silence. Because she had heard my voice. Not scared. Not shaking. Just honest. And that honesty undid her.

She slid down the wall, hands clenched in her lap. Wept quietly. Didn't knock. Didn't come in. Because something sacred was happening behind that door. And she knew—deep in her chest—that if she interrupted it, the truth might retreat again.

So she stayed.

And let it be what it needed to be.

Inside my room, I sat completely still. The sentence glowed in the low light. *He raped me.* I didn't erase it. Didn't edit it. Didn't run.

I just breathed.

The air didn't taste like fear anymore. It tasted like ash. But even ash can mean the fire is over.

I stood and walked to the closet. Pulled out the duffel bag. Set it on the bed. Checked inside, Cash. Clothes. Toothbrush. Deodorant. Socks. Journal. Everything I needed to leave. But I wasn't leaving tonight. Not because I was scared. But because now, I didn't need to escape in silence.

I was getting ready to speak.

Out loud.

To someone who mattered.

To someone who could stop him.

This time, I wasn't just surviving.

I was preparing for war.

## 11 THE BATTLE BEGINS

*"Sometimes war looks like walking out the door." – Cassandra Wade*

**The next morning, the house was too quiet.**

No footsteps. No voices. No clinking of breakfast dishes. Just silence so complete it felt suspicious, like the whole house was holding its breath.

I sat on my bed, staring at the emergency bag I hadn't unpacked. The journal rested beside it—open to the page I'd written the night before.

*He raped me.*

I traced the words with my finger. They didn't feel foreign anymore. They felt rooted. They felt like truth. And the truth had a name. One I hadn't spoken. Not out loud. Not yet.

A soft knock broke through the stillness.

"Div?" Harmony's voice—barely more than a breath—carried through the door.

I hesitated. My legs felt heavy, like they knew what was coming. Still, I stood and opened the door.

Harmony stood there—eyes red, shoulders clenched, lips pressed so tightly it looked like pain.

She didn't speak at first. Just walked in and sat on the edge of my bed like she'd rehearsed it and forgotten her lines halfway through.

The journal was still open. She glanced at it—her gaze skimming the page but not staying. Like she couldn't let herself read it again. Like she already knew.

"I heard you," she said quietly.

I nodded. "I know."

She took a breath that stuttered halfway in. "I read your letter to your mom. I didn't understand it then. But now…"

The silence tightened around us. A noose of unspoken truths.

Harmony turned to me, her voice almost a whisper. "Who?"

My throat closed. I swallowed hard.

"Divinity… who did it?" she asked again. Then her face twisted. "Was it Chris?"

I sat down beside her slowly. My body felt like it was bracing. "No. Why would you think Chris?"

"Because—even though he broke your heart—he's been around. Lingering. Like a puppy who got kicked but refuse to leave."

"He's harmless," I said. "He's been there."

I didn't want to make her feel like she hadn't—but I also couldn't let her protect the wrong person. Not now.

My hands shook in my lap. "You already know," I said.

"No, I—"

"Yes, you do." Louder this time. Sharper. "You saw it. You just didn't want to."

Harmony shook her head, slower this time. "I don't… I don't understand—"

"Your brother."

The words landed like glass shattering on tile.

"Darnell."

The name landed like a grenade.

Harmony went rigid. Every bit of color drained from her face as if her blood had forgotten where to go.

"No…" she whispered.

I nodded, my eyes burning but steady. "Yes."

She shook her head—slower at first, then faster, like shaking could undo the syllables she'd just heard.

"Div… that's my brother. You can't—he wouldn't—"

"He did," I said, voice trembling. "More than once."

Harmony's entire face changed—collapsed inward like something cracked behind her eyes. She looked at me. Then the journal. Then back again, her mouth moving but forming nothing.

"I didn't know," she whispered. "I didn't know."

"I know." I swallowed the sob rising. "I never blamed you."

She rubbed at her cheeks with shaking hands. "How could he—how could he—?"

She choked on the rest. Couldn't push it through.

I didn't make her.

We sat in the silence together, two best friends with a truth wedged between us—too sharp to carry, too solid to ignore.

Harmony leaned forward, elbows on her knees, head cradled in her hands. Her breathing came in short, rapid bursts like she was trying to outpace her own thoughts.

I watched her. Unsure whether I was supposed to hold her or guard myself.

There's no blueprint for moments like this—when the person you love most sees the truth for the first time and realizes the monster lived in their house.

"Say something," I whispered.

"I don't know what to say." Her voice was muffled, soaked in panic. "I don't even know how to feel."

"You don't have to feel anything for him," I said quietly. "You don't owe him that."

Harmony lifted her head. Her face was raw, streaked with salt. "He changed my diapers. He taught me to ride a bike. He used to walk me to school like he was proud to be my brother."

She pressed her fist hard to her forehead. "How can he be both of those people?"

"I don't know," I said, my voice flat with exhaustion. "But he is."

Harmony stood suddenly, arms folding tight around herself. She paced to the window but didn't look out—just stood there like the world outside had nothing to offer.

"I keep thinking back," she murmured. "The jokes he made. The stuff that sounded off but I laughed anyway. The way you'd go quiet when he walked into a room."

Her breath broke. "And I still didn't see it."

"You weren't supposed to," I said. "He made sure of that."

She turned to me—eyes puffy, skin blotched, trembling with rage.

"I should've protected you."

"No." I didn't let her carry it. "He should've."

We locked eyes.

Two girls—connected by love, ripped apart by betrayal—trying to hold each other up without falling over.

"I want to hurt him," Harmony said, sudden and fierce. "I want to scream. Break something. Make him feel what you've felt."

I stepped closer. My voice was steady.

"Then help me tell."

Her breath caught in her throat.

"I'm going to tell, Harmony. Tia. I'm done protecting him."

She nodded slowly. "I'll be with you. Every second."

"You sure?"

"Yeah. I don't know what comes next. But I'm sure of you."

We stood in the center of the room, something heavy and beautiful between us.

Not just pain.

Power.

A knock at the door cracked through the quiet like a gunshot.

We both froze.

"Girls?"

Tia's voice came from the hallway—soft, concerned, but carrying the edge of a mother who knew something wasn't right.

Neither of us answered.

I stood, slow and shaky, wiping the wet from my eyes with the back of my wrist. I crossed the room and cracked the door open.

Tia's face was lined with worry. Her eyes swept past me to Harmony, who still sat rigid on the bed, red-eyed and stunned.

"What's going on?" she asked, her brow folding in.

My mouth opened. Then closed.

This was the edge.

But I wasn't ready to fall over it just yet.

"We're just... talking," I said.

Tia didn't buy it—not entirely. I could see it in the way her mouth tightened, the way her eyes tried to connect invisible dots.

But she nodded. "Okay. Just checking in."

She turned, slowly, and walked back down the hall like someone who knew a storm was coming but didn't know from which direction.

The moment her footsteps faded, Harmony looked up.

"We have to tell her," she whispered.

I nodded. "I know."

The house was too quiet for what it held.

Harmony hadn't moved from the bed. Her fingers trembled in her lap, her lips repeating Darnell's name like it might rewrite the truth if she just said it enough.

I sat beside her, staring at the door. Waiting.

Then—

The jingle of keys. A laugh.

The front door opened.

Darnell's voice drifted up like poison.

"Yo, why's it so quiet in here? What, y'all mourning the school year already?"

I went cold. Harmony stood—fast and full of fire—and walked out.

I followed.

She stopped at the top of the stairs. Darnell stood in the kitchen below, water bottle in hand, smirking like nothing had shifted.

He looked up and grinned. "What's with the faces? Somebody die?"

Harmony's voice sliced the air.

"You're disgusting."

Darnell blinked. "What?"

She started down the stairs like each step was a strike. "Don't play dumb, Darnell. I know. I know what you did."

"What are you talking about?" he asked, but there was a tremor under the words.

Harmony didn't hesitate. "You violated her. Hurt her. And you came back here like it was nothing. Like you belonged in this house. Like you were safe to be around."

His face cracked. "Wait—whoa, you're serious? She told you that? That lie?"

Harmony's rage broke like a wave. "It's not a lie! I read it. I heard it."

"What did she say, huh?" Darnell's voice rose, panicked and posturing. "She's confused. She's been through stuff. You really believe that after everything I've done for this family—after all the years I've protected her?"

"Protected?" Harmony screamed. "You destroyed her!"

Tia's door flew open. She appeared, eyes wide, breath short.

"What is going on?!"

"Ask him!" Harmony shouted, finger shaking as she pointed. "Ask your son what he's done!"

Tia's gaze darted between us—panicked, frozen.

"What are you talking about?"

I stepped forward. Slowly. Carefully. Like one wrong word might shatter the whole room.

"She's talking about me," I said. My voice cracked, but I didn't lower it.

"Darnell. He didn't just hurt me. He raped me."

Silence.

Complete.

Brutal.

Tia stared at me like the words hadn't landed yet. Like her ears heard them but her heart couldn't process the shape of them.

Darnell let out a laugh that was all nerves and denial. "Ma—come on. Don't listen to this. She's confused. She's making it up. You know I'd never—"

Tia raised her hand.

Sharp.

"Stop."

One word. Low. Controlled. But her whole body trembled beneath it.

She turned to me. Her eyes shimmered, but the tears hadn't fallen yet.

"Is it true?"

I nodded once.

"I didn't tell you because I didn't want to break this house," I said. "But it was already broken."

The words came out flat, but inside me they cracked like glass.

Tia's face collapsed in on itself. "Oh God…"

"I'm sorry," I whispered. "I didn't know how to protect you from this."

And then her voice changed.

She turned to Darnell, and it wasn't thunder. It was fire.

"Get out."

"Ma—"

"GET OUT OF MY HOUSE!"

She was shaking now, but the words poured out like a flood. "You were accused before. You swore the girl lied. Said you dated. I believed you. And now this? What kind of mother lets her son walk back in here after that—and lets him do it again? To someone I love?"

She covered her mouth for a moment—like she wanted to swallow the grief before it choked her. Then she pointed again.

"GET. OUT. OF. MY. HOUSE. NOW."

Darnell staggered back. His mouth moved, but no words came that could save him.

He left. Slamming the door like a tantrum. But it was done.

Tia collapsed into the nearest chair, her hands shaking as the tears finally came.

Harmony stood off to the side, arms crossed, face blank with too much feeling to hold.

And me?

I didn't cry.

I walked to the stairs, picked up my emergency bag.

"I have to go," I said. Quiet. Not shaken. Just done.

"I have to go."

My voice didn't shake.

But the weight in it shifted the room.

I slung my bag over my shoulder. Turned toward the door.

"Wait—no," Harmony said, rushing to me. "You can't just leave. Not like this."

"I have to."

"Where will you go?"

Tia's voice rose behind her. "You're still under my care, Divinity. You can't just walk out. Worse can happen out there—"

"Worse already happened."

I turned around. "I have a plan. I've had one for months. And aside from death, nothing worse can happen to me than what already did."

I looked at them both—my second mother, my best friend—and felt the air around us change. Not colder. Just thinner.

"I didn't say anything," I told them, "because I didn't think anyone would believe me. But now that it's out—now that it's real—I can't stay here and pretend it's over just because he's gone."

My voice started soft but sharpened.

"He's not the only thing I have to leave behind. The walls here... they remember. Every hallway echoes. I still hold my breath when I walk past his room."

Tia's voice splintered. "You don't have to leave. We can fix this. We can—"

"You can't fix what happened to me."

"And I can't heal in the place it happened."

Harmony wiped her face. "But we need you."

I looked at her. Held her gaze.

"I need me more."

I opened the door.

Cold air rushed in—not cruel, just real. Like the truth.

"I love you both," I said. "But this part of my story—I have to walk it alone."

Tia begged. Pleaded. Offered help.

But I kept walking.

The sky had started to dim by the time I reached Chris's. I didn't text. Didn't knock.

I just stood there, bag on my back, heart open but stitched with threadbare grace.

Chris opened the door and froze.

"Div..."

His voice broke over my name. He didn't step forward. Just looked at me like he was afraid if he blinked, I'd disappear.

"I told Harmony," I said, voice soft but scraped thin. "And Tia. I said it out loud."

Chris stepped onto the porch and closed the door behind him—slow, careful.

He didn't ask what happened.

He didn't need to.

He just stood beside me like he had always promised he would.

"I'm leaving," I said.

He studied me, jaw tight. "Where?"

"I don't know."

He nodded—slowly, like every bone in his neck resisted it.

"You sure?"

"No."

I let out a breath that caught somewhere between a laugh and a sob. "I just know I can't stay."

Chris nodded again. Firmer this time.

Chris sat beside me. We stared out at the street like it might answer a question we hadn't dared ask.

After a moment, he said, "There were signs. I saw them. How you tensed up around him. How quiet you got when he was near. I didn't want to believe what I was seeing, so I told myself I was imagining it."

He shook his head. "I should've said something. I should've asked."

I looked at him. "You didn't fail me."

"I still feel like I did."

"But you didn't run. You stayed. That's what matters."

He gave a slow nod, jaw clenched, eyes glassy.

"Do you need anything? Do you want me to come with you?"

That question—so simple—unraveled something in me. Not in a way that broke me. In a way that reminded me I wasn't alone. But I shook my head.

"I need to do this myself."

He rubbed the back of his neck, looking at the street like it might offer him something to hold onto.

"You're the strongest person I've ever met," he said. "But if you ever need to stop being strong, I got you. You hear me? Doesn't matter where you are—I'll show up if you call."

"I know."

He pulled a folded envelope from his back pocket and held it out.

"It's everything I had saved. For college. For sneakers. Whatever. It's yours now."

My pride flared up—but only for a second. This wasn't about pride. I took it. "Thank you."

Chris sat down beside me. We stared out at the street like it was holding its breath.

After I left Chris, I walked until the city blurred.

Not toward anything—just away.

Every step felt heavier. Not just from the weight of the bag on my back, but from the silence I'd finally broken.

I hadn't eaten since breakfast. My body throbbed with exhaustion. My mind refused rest.

The motel sat off a cracked highway—peeling paint, flickering neon. The woman at the desk didn't ask questions. Just took my cash and handed me a key.

Room 16.

I locked the door. Twice. Then I dragged the dresser in front of it. The room smelled like mildew and half-forgotten stories. The lamp buzzed. The air was stale. But it was mine.

I collapsed onto the stiff mattress and whispered into the dark, "Thank you."

I didn't pray.

I didn't cry.

I just slept.

A deep, dreamless kind of sleep. Until it wasn't dreamless anymore.

I was in the old kitchen. The one from before. Before death. Before silence. Yellow walls. Cinnamon in the air. My mother stood at the stove, humming like always.

"Blessed assurance..."

"Mama?"

She turned. Flour on her cheek. That tired-soft smile I'd memorized in pieces.

"Hey baby," she said.

I moved toward her, voice trembling. "I miss you."

She smiled, sad and warm. "I know."

I wanted to tell her everything. About Darnell. About leaving. About how tired I was.

But she raised a hand.

"Divinity... listen."

Her voice held something deeper than instruction. It held warning.

"You're strong. But don't confuse running with healing."

I flinched.

She touched my face—just like she used to. "You don't have to go back," she said. "But think, baby. Think all the way through."

"Tia loves you. So does Harmony. The world's taken enough from you. Don't let it take your softness too."

I couldn't speak.

She leaned in close, forehead to mine. "I'm proud of you. You told the truth. You walked through the fire. Now don't burn down what's left trying to feel safe."

She was fading.

"Wait—Mama—"

"Think, baby," she called. "Don't just survive. Choose where to grow."

The kitchen dissolved.


I woke.

The motel hummed faintly. The light flickered once, then steadied.

I sat up, slow. My hands were curled into fists against my chest.

Her voice still echoed through me. Like a thread sewn into the lining of my ribs.

I moved to the window and pulled back the curtain. The world outside had shifted—washed in early hues of gold and bruised blue. Streetlights flickered, unsure of whether to surrender to the morning. But above all of it—The sun was rising. Not loud. Not fast. Just steady.

Like it had never stopped rising. Even when I stopped looking. I pressed my forehead to the cool glass and whispered,

"I'm thinking."

And for the first time...

I meant it.

## 12. NOTHING'S FREE

*"You were bought at a price." – 1 Corinthians 6:20*

**It had been eight months.**

Two hundred and forty-three nights. I kept count at first—then I stopped. Because eventually, counting didn't help when the nights were cold, the sidewalks hard, and hunger followed me like a shadow.

I was sixteen, nearly seventeen now. Not grown. Not a child. Somewhere in between. Somewhere lost—like the space between the neon lights and the sunrise.

The streets had taught me how to sleep light and walk fast. How to keep one hand in my coat pocket wrapped around my cash. How to make eye contact just long enough to prove I wasn't an easy target.

I learned which alleys were safe to nap in during the day and which corners to avoid after sunset. Summer made me sweat and stink. Fall made me ache. Winter had almost broken me. A few times, I thought I might not wake up from the cold.

But I always did.

Barely.

Harmony called often. So did Tia. The calls came at random times— early mornings, midnight, once even in the middle of a thunderstorm when I had ducked into a bus shelter just to stay dry. They never begged. They never yelled

They just said the same things in different ways,

"We love you."

"Please come back."

You don't have to talk. Just stop by. Just be safe. They'd leave me a voicemail where they left the food. A bag behind the gas station dumpster. A sandwich near the church steps. A bottle of water in a shoebox behind the flower shop.

I'd go when I was desperate. Never when they were there. I kept the phone on. Low brightness. Never used unless necessary. It was the only piece of my old life I hadn't let die.

I heard that Darnell never returned to the house. Tia wouldn't let him back in. She'd locked the door behind him and kept it that way. She changed the locks on the door but left me a key in one of the food stashes. Because I never filed a report. Never went to the police. Never told a counselor or a hotline or a doctor so he never paid the true price for his crime.

I told my truth once. That had to be enough. The thought of him still being out there haunted me. Afraid I would run into him at any moment.

I wasn't completely alone at first.

Her name was Sam—short for Samantha. She'd been on the streets since she was fifteen. She was eighteen when I met her. Tough, wiry, sharp-tongued. She was dark skinned. She had these dark eyes that looked like they'd seen everything, and probably had. Considering all she had been through she was still beautiful.

I met her my second week out. I was sitting outside a laundromat, cold and stupid, clutching a half-empty water bottle like it was some kind of lifeline. She walked right up to me, looked me over, and said, "You're new."

I nodded, even though I hated how easy it was to read me. Sam sat down like she didn't have anywhere better to be and share half a granola bar.

"Rule one," she said. "Don't sleep in the same place twice in a row. Rule two, always keep a piece of metal in your sock. Rule three, people will offer you things. Most of them will cost you later."

I didn't ask how she knew all that. I just listened. Because she knew how to survive. And back then, I didn't.

We were inseparable for months. We shared food. Found corners to rest where no one would bother us. She showed me which shelters were safe and which ones felt like cages. She taught me how to barter, how to blend in, how to disappear.

Sometimes we'd just walk—miles at a time—saying nothing. The silence between us felt safe. She never asked what I was running from. And I never asked what she had left behind. That's how it worked.

Then one day...

She was just gone.

We were supposed to meet behind the church, near the food pantry.

She never showed. I waited all night. Morning came. Still nothing.

I checked every spot we'd slept, every alley we'd shared.

I asked around. No one had seen her. And just like that—Gone. No goodbye. No note. No trace.

Sometimes I wonder if she made it out. If she got picked up, or saved, or taken. Sometimes I worry she didn't. I still hear her voice when I zip my coat.

*Rule one: don't sleep in the same place twice.* I still tuck a piece of metal into my sock. Just in case.

After she disappeared, I was back to being alone. I felt safer on the streets with her there, because we had each other's back. But now? It's just me.

I continued to look for Sam every day. And nothing. At first, I thought maybe she just moved on. Maybe she found someplace better. A room with a lock. A job. A warm hand to hold. But deep down, I didn't believe that.

Some nights, I'd lie awake under an overpass, staring at the belly of the city—its steel beams and rusted bolts—and wonder if that was the last place she'd slept too.

Other times, I'd pass a girl with a hood pulled tight, and my heart would lurch. I'd hurry over—just in case. But it was never her. She became another ghost in a city full of them. And yet, she never really left me.

I still walked the same paths she'd taught me. Still counted exits and shadows. Still heard her in the back of my mind.

I stopped talking about her. Stopped asking around. But the absence? It stayed. Heavy. Quiet. Always there. Like a story that refused to end— Because no one had told the last line.

One night, the ache in my stomach was too much to ignore. I hadn't eaten in almost two days. The last granola bar Harmony left me was long gone. I'd even considered stealing something from a corner store, but fear always stopped me at the door.

I was sitting outside the 24-hour laundromat, head on my knees, arms wrapped around my backpack, when a car pulled up slow.

A sleek, black coupe with tinted windows. The passenger side window rolled down.

A smooth voice called out,

"You good, little mama?"

I didn't look up. Didn't respond. I'd learned not to. But the man got out anyway.

He was tall. Light brown skin. Neatly braided cornrows. Clean jeans. Expensive sneakers.

And his voice?

Calm. Warm. Like silk dipped in sugar.

"I'm not trying to bother you," he said, holding up his hands. "Just looked like you might be hungry."

That word hit my stomach like a slap. He held up a wrapped sandwich from the deli across the street.

"I bought two."

I watched him for a long moment. Then nodded slowly. He handed it over. Didn't ask for anything. Didn't even sit beside me.

He just stood there and said, "Name's Kyson."

I didn't give mine.

He didn't ask.

He just said, "If you ever get tired of sleeping out here, I got a spare couch. Clean. Safe. No strings."

Then he got back in the car and drove off.

No second look.

No slick lines.

Just silence—and the warmth of his offer still hanging in the night air like smoke that refused to fade.

I sat with the sandwich in my lap long after the car disappeared. I didn't eat it right away. My hands turned it over slowly, thumbs brushing across the deli's waxy wrapper. The logo was fading at the corners, printed in red, slightly smeared from the steam.

My stomach growled—loud and sharp, like a warning shot. Still, I hesitated. I hated this part. The part where I needed. Where I accepted. But my body didn't care about pride. I peeled back the wrapper, slow and cautious. Sniffed it once. Turkey. Cheese. Mustard. Still warm. The scent alone made my mouth water.

The first bite burned. Not because it was too hot. But because I hadn't realized how close I was to breaking. How close I was to passing out from hunger. It was soft and salty and perfect. I closed my eyes as I chewed, something between gratitude and shame bubbling in my chest. I hated that it tasted good. I hated that I felt relief.

I hated needing kindness from strangers who might turn on me the next second. But Kyson hadn't asked for anything.

Not my name.

Not my story.

Not my body.

That hit harder than the sandwich.

Darnell had offered protection like a collar. Tia had offered love with conditions. Even Harmony's care had been stitched with guilt and confusion. But Kyson? He just gave. And left.

I ate every bite. Fast. Messy. I licked mustard from my fingers and swallowed the last of the bread like it might be the last thing I ate all week. Then I wiped my mouth with my sleeve. Leaned back against the cold brick wall. And thought about him. Kyson. Not just the sandwich. Not just the offer. But the fact that—for once—kindness didn't come with a price tag.

There was something about him. Not just the smooth talk or the clean look. It was the way he didn't push. The way he handed me food like it wasn't a favor but a gift—something I was allowed to have without owing him anything. He hadn't stared too long. Hadn't tried to follow me. Hadn't asked my name. That was the part that stuck with me. Most men who approached me in the dark always wanted something.

Kyson had just… given.

And then left.

Three nights later, I was huddled behind the back of a liquor store trying to stay warm under a broken awning when I saw the car again.

Same sleek black coupe. Same soft hum as it rolled up to the curb. This time, I stood first. Kyson stepped out with a bag in hand—this time from a McDonald's.

"You remember me?" he asked.

I nodded.

He smiled, a little surprised.

"Didn't think you would."

"I did."

He handed me the bag.

"No pressure," he said. "But you can eat it somewhere warm if you want."

I looked at the car.

Then back at him.

Kyson leaned against the hood, not moving closer.

"I meant it the other night," he said. "I got a couch. Nobody else is there. Not even a cat. Just a couch, some heat, and a working lock."

I hesitated.

I knew better than to trust strangers. But I also knew what it felt like to sleep in the rain. To wake up with cramps from hunger. To feel like I might die and no one would know my name.

"I'll come for an hour," I said.

Kyson smiled and opened the door.

"No rush," he said. "You leave when you want."

I slid into the passenger seat, holding the bag tight in my lap. And for the first time in months, I let my shoulders drop.

Just a little.

Just enough to breathe.

Kyson's apartment was on the second floor of a worn brick building with metal stairs that creaked under our weight. The hallway smelled like old carpet and lemon disinfectant. Two doors down, someone argued behind a closed door. A baby cried faintly on the floor below.

But when Kyson unlocked his door and stepped inside, everything changed.

It was… nice.

Cleaner than I expected.

Dim lighting. A small leather couch. A TV mounted to the wall. A faint smell of cologne mixed with vanilla candles burning low in the corner.

It didn't feel like danger.

It felt like relief.

I stepped in slowly, eyes scanning every corner. I didn't sit right away. I stood near the edge of the rug, holding the bag like it might vanish if I blinked. Kyson dropped his keys in a dish by the door and moved to the kitchen, which was small but tidy—plates drying in a rack, spices lined neatly on a shelf.

"You can sit," he said, opening the fridge and grabbing a bottle of water. "Couch is yours."

I nodded once and lowered myself slowly onto the edge of the cushion. It creaked softly under my weight. I set the bag on my lap and peeled it open. Fries. A burger. Two ketchup packets. My stomach twisted with gratitude and hesitation.

I glanced at him—Kyson leaned against the counter, sipping his water, phone untouched in his hand.

He wasn't watching me.

Not in that way.

Not like Darnell used to.

He didn't hover or crowd the space. He just existed in it, quiet, calm, like someone used to being alone.

I unwrapped the burger, my fingers stiff from cold. The scent hit me fast—grease, heat, something fried. I took a bite and it practically melted. Hot. Fresh. Real.

I chewed slow at first, then faster. Kyson didn't comment. When I reached for the fries, I finally spoke. "Why'd you help me?"

He looked up, blinked like he hadn't expected the question. "Cause someone helped me once."

That was it. No sermon. No sad story. Just a sentence that sat between us, soft but heavy.

I ate the rest in silence, eyes flicking toward him now and then. He moved like someone with nowhere to be. He didn't fill the room with noise. He let it be quiet.

And in that quiet…

I exhaled.

He waited.

Only when I finished and leaned back with a small sigh did he finally say, "So… how long you been out there?"

I hesitated.

Then shrugged. "A while."

He nodded like he understood. Not the way people nod when they're trying to be polite—but like he'd walked that street before.

"People think it's easy, huh?" he said. "That you just go home or go get help and it's all fixed. But they don't know."

"No," I said. "They don't."

Kyson leaned forward, elbows on his knees. "Well… I do."

I looked at him.

He didn't smile.

Didn't soften his tone.

Didn't perform empathy the way some adults did—over exaggerated and hollow. He just nodded, slow. Like someone who had earned their stripes and kept them hidden beneath the surface.

"I've been where you are," he said. "I get it. You want somewhere safe. No strings. Just rest."

I nodded again. My body still tense. But less so.

"You can stay here tonight," he added. "I'll sleep in the other room. You take the couch. Door locks from the inside. Nothing's gonna happen to you here."

That last sentence made me flinch—but not from fear. From the way it sounded like a promise. Like a kindness. Like a lie dressed in comfort. Because how many times had I heard those words before? How many

140

times had they meant the opposite?

But Kyson didn't press.

Didn't lean closer.

Didn't wait for approval.

He just stood slowly, stretched, and grabbed a folded blanket from the hallway closet.

"Laid out some extra stuff if you want it," he said, setting it on the arm of the couch. "Bathroom's down the hall. Light switch sticks a little."

Then he disappeared into the other room, the soft click of the door closing behind him echoing louder than it should have.

I sat there for a while. Silent. Still. Listening.

No footsteps. No creaking floorboards. No surprises.

Just quiet.

And that quiet?

It didn't feel like danger.

It felt like rest.

I curled up on the couch, the blanket pulled to my chin. The fabric smelled like detergent and faint wood smoke, soft enough to almost fool me into thinking I was somewhere familiar. Somewhere safe.

I didn't change clothes. Didn't remove my shoes.

I kept my backpack clutched to my chest like a second skin.

The lights were off, except for the one over the stove that Kyson had left on. It cast a dull glow across the room, just enough for me to see the outline of the coffee table, the wall-mounted TV, the row of dusty books tucked into a shelf beside the couch.

My eyes stayed open. Not because I wasn't tired. But because tired didn't matter when your mind couldn't slow down. Even here, in this quiet apartment with its closed doors and soft air, I couldn't stop the noise inside me. I thought about Tia. I thought about Harmony. I thought about Sam, and the way she'd vanish and reappear like a stray cat—until one day she didn't come back at all. I thought about the way my mother's voice sounded in dreams, always singing, always reminding me who I was even when I couldn't see her face.

I thought about the sound of Darnell's laugh and the slam of the door behind him the day he left.

And I thought about how it still wasn't enough. Not to undo anything. Not to erase what had happened. Not to fix the way I flinched when kindness felt too close.

My stomach turned. But it wasn't hunger. It was the ache that never left. The ache that came from knowing home didn't mean the same thing anymore.

I turned on my side and faced the couch cushions.

My eyes finally started to close.

And just before sleep took me, I whispered into the dark,

"Don't let this be a mistake" I didn't know it yet – but the price of that blanket and burger was coming.

I woke to the soft scent of breakfast. Not the street smells I was used to—grease, car exhaust, mildew—but real food.

Eggs. Toast. Coffee.

For a moment, I forgot where I was.

The blanket was still draped over me, and my bag was untouched in the corner where I'd left it. The sun filtered through the blinds in slanted golden stripes across the floor.

It felt almost… normal.

I sat up slowly, stretching. My body ached less than usual. My stomach wasn't screaming. My fingers weren't numb.

It was the first time in months I hadn't woken up afraid.

Kyson was in the kitchen, back turned, humming along to an old R&B song on the radio. He had a plate in one hand, flipping something with the other.

He glanced over his shoulder and smiled.

"Mornin'. You sleep okay?"

I nodded. "Yeah."

He pointed to a clean plate on the counter. "Made you some eggs and toast. No meat—I didn't know what you liked."

I walked over, cautiously, and picked up the plate.

"Thanks."

"No problem. You allergic to anything?"

I shook my head.

"You drink coffee?"

"A little."

He poured me a cup and handed it over like we did this every day. Like I wasn't a runaway. Like he wasn't a stranger.

We sat at the table. Kyson kept the conversation light—asked about music, if I liked movies, what my favorite food was.

I answered sparingly.

But I listened.

And that was enough for him.

"You ever think about going home?" he asked casually, not looking up from his coffee.

142

I stiffened.

"I don't have a home."

Kyson nodded like he understood completely.

"That's alright. You do now."

I didn't respond.

But my walls dropped another inch.

After breakfast, I started gathering my things.

"I should go," I said quietly.

Kyson leaned back in his chair, rubbing his chin. "You sure?"

I hesitated.

It was the first time I didn't know.

He stood and crossed the room, opening a cabinet above the TV. He pulled out a toothbrush, a pack of unopened socks, and a small bottle of lotion.

"I got these last week. Figured someone might need 'em."

He placed them on the table without pressure.

I blinked, unsure how to respond.

He walked past me toward the door.

"You don't have to go," he said. "But you can. I'm not holding you here."

And somehow, because he said that—it made me stay.

I stayed another night.

Then another.

And when Kyson offered me a drawer in the bedroom, I didn't say no. When he gave me a hoodie that smelled like laundry and cologne, I wore it. When he said I could stay as long as I wanted, I believed him. Because what I needed most wasn't just food or shelter. It was the feeling of being chosen.

Seen.

Safe.

I didn't see the change yet.

Didn't notice the way he started keeping track of when I came and went. Didn't feel the shift in tone when I asked to go for a walk alone and he said, "Why would you need to go anywhere?"

Not yet.

Because I was still catching my breath.

Still listening.

Still mistaking comfort for care.

A week passed.

I no longer counted the nights on concrete. I didn't flinch every time I closed my eyes. I started folding my clothes and placing them in the drawer Kyson gave me, alongside his.

I soon realized that everything with Kyson had been a lie. The person he portrayed to be—the gentle man with the soft voice, the warm food, the patient posture—wasn't real. He had played a role, like someone rehearsed in how to earn trust, how to listen just enough to make you think you were safe.

But safety had never been the plan.

Kyson was a glorified pimp. Only, his girls didn't stand on corners or lean into open car windows. He was smarter than that. Cleaner. More polished. He ran his business behind closed doors, kept his girls fed, clothed, and just afraid enough not to run. Multiple apartments around Brooklyn. He was a genius if you really thought about it.

He didn't yell. He didn't strike. Not at first. He asked questions. Listened closely. Picked up on every crack in your voice.

And if you had no one? If your story had gaps? If your fear showed too easily? He'd know you were his.

Kyson had studied me. Noticed how I flinched when a door closed too fast. Noticed how I clutched my bag to my chest like a lifeline. Noticed how I never mentioned family. Never used a last name. Never said the word "home."

That's how he knew. That I had nowhere to go. No one who would come looking.

He never asked for anything. Not right away. He let me settle in. Let me feel like I belonged. But little things changed. He started keeping tabs on when I left the apartment. Asking where I went. Who I saw. He wanted to know if I still talked to anyone from "before."

One night, he stood too close. Not in a threatening way. But in a way that said, I see you. I own this space you're standing in.

And still—I stayed.

Because the world outside was cold, and hunger was real, and Kyson gave me three hot meals and a door that locked from the inside. But deep down, I had started counting again. Not days on the street. Not hours of sleep.

But signs.

The way his compliments turned into suggestions.

"You're beautiful, you know. You could make money just being you."

The way his comfort turned into control.

"You don't need to leave. Everything you need is right here."

The way his gifts came with silence when I didn't thank him fast enough.

I remembered what Sam used to say. *Rule Three. People will offer you things. Most of them will cost you later.* I wish I had taken that rule seriously. But I didn't. Because Kyson hadn't taken anything.

Not yet.

He just made it clear—eventually—that everything came with a price. And soon, I'd have to decide if I was willing to pay it.

One night, something changed.

We'd just finished eating—takeout again, Chinese this time. I stood at the sink rinsing my plate while Kyson sat behind me on the couch, channel surfing and laughing at something on the television.

I dropped my plate too fast. It clanked loud against the porcelain.

"Sorry," I called.

Silence.

Then—his voice, flat. "You gonna clean it?"

I turned, confused. "Yeah. I was going to."

He stood slowly.

His expression wasn't angry.

Just... different.

Harder.

"Don't get lazy," he said.

I blinked. "I wasn't."

He took a step closer.

"You like having a place to stay, right?"

Something cold brushed down my spine.

"Yeah," I said, quieter now.

"Then show me you appreciate it."

He smiled.

But it didn't reach his eyes.

I nodded slowly, turning back to the sink. Scrubbed the plate like it mattered more than anything. My breathing shallow. My hands shaking just slightly beneath the running water.

That night, I lay on the couch, blanket pulled tight—not for warmth, but for protection.

And I didn't sleep.

Not fully.

Because something had shifted. Something quiet and invisible, but unmistakable. I felt it in the way he looked at me without really seeing me. I felt it in the way the apartment seemed smaller now, like the walls had moved in while I wasn't watching. This wasn't a rescue.

It was a setup.

And it had just begun.

The next night, the tone changed again.

It started normal—leftover lo mein, another movie on mute, Kyson tapping on his phone while I curled up on the couch in his hoodie, pretending everything was still okay. He stood behind the couch with a bottle of soda in one hand, watching me.

Too long.

"I been thinking," he said casually.

I looked up.

He wasn't smiling.

Not really.

"I've helped you. Fed you. Kept you off the street."

He said it like he was listing receipts.

Like I owed him.

"I appreciate that," I said carefully, sitting up straighter.

"Do you?" he asked.

There was no warmth in his voice.

Just calculation.

"Yeah. I do."

He stepped around the couch, slow and steady, like someone testing the weight of the floor.

"You know how many girls out here would kill for a spot like this?" he asked, eyes locked on mine.

I didn't answer.

"You got a bed. A door that locks. Hot meals. Ain't nobody hurting you here."

Still, I said nothing.

He crouched slightly, his tone dropping. "But nothing's free, little mama."

My stomach turned.

There it was.

The cost.

"What are you saying?" I asked, voice barely steady.

"I'm saying you can stay," he said, smiling now—soft, slick. "You can have this. But you gotta be useful."

I stood up slowly. "Useful how?"

Kyson laughed like it was a dumb question.

"You're pretty. Quiet. Nobody gonna hurt you. Not if you're with me."

My chest tightened. I backed up a step.

"I'm not for sale," I said.

Kyson's eyes narrowed. "You already sold. You just didn't read the receipt."

Silence.

Heavy.

Cold.

I stared at him—really saw him for the first time. The smooth voice. The calm tone. The fake safety. It had all been a lie. A net. And I had walked right into it.

Kyson stood fully now, towering.

"But don't worry," he said. "You don't gotta do anything yet. Just think about it. Door's not locked."

He smiled like it was a kindness.

Like he hadn't just branded me with ownership.

Then he turned and walked out the door, closing it softly behind him.

I didn't move for a long time.

Just stood there in the center of the room, the plate of cold noodles on the table, the hoodie clinging to my arms like guilt. The quiet wasn't peace anymore. It was a warning.

"Door's not locked."

That's what he said. Like it was a test.

Like he was daring me to try.

I picked up my bag from beside the couch—light, half-unzipped, but always packed. My fingers wrapped around the strap slowly, like the motion alone might set off an alarm.

I crept to the door.

Listened.

The apartment was still.

The hallway outside even stiller.

I turned the knob slowly—one inch, two—until the click sounded like a gunshot in my chest.

Then I pulled.

The door opened.

And I froze.

Cash was there. Leaning against the wall like he'd been waiting hours. One foot propped against the baseboard, a toothpick bobbing gently between his teeth. Hoodie zipped to the neck. Eyes dead still.

But here's the part that made my stomach drop—

I hadn't heard him come up. Not one creak on those stairs. Not a door. Not a breath.

Which meant… He'd been there the whole time. Just waiting.

I barely ever saw Cash—but what I did know was he didn't play, especially when it came to Kyson. From what I could tell, he was the muscle. And he was scary. His eyes were dark, like he'd already lived through more than most men survived. He stood about six feet tall, stocky, and solid—and I knew if he was here, I was trapped.

He didn't smile. Didn't nod. Didn't pretend.

Just said, "Where you going?"

My throat tightened.

"I was… just getting air," I said.

He tilted his head slightly. "You sure that's a good idea?"

I looked down the hallway.

The stairs were only a few feet away.

But it felt like a mile.

"I just need to clear my head," I said, trying again.

Cash stepped forward—not fast. Not loud. Just enough to block the doorway.

And when he spoke next, it wasn't a suggestion.

"You ain't ready to leave."

My chest caved in.

There it was.

The truth I hadn't wanted to see.

There was no "choice."

No unlocked door.

Kyson hadn't been generous. He'd been grooming.

And Cash?

He was the fence around the trap.

I swallowed hard, fighting the tremble in my hands.

"Kyson said the door wasn't locked."

Cash smirked, cold. "Yeah. It ain't. But that don't mean you walk through it."

He stepped back just enough to gesture inside.

"Go on. Get back in. Streets don't treat girls like you nice no more."

My feet didn't move.

So he added—softer now, but colder,

"Unless you want things to get harder for you out there than they already were."

148

I backed into the apartment.

Closed the door.

The click behind me sounded heavier this time.

Like chains.

I stood in the middle of the room, door shut behind me, Cash's shadow still etched into my mind like a bruise.

I didn't drop my bag.

I didn't sit.

I just stood there.

Still.

Frozen.

The kind of stillness that comes when your body realizes you're not just tired—

You're trapped.

And this time, no fire escape.

No train station.

No couch to curl into and cry.

Only walls that smelled like fake safety, and candles that masked something rotting.

I walked slowly to the bathroom, closed the door without locking it. Because locks didn't matter here. I stared at my reflection. The girl in the mirror was me. But not. Her eyes were wild. Her lips were trembling. She looked like someone who had been almost saved, and then tossed back into the water with her lungs full of hope.

I pressed my hands to the sink, trying to breathe.

One breath.

Two.

The third didn't come.

I bent forward, gasping soundlessly. My fingers dug into the porcelain like it could hold me up. Like it could stop the panic crashing through my chest.

I wanted to scream. Not loud. Not long. Just enough. Just enough to rip a hole in the air. But I didn't. Because I remembered Sam.

*Rule Three: People will offer you things. Most of them will cost you later.*

And I hadn't listened.

I sank to the floor and let my back slide down the cool tile. Clutched my bag to my chest.

And for the first time in months— I cried. Not silently. Not stoic. But loud. Ugly. Like a kid. Because that's what I was. Just a girl. A kid who wanted to feel safe.

And now?

I couldn't even walk out the front door.

I don't know how long I stayed there. Long enough for my face to swell and my breath to slow. Long enough for the air to go still again.

Then—

The front door opened. Footsteps.

Kyson's voice, cheerful and smooth,

"Yo, I picked up that snack you like. You still up?"

I didn't move.

Didn't answer.

A soft knock at the bathroom door.

"Everything good?"

Silence.

Then his voice, more gentle. Like warm syrup.

"You ain't mad about earlier, are you? I was just playing, baby girl. Just trying to keep the place in order."

I closed my eyes. Held my breath. His voice kept going, like a lullaby made of poison.

"You know you're good here. You know I'd never let nothin' happen to you."

The lie slid under the door, wrapped around my legs, tried to pull me out of the dark.

"You're safe with me. You know that, right?"

I pressed my forehead to my knees. Didn't speak. Didn't move. Because now I knew what he really meant when he said safe.

He meant silent.

He meant obedient.

He meant owned.

## 13.  SOFT CAGE

*"Safety isn't always peace. Sometimes it's just fear in a prettier dress."*
*– Divinity's Journal*

**Weeks passed, and nothing got better.**

But they didn't get worse either. Not exactly. I told myself that was something to be grateful for.

Kyson wasn't cruel—not the kind people notice. He didn't yell. Didn't hit. Didn't lock the doors. He said the door was always open, that I could leave anytime. But we both knew that wasn't true.

Because when someone gives you everything—shelter, food, a toothbrush and sock —then walks around like they expect nothing in return, you learn to read the spaces between the words.

 And in those spaces?

I was a prisoner.

Like generosity could erase captivity.

A quiet, fed, well-rested prisoner with clean sheets and dim lighting and no bruises to prove it.

The days blurred into each other, like brush strokes on wet paint. I couldn't tell Mondays from Fridays. Couldn't remember the last time I saw the sun without glass between us. Kyson kept the blinds closed. Said sunlight made the apartment too hot.

The only time I felt fresh air was when he cracked the window during his morning smoke—just wide enough for the smoke to drift out, never wide enough for me to breathe.

Breakfast came late. Usually around noon. An Egg sandwich wrapped in wax paper, or reheated rice from the night before. Sometimes just a pack of crackers and a Capri Sun.

I ate quietly on the couch while Kyson channel surfed for sports highlights.

He brought groceries sometimes, let me cook if I wanted.

But he always reminded me, "You don't have to. Just relax. You've been through enough."

I folded our laundry like it was a job—shirts that weren't mine, hoodies he let me borrow, socks I'd never bought but kept washing anyway. It gave my hands something to do. Something that felt useful.

At night, he'd watch movies while I sat beside him, legs tucked under me, blanket pulled high. Sometimes he laughed too loud. Sometimes I pretended to laugh too. Just to fill the space.

He had a way of making silence feel like a decision I was making—not something he had designed.

My phone had died a long time ago. No charger. I mentioned it once. He said we'd get one, "next time we're out." But we never went anywhere. I stopped asking. I hadn't spoken to Harmony. Or Tia. Or Chris. I hadn't spoken to anyone outside these walls. And somehow, the longer I stayed, the more it felt like maybe I didn't exist anywhere else. Like everything before Kyson was fading, shrinking.

He never asked me about the past. And maybe that's what made it worse. Because pretending the past didn't matter made it easier to forget I had one. He'd say things like, "You're safe now." And sometimes I believed it. But other times—late at night, when the TV was off and his footsteps stopped echoing down the hall—I'd lie awake and wonder,

*If I screamed, would anyone hear me?*

*Would anyone even know I was gone?*

But soft cages have rules. Even if no one writes them down. Even if no one says them out loud.

It started small. Kyson came home one night with a shoebox tucked under his arm. "Found something I thought you'd like," he said, setting it on the couch beside me. Inside was a pair of white sneakers—name-brand, spotless, still with tissue paper stuffed inside the toes.

"They're your size," he added, as if that made it less suspicious.

I hesitated. "Where'd you get these?"

He shrugged. "Friend owed me a favor."

That line again.

I slipped them on. They fit perfectly.

"See? I got taste," he said, grinning. "Told you I'd take care of you."

I nodded, smiling just enough to make him believe it.

That night, he cooked dinner himself. Real food. Chicken and yellow rice. Even set out two plates instead of eating from the container like usual.

"You're different," he said across the table. "You don't talk too much.

Don't ask for anything. You make this place feel... peaceful."

I didn't know what to say. So I just kept eating.

"I've had girls stay here before," he continued. "A lot of 'em get greedy. Start acting like I owe them something."

I paused.

He noticed.

"Not you," he added quickly. "You're not like that. You're grateful."

He smiled again.

But this time, the smile came with weight.

Like gratitude was currency. Like my silence, my smallness, my acceptance of everything—that was the payment he wanted.

After dinner, I tried to help clean. He waved me off.

"Nah. You're not here to work on dishes. Just be good."

*Be good.* I carried that phrase to bed with me. It echoed louder than the radio. Louder than the neighbors. Louder than the voices in my own head. Be good. Be grateful. Because nothing's free. Not even comfort. And while he never asked for anything outright... I could feel the tension pulling tighter every day.

That night, I couldn't sleep. Not because the apartment was loud—Kyson kept it quiet, the TV turned low, the lights dimmed just enough to cast soft shadows across the walls. But something inside me had shifted. The shoes were by the couch, clean and white and expensive-looking. I hadn't taken them off since dinner until now. I stared at them like they might change shape.

*"Just be good."*

That line kept replaying in my head like a broken record. I lay on the couch, blanket pulled up to my chin, staring at the ceiling fan turning slow and silent. I could hear Kyson breathing in the next room, steady and even. I hated how safe it sounded. Because I didn't feel safe. I felt studied. I closed my eyes. And slipped into sleep.

The dream came fast this time—no slow fade, no fog. One minute, I was lying on the couch. The next, I was standing in an alley. Wet bricks. Humid air. A flickering streetlight overhead.

And Sam.

She was sitting on a milk crate in the corner, legs crossed like always, her black hoodie zipped all the way up, face half-shadowed.

She looked just like I remembered her—dark skin glowing under the lamplight, eyes sharp, unblinking.

"Been looking for you," I whispered.

She didn't smile.

"You waited too long," she said.

My throat tightened. "I didn't know where to go."

"You think this is safety?" she asked. "Think cause he feeds you and gives you clean shoes, that makes him real?"

I didn't answer.

She stood.

Walked closer.

"I told you. Rule three," she said. "They don't always hit. The ones that don't? They own you in silence. And it only gets worse."

I blinked. "He said I could leave—"

Sam cut me off. "Then why haven't you?" Her voice cracked. Not from anger. From knowing. "You gotta get out. Now. Before he decides you don't get to."

The dream cracked like glass around me.

Her face blurred. Her voice echoed,

"Get out before he chooses for you."

I sat up, gasping—chest heaving, face damp with sweat. The living room was dark. Still. But I wasn't. I stared at the door. At the bolts. At the shoes by the couch. And I knew—Sam was right. This was the warning. And I wouldn't get another.

The next morning, I moved slower than usual. Kyson noticed.

"You okay?" he asked from the kitchen, stirring oatmeal with a plastic spoon.

I nodded. "Just didn't sleep well."

He smiled like he didn't believe me, but didn't press. He never did when he didn't need to. But something had shifted. Everything about the apartment looked the same—blank walls, soft music, the scent of cologne and toast—but it all felt different now. Too still. Too intentional. A quiet performance of peace.

I ate my food, thanked him like always. He grinned like he'd earned a prize. But Sam's voice echoed in the back of my mind. Her warning. Her eyes. Her urgency. I needed out. Even for a second.

After lunch, I drifted toward the front door, letting my fingers graze the frame like I was just curious.

"Mind if I step outside for a little?" I asked casually. "Just need some fresh air."

Kyson looked up from the couch, remote resting in his lap.

"Fresh air?" he said with a smirk. "Why? You got everything you need right here."

The smile didn't reach his eyes.

I paused.

Then shrugged. "Just been a while since I felt the sun, that's all."

He stood up slowly, walking over like he wasn't mad—just amused. "C'mon now, you know it's not safe out there. You said that yourself. We got air in here. Open a window if you want." I nodded, swallowing the lump in my throat.

He kissed the top of my head like I'd asked something silly. "Ain't no need to be out there when you got everything you need right here."

I sat back down on the couch. He turned on a movie—something loud and senseless—and slid in beside me.

"See?" he said, "Better than any walk."

I nodded again, eyes fixed on the screen but seeing nothing. Only the door. And Sam's voice from the night before. *"You gotta get out. Now."* And this time, I didn't just believe her.

I started planning.

The TV hummed in the background, some movie Kyson picked— loud enough to fill the silence but not enough to quiet my thoughts. My eyes were on the screen, but I wasn't watching. I was with Sam. I could see her now, clear as day.

That night we lay under the broken scaffolding behind the dry cleaner, her arms folded behind her head like she wasn't sleeping outside. Like the sidewalk didn't bite at her spine.

The moonlight made her skin glow—deep and dark like polished mahogany—and her voice cut through the stillness like a knife wrapped in silk.

"You ever get stuck with someone who makes it look like they saving you?" she asked me, eyes on the sky.

I was seventeen and stupid. "Saving you's a good thing, isn't it?"

Sam scoffed, slow and bitter. "Not when they remind you every second that they did."

That hit me hard, but she wasn't done.

"They make you think it's love. Or kindness. Or maybe God answered your cry. But really? They just wanna own you. Make you scared of bein' hungry so you stay fed. Make you scared of bein' alone so you stay near. That ain't love, Div."

I remember asking, "But how do you know when it's real?"

Sam had gone quiet for a while. Then she said something I didn't get back then, but it echoed now like prophecy,

"If you gotta ask if you're free? You ain't."

The movie ended. Kyson hadn't even noticed I hadn't laughed at a single scene. I sat curled on the far end of the couch, knees drawn to my chest.

Sam's voice played louder than the end credits. I remembered her hands—rough from sleeping rough, but always warm when she handed me half her sandwich. I remembered the day she gave me her extra socks when mine were soaked.

She never made me feel like I owed her. She never asked me to prove I was worth her kindness. And now she was gone. And I was here. In a quiet, polished trap. I curled tighter into myself. And for the first time in weeks, I whispered aloud,

"I miss you, Sam."

Just those words.

And nothing after.

One night, everything shifted. Up until then, Kyson hadn't crossed that line. He controlled what I ate, when I slept, who I saw. He monitored my movements, silenced my needs. But he hadn't touched me—not like that. Not yet. I think, deep down, I wanted to believe he wouldn't. That maybe he was just lonely, just broken in the same places I was. But that was a lie I told myself to sleep. And that night? That lie shattered.

He was in the kitchen, rinsing out his takeout container, when he said it. Calm. Like he was asking what I wanted to watch.

"Why don't you sleep in the bed tonight?"

I blinked. Confused. Cold all at once.

"Are you sleeping on the couch?" I asked, though I already knew the answer.

He smirked.

"Nah, shorty. I'm sleeping in the bed too. It's time we start doing some adult things. "You've had time to rest," he said softly, like he was handing out grace. "Now it's time to start… doing your part."

It wasn't a suggestion.

It was a sentence.

I froze, tears already slipping free before I could stop them.

"Please… I'd prefer not to."

That's when the shift came.

His face hardened.

No more soft smiles. No more charm.

He grabbed me—fist knotted in my hair—and yanked me so fast my feet barely touched the ground.

"Get in the room."

The words were sharp. Final.

I stumbled forward, sobbing now, my pleas small and useless in the shadow of his fury. I focused on the spot on the floor where the first physical abuse started as he dragged me in the room.

And that was the first night. The first time the mental prison became a physical one. The beginning of something darker than I'd ever known.

I curled into myself afterward, shaking, broken in ways I didn't know could still break. I lay there while he slept beside me, as if nothing had changed.

But everything had. And I knew in my bones—quiet and shaking beneath the weight of silence—

I had to get out.

Again.

Because if I stayed?

There wouldn't be another chance.

The next morning, the sun came up like it didn't know what happened. Like the world could keep spinning while I lay there, hollowed out, barely breathing beside the man who had stolen the last piece of me I didn't even know I'd been saving.

Kyson moved around the apartment like he always did—brushing his teeth, humming while he cooked eggs, flipping through the TV channels like nothing was different.

But it was.

Everything was different.

I stayed on the couch that morning, still wrapped in the same blanket I'd slept under in his bed. My legs wouldn't move. My voice wouldn't come.

He brought me a plate of food and sat it on the coffee table with a grin.

"Eat up, baby girl," he said. "You need your strength."

I nodded.

But I didn't touch it. That's when it started.

The switch.

He began kissing my forehead again. Telling me how special I was.

How soft I made his life feel. How lucky I should feel to have a man who "takes care of everything."

How this was love.

"You just not used to being loved the right way," he said, brushing his fingers against my jaw like he hadn't bruised it hours earlier.

That afternoon, I stood in the bathroom and stared at my reflection. My face didn't look different. No blood. No cuts. Just the smallest swell on my cheekbone that could pass for anything.

But my eyes— My eyes had turned to stone. I didn't cry. I didn't scream. I just... stared.

I had stopped counting days again. Because now, the time didn't matter. Only the plan. And so I started over—slowly.

I memorized the lock again. I watched when he left, how long he was gone, which drawer he kept the keys in when he got lazy.

I stopped reacting. I became the girl he met the first day on the curb— quiet, grateful, small.

And every night, I rehearsed what I would say to get past Cash. What lie might be good enough. What face I needed to wear. I even looked at my shoes—scuffed and worn, but mine—and whispered to them, "Soon." Because this time? I wasn't running away from home. I was running toward myself.

It happened on a Tuesday. Kyson had left in a rush—some phone call about "business," muttering to himself as he grabbed his keys and slammed the door behind him. Cash wasn't at the post outside. For once, the hallway was empty.

It was the moment I'd been waiting for. I slid on my sneakers without socks, stuffed my toothbrush and the few clothes I still had into my bag, and unlocked the door with the quiet patience of someone who had practiced it a hundred times in her head. I crept down the stairs. Every step was a scream in my ears. At the bottom, I paused. Listened.

Nothing.

Freedom.

The sun hit my face as I stepped outside and for a second, I thought I might actually cry from the light. I didn't run. I walked. Fast but steady. No panic in my face. No rush in my pace. Until I turned the corner and came face-to-face with him.

Cash.

Leaning against a car. Eating sunflower seeds. He looked at me like he'd been expecting it.

I froze.

He spit a seed shell onto the curb and grinned.

"You lost, shorty?"

I tried to play it cool. "Just going for a walk."

Cash shook his head slowly.

"Nah. That's not how this works."

"I thought the door wasn't locked."

"It ain't." He tossed another seed in his mouth. "But the street is."

Before I could blink, he stepped in front of me. His hand didn't touch me. But it hovered just close enough.

"Go back," he said, voice low. "Don't make this ugly."

I did.

I turned around, walked back up the stairs, back through the door, and into the apartment where the air felt heavier than ever. The silence after failure was worse than the silence before.

When Kyson came home, he didn't ask where I'd gone. But everything about him had shifted. He moved closer when he spoke. He watched me more when I ate. He didn't yell. He didn't touch me that night. But something in his eyes told me that my mistake hadn't gone unnoticed. That's when I knew.

There would be no escaping unless he let me. And the only way he would let me... was if he believed I didn't want to stay.

So I stopped resisting.

I started nodding more, smiling sometimes, laughing when he told jokes. I didn't give in.

I adapted. I learned what time his phone buzzed and which names came up on the screen. I listened for what corners he mentioned in phone calls and which girls he said were "doing good."

I started to map the network. Because Kyson wasn't just one man. He was a system.

A quiet web stretched across the city. And if I wanted to leave without being caught, without being dragged back like the others—I had to think like him. I had to be smarter than him.

This time, the plan wouldn't be to run. It would be to outplay. To make him trust me enough to hand me the key himself. And until then?

I smiled.

I obeyed.

And I learned everything I could about his world. Because if I was going to get out... I'd need to disappear through the cracks he didn't know were there.

He was in the kitchen again—same easy smile, same sweet voice. Like the night before hadn't happened. Like the shift in his tone, the way he watched me wipe down the counters like I owed him, had never existed.

He slid a shopping bag across the table—new clothes. A soft sweater. A dress I never asked for.

"Got you something," he said. "Figured you could use a little upgrade."

I opened it slowly, forcing a smile. "Thanks."

He watched me too closely. "You like it?"

"Yeah. It's nice."

Kyson leaned back in his chair, arms folded. "Thought maybe you could wear it tonight."

I hesitated. "Tonight?"

"Yeah. We might have some company. A friend of mine wants to meet you."

My stomach dropped.

"A friend?" I repeated, trying to keep my voice level.

He nodded, still smiling. "Real generous dude. Treats girls like queens. You wear that dress, he'll take care of you. Might even put something in your pocket."

There it was.

The wall behind the gifts. The hook hidden beneath the silk.

I didn't answer.

Kyson stood and walked around the table, resting his hand on my shoulder. "You ain't gotta be scared. Just be sweet. You're good at that."

His hand lingered.

I didn't breathe until he walked away.

Later that day, I waited until Kyson was in the shower. I didn't move toward the door this time. I just sat at the edge of the bed, bag beside me, the dress still folded on the table like a question I hadn't answered. I was tired of answering.

The sound of the shower running was almost calming, until I heard it stop. I sat up straighter.

Kyson stepped out a few minutes later, towel slung over his shoulder, a fresh shirt in his hands. He didn't even glance at me. Just hummed as he moved around the room, casual, like we were any couple getting ready for a night in.

Then he looked at me.

"You might want to change soon. He'll be here in an hour."

I blinked. "He?"

Kyson smiled—warm, easy, practiced.

"The friend I told you about. Just chill, shorty. He cool. He just wanna meet you."

I stared at the dress again.

Kyson leaned down, kissed the top of my head, and walked off toward the kitchen. Like he hadn't just sold me in a sentence. Like my body was something he could offer because he'd fed it. I sat still for a long time, the dress heavy in my lap, my throat tighter than it had been in days.

And I realized—

The cage wasn't soft anymore.

It was steel.

And tonight, the door was wide open... but only for him.

## 14. TIME TO CHANGE

*"I will give you a new heart and put a new spirit in you."* – *Ezekiel 36:26*

**It had been about two months since the first "meet."**

I called it surviving. Just doing what I had to do. I told myself Kyson was helping me. Protecting me. Loving me—in the only way someone like me deserved. It was the story I fed myself so I could keep playing the part.

He bought me clothes. Kept a roof over my head. Fed me when no one else would. And when he started sending me to "meet" men, to "handle" things—I told myself it was a small price to gain his trust.

But there was nothing small about it.

The "meetings" happened at least three times a week. And when there weren't any? I had to sleep in the bed with Kyson. He told me I was beautiful. That I had power. That he was showing me how to use it.

But I wasn't powerful.

I was owned.

And I knew it.

Kyson didn't even pretend anymore. The sweet voice? Gone. The warm eyes? Gone. Replaced with commands barked over his shoulder. Sharp looks if I didn't move fast enough. Cold silence when I got something wrong. I wasn't his "baby girl" anymore. I was his product.

Eventually, he gave me more freedom. I could go outside—but never alone. Cash was always there. Shadowing me like a leash I couldn't shake.

I tried.

Looked for exits in corner stores. Back doors in alleys. Escapes that didn't look like escapes. But everywhere I turned, Cash was there.

Kyson told me where to go. What to wear. Who to see. If I was gone too long, Cash came inside looking for me.

If I didn't bring back what Kyson expected?

162

He got cold.

Then violent.

He didn't need to say the threat out loud. It was in his fists. In the cold gleam in his eyes. In the way his hand hovered just long enough for me to brace myself.

The first time he hit me, it wasn't a slap.

It was a punch.

Quick. Brutal. No warning.

Because I said the wrong thing to the wrong man.

That was the first time I saw stars. The first time I bled from my mouth. He apologized after. Held me while I cried. Brought flowers the next day.

"You know I hate having to remind you."

And like a fool—like someone desperate to be loved—I nodded.

But I wasn't desperate to be loved anymore. I was desperate to be free. I had to believe that escape was coming. Because if I didn't? Everything I'd endured meant nothing.

And that would've broken me.

Over time, I learned how to smile through it. How to quiet the shaking in my hands with cheap liquor. How to silence my soul with nights I didn't remember.

By the time I turned nineteen, my eyes were hollow. My voice, a whisper. My body moved on autopilot.

But my spirit?

Gone.

I didn't sneak and check messages from Harmony anymore. Or Tia. Didn't want to hear the voices of the only people who had once offered me safety. I'd been gone too long. Too far. Too dirty to come back.

Or so I thought.

It had been over a year since I'd seen the house.

Harmony's house.

Tia's house.

Home—or what used to be.

I didn't plan to go back. I didn't even know why my feet brought me there that day. Maybe it was muscle memory. Maybe it was the ache that bloomed out of nowhere when I saw a mother walking her daughter down the block—matching ponytails, matching laughter.

I crossed the street fast and ducked behind the tall hedges across from the house.

Close enough to feel it.

But hidden.

Cash was a few paces behind. Watching, always. Not interfering. Not yet. The front door was still olive green—Tia painted it after my mom died. The top of the steps still held the wind chimes. Harmony's bike leaned against the side fence, a little rustier now.

It all looked the same.

But I didn't.

I stood there for almost ten minutes. Just staring. I remembered late summer nights on those steps, popsicles melting, us talking about boys like we knew what love was.

I remembered movie marathons in the living room, wrapped in blankets, dreams bigger than our small hearts could hold.

Tia humming in the kitchen, gospel playing low while she stirred a pot like it was sacred.

I remembered feeling safe. Even inside the trauma. Even after the loss. I had been held.

And I didn't know it.

Didn't value it.

Didn't understand that sometimes, the safest place is the one that makes space for your silence—until you're ready to speak. But instead of speaking? I ran. Straight into the arms of someone who turned me into a shadow.

Tears burned the backs of my eyes, but I didn't let them fall. I couldn't afford the weight of regret now. But it was there.

Heavy.

Because here's what no one tells you, you don't always know when you're making the wrong choice—not until it costs you everything. And back then, when I thought it couldn't get worse? That was a lie.

Things had gotten worse.

So much worse.

Cash leaned against the passenger side of the coupe, arms crossed, his eyes never leaving me.

He chewed a toothpick like it was a clock ticking down, slow and steady.

His posture didn't shift, but his gaze narrowed.

Inside the car, Kyson sat behind the wheel, engine off, radio low. He tapped his fingers on the leather steering wheel, eyes locked on the girl in the bushes who hadn't moved in ten minutes.

"She's getting bold," Cash muttered.

Kyson didn't respond.

Cash spit the toothpick to the ground. "Too bold. You gonna check her?"

Kyson finally looked over. "She's just remembering. That house got ghosts."

"Yeah, well… ghosts make people brave."

Kyson smiled—but it didn't reach his eyes.

"She ain't got anywhere else to go."

Cash shrugged. "Everybody got somewhere to go if they're desperate enough."

There was silence.

Kyson stared back toward the house, jaw flexing. He watched me, the way my arms curled around my ribs, the way I kept glancing toward the stoop.

"She won't run," Kyson said flatly.

"You sure?" Cash asked.

"She knows what's waiting out here," Kyson replied. "She knows the streets'll chew her up without me."

Cash didn't argue.

But he didn't agree either.

Just pushed off the car and nodded toward me. "She stays five more minutes, I'm pulling her back."

Kyson waved a hand lazily. "Let her grieve. Let her pretend."

Then he added, quieter, almost to himself,

"Let her remember what she gave up. That way, she won't try to take it back."


I stood there a little longer, heart pounding like it understood this was sacred ground.

Then I whispered under my breath,

"I'm sorry."

I didn't know if it was for leaving. For breaking their hearts. For breaking my own. Maybe all of it.

Then I turned and walked away—before anyone saw me, before I changed my mind, before I forgot how much it hurt to remember, before I put them in danger.

The moment I turned the corner and left the brownstone behind, I felt the car roll forward.

It hadn't moved the entire time I stood watching the house—but now, the engine hummed back to life, slow and deliberate.

Kyson was behind the wheel. Cash was in the passenger seat.

I didn't look at either of them.

I just walked to the curb, opened the back door, and slid in.

The silence inside the car was thick. Cash didn't turn around. Kyson's hands gripped the steering wheel like it was the only thing keeping him calm.

We drove.

No music. No small talk.

Kyson didn't ask where I'd gone.

He didn't have to.

When we pulled up outside the apartment, the air felt colder somehow. Like even the building knew what kind of storm was brewing.

Kyson parked but didn't get out right away. He tapped the steering wheel once. Then again. Then said, without turning around, "You miss home, shorty?"

I stared out the window.

He chuckled to himself. "Funny thing about homes... the doors only swing one way."

No one moved for a beat.

Then Cash got out first. Waited. Watched.

I stepped out, bag clutched tight against me. Kyson followed, closing his door a little too gently.

We climbed the stairs in silence.

Inside, Kyson locked the door behind us, turning the bolt with that slow, deliberate click. He poured a drink. Sat on the couch. Looked at me for a long time.

"You thinking about leaving again?"

I didn't answer.

He laughed—a low, quiet sound. "That door stays open, you know that. Ain't nobody keeping you here."

He took a sip.

"But if you go back over there..." He gestured out the window. "...you think they're gonna take you back? After the things you've done?"

My chest burned, but I didn't let it show.

"You're lucky, shorty," he said. "Most girls don't get this kind of setup. And you? You walk away like it's nothing."

He stood now. Walked toward me, slow and steady.

"You don't know how good you got it."

I didn't flinch.

166

Not this time.

But inside, I was unraveling.

Because I wasn't sure anymore if escape was even possible.

Everything felt dimmer. The lights hadn't changed. The couch was still slouched. The candles still burned low. But I wasn't the same. I didn't take off my shoes. Just stood at the window, arms folded tight, watching the wind rattle the trees.

I kept seeing the chipped green door. Harmony's bike. That life. I had touched it again—for just a second. And it hurt more than I expected.

I didn't miss home. I missed being someone who could walk through that door without shame. Without secrets stitched into her skin.

And then the shame hit.

Hard.

Because I had thought about staying. Thought about knocking. Thought about telling Harmony everything.

But I didn't.

I turned around.

And the worst part? Kyson was right. That door didn't swing both ways. Not anymore. Because even if they opened it—even if they begged me to stay—I wasn't sure I'd ever feel clean enough to walk through it.

I sat down slowly on the edge of the couch, bag still clenched in my lap, and whispered into the still air,

"Why didn't I run when I had the chance?"

But I knew the answer.

Fear.

Control.

The lie I'd been told over and over again, That I was lucky. That I had it good. That no one else would want me now. That I was his. Not a girl. Not a sister. Not a daughter. Not a friend.

Just his.

A door slammed somewhere in the apartment, dragging me out of my thoughts. Kyson's laughter cut off. His footsteps came down the hall.

I didn't move.

I just kept breathing slow and steady.

Because now I understood something Sam once said to me,

"They don't always use chains. Sometimes, they use comfort."

And this?

This was a cage lined in pillows and promises.

But it was still a cage.

I hadn't felt right for a few weeks. I was tired more than usual. My appetite was off. My mood swung wide. Some nights I couldn't sleep. Others, I slept straight through the sunrise and woke up disoriented, drenched in sweat.

At first, I chalked it up to exhaustion. The grind. The weight of pretending. Then the nausea started. Then the missed period. Then the gut feeling I could no longer ignore.

I went to Dollar Tree and grabbed a pregnancy test while Cash was in the car. I got some other things to make it look like I went for something else. I stopped again at McDonalds and went to their bathroom. I took the test there because there was no way I could take it at Kyson's place.

It was a Friday afternoon. The bathroom smelled like bleach and stale air. I locked the door and sat on the edge of the toilet with my heart in my throat.

Three minutes.

I watched the test like it might blink. And then it showed.

Two lines.

Bold. Pink. Unmistakable.

Pregnant.

My hand flew to my mouth. Not from joy. Not from surprise. But from terror. I wasn't supposed to be someone's mother. I wasn't even someone's daughter anymore—not really.

And Kyson?

If he found out…

I knew what he would say.

Whose is it?

You trying to trap me?

You gonna slow down and cost me money now?

I couldn't imagine a world where he took the news with anything but rage.

So I didn't tell him.

I wrapped the test in toilet paper, shoved it deep into the trash, washed her hands, and walked back out like nothing had changed.

But everything had.

That night, I lay awake on the couch, hand resting over her stomach. I wasn't showing yet. No one would know. But I did. And for the first time in a long time… I wanted to live.

Not just survive.

I didn't know what kind of future I had, or if I could even keep this baby. But in that moment, I wanted to try.

I didn't drink that night.

Didn't numb the ache. I just curled up under the blanket and whispered into the dark,

*"I don't know if I'm strong enough for this."*

And somewhere deep inside, something whispered back,

*But you're not alone.*

That night, the television blinked colors across the wall while I drifted into sleep.

And then—

The dream came.


I was back in my childhood bedroom.

The one with the pale-yellow walls. The bookshelf my mother built herself. The tiny radio she used to play gospel from every Sunday morning.

Everything smelled like lemon oil and fresh sheets.

I turned toward the window, and there she was.

My mother.

Not younger.

Not older.

Just... whole.

She stood by the dresser, backlit by soft light, folding a baby onesie I didn't recognize. Her hands moved slow and steady, the way they always did when something was on her mind.

"Mommy?"

She didn't look at me right away.

"You're in trouble, baby," she said gently.

My chest tightened.

She turned, eyes meeting mine—soft and deep and filled with something I couldn't name.

"Something's coming," she whispered. "Something that won't wait for you to be ready."

I shook my head. "I know. I know it is. But I don't know where to go."

"You do," she said.

"Mommy, I can't just leave."

Her voice grew firmer. "Then you'll have to choose. When it happens—you'll have to choose if you want to survive it or stay in it."

I felt myself crying, but in the dream, no tears fell.

"I don't feel strong."

"You're stronger than me," she said. "And I was strong."

She walked to me then, placed her warm hand over my stomach.

"You're not just fighting for you now. You hear me?"

I nodded.

She leaned in close, forehead to mine.

"You have to go. Now, if you can. If not—get ready."

Her voice—her body—began to fade.

I tried to hold on.

"Mommy?"

But she was gone.

Just the hum of static.

Just the soft wind from the window.

Just her voice echoing in the dark,

"Choose to live, baby."

I woke up gasping.

The television was still flickering. My blanket had slipped halfway to the floor. I sat up slowly, heart pounding, the words still burning in my ears.

Something's coming.

You have to go.

If not… get ready.

I stared at the ceiling for a long time. Felt the baby—still just cells and hope—somewhere deep inside. And I knew the truth, there would be no saving me later. I had to save myself now.

The days after I found out were fragile. I moved through them like glass—careful, quiet, deliberate. I stopped drinking completely. Told Kyson it was making me feel sick. He didn't question it at first. Didn't care, as long as I kept doing what he asked. As long as I showed up, smiled, and came back with cash.

But I started saying no more often.

Started coming home early. Started asking for breaks. Started hiding my money. My movements grew slower. My body more tired.

And the fear?

It never left. It clung to me like a second skin.

I kept the pregnancy a secret for six weeks.

Almost two months of silence.

Two months of whispering apologies to a baby I wasn't sure I could keep, but already felt tethered to.

Two months of hiding my pills in the trash, my nausea behind bathroom stalls, my dreams behind my eyes.

But secrets don't stay buried. Not in a place where control is everything.

It happened on a Wednesday night. Kyson had just come home— tight-jawed, storm-eyed. Something hadn't gone right. Money was short. His temper already lit. I was curled on the couch, trying not to breathe too loudly.

A bowl of uneaten soup sat on the table beside me.

"You sick again?" he asked, tossing his jacket onto a chair.

"I think I caught something," I said, my voice low.

He stared too long.

Walked over.

Picked up the bowl.

Sniffed it.

He slammed it back down.

"You haven't eaten all day?"

"I wasn't hungry."

"That ain't normal, shorty."

I didn't respond.

He narrowed his eyes.

Then looked at me—really looked. My oversized sweatshirt. The way I curled protectively around myself. The faint softness rising just below my ribs.

His voice dropped.

"You pregnant?"

My whole body stilled.

He didn't yell.

Didn't move.

Just stood there, his voice flat.

Accusing.

Deadly.

"Answer me."

My breath caught. "I don't know."

"Don't lie to me."

"I'm not," I whispered. "I just—I wasn't sure how to tell you—"

Before I could finish, he moved.

Fast.

A flash of rage.

A fist.

It caught me hard in the side, just below the ribs. I crumpled. The pain knocked the wind from my lungs, my voice from my throat. I hit the floor on my knees, hands grasping at nothing.

My head rang.

My body pulsed with shock.

I didn't cry out.

Didn't scream.

Just tried to breathe.

And in that moment—face pressed to dirty floorboards, one hand over my belly—I knew, this was no longer about escape.

This was about survival.

"I take care of you," he snarled. "I feed you. I keep a roof over your head. And this is how you repay me?"

I tried to crawl away, but he grabbed a fistful of my hair and yanked me back.

I screamed and threw my arms around my belly, leaving my face wide open.

The second blow hit my jaw.

Something cracked.

Blood sprayed from my mouth across the floor.

The third—

My stomach.

A flash of white.

Then nothing.

I don't know when he stopped hitting me—

Because I left my body.

I was floating.

Heavy and weightless at the same time.

I could hear everything.

But I couldn't move.

Couldn't speak.

Could barely breathe.

My breaths were so shallow, anyone watching would've thought I was dead.

And maybe—

I was.

Sirens.

Blurred voices.

White lights.

Pain blooming everywhere like fire under skin.

Then darkness swallowed me whole.

Kyson didn't call 911. He didn't cry. He didn't stop to check if I was alive. This was how he handled his problems.

He dragged my limp, bloodied body to his other car, the one without plates.

Told Cash, cold and flat, "Take care of it."

Cash didn't ask questions.

He never did.

They drove ten blocks to a deserted corner near a long-abandoned bus stop.

Then they rolled me out like yesterday's trash. Onto the pavement. Like I was nothing. And they drove away.

I laid there—barely conscious, pain screaming beneath my skin—twenty, maybe thirty minutes. Trying to move. Trying to breathe. Trying not to die.

Then I heard footsteps.

A woman walking her dog.

She paused—thought I was a pile of clothes.

Until she heard me.

A broken, desperate whisper.

"Help… me…"

She froze.

Turned.

Saw the blood.

Dropped her dog's leash and screamed. She ran to me, dialing 911 with shaking hands. She knelt beside me, touched my forehead gently, and prayed loud enough for heaven to hear.

"It's okay, baby. You're gonna be okay. Just stay with me. Stay with me."

Somewhere in the fog, I managed to whisper, "I'm pregnant."

She gasped.

"Jesus, no…"

The paramedics arrived ten minutes later.

My pulse was faint. Both eyes swollen shut. Lip split. Bruises dark across my neck, arms, ribs. And my stomach—my stomach was hard with trauma.

Internal bleeding.

They suspected the worst.

They cut my clothes off in the back of the ambulance. Started compressions. I never opened my eyes.

At the hospital, while surgeons rushed me into emergency surgery, a nurse searched through the small wallet that had somehow stayed in my back pocket.

A crumpled ID card.

One emergency contact.

Inez Santana.

The nurse made the call.

Tia was folding laundry when the phone rang. She almost didn't answer. The number was unfamiliar. But something in her spirit stirred.

Twisted.

When she picked up—

The voice on the other end shattered her.

The nurse spoke gently. "Your daughter Divinity is in surgery. She's sustained major injuries, from a physical assault. She's in critical condition."

Her knees buckled. The phone slipped from her hand. Harmony caught it mid-fall. Snatched it to her ear.

"What happened?" she cried. "Where is she?" The nurse told her what hospital and Harmony and Tia was there within the hour.

Once they reached the hospital they were ushered into a waiting room with beige walls and ticking clocks. Tia's hands trembled as she filled out the paperwork for me. Harmony sat with her head in her hands, whispering over and over, "She said she wasn't coming back. She said she couldn't. We should've tried harder. We should've-"

"Don't." Tia said, voice breaking, "Don't you blame yourself. We loved her everyday she was gone. We prayed for her every night."

And they waited. Waited to see if the girl they both loved would ever wake up again.

My body lay motionless under crisp hospital sheets. Tubes down my throat. Monitors blinking. My belly wrapped in gauze. Inside me, life still flickered-barely. And in the quiet dark of unconsciousness, I dreamed. This one felt divine.

I was standing in a field. Golden. Endless. The air warm, light wrapping me like silk. In front of me stood a woman I hadn't seen in years.

My mother.

Alive.

Whole. Smiling. I stepped forward, mouth trembling.

"Mommy?" My mother nodded, eyes soft and full of something deeper than peace.

"Baby, it's time to come home." She said.

"I-I messed everything up," I whispered. "You wouldn't even recognize me now."

My mother stepped forward and touched my cheek.

"I've never stopped seeing you."

I broke. Collapsed into her arms like a child. My mother held me tight, whispering, "God didn't leave you. He was there in every step. Every tear. Every scream. You were just hurting too much to hear him."

"I don't know how to come back."

"You don't have to. Just say yes. Say yes to healing. Say yes to living. Say yes to grace."

I pulled back, tears soaking my face.

"Do you think He'll still want me?"

My mother kissed my forehead.

"He never stopped."


Back in the hospital bed, my fingers twitched. The surgery was over.

My lips parted. A single tear slipped down my cheek.

I was coming back.

The light in the room was too soft to be real. At first I thought I was dreaming again but then I heard the beeping- slow, steady.

I blinked.

My eyes stung. My throat felt like sandpaper. I tried to move, but every muscle screamed.

And then I saw her.

Tia.

Her face was blurry, but I'd recognize that voice anywhere.

"Divinity... baby—"

She rushed to my side. Her hand gripped mine like it was the only thing keeping her standing.

I blinked again, and behind her was Harmony.

My Harmony.

She looked older. Tired. But still her.

She reached for my other hand, her lip trembling. "Oh my God, Div... we thought we were going to lose you."

Tears spilled from my swollen eyes before I could stop them.

"I'm… I'm sorry," I whispered, my voice barely a thread. "I didn't know where else to go…"

"You don't have to be sorry," Tia said, brushing hair from my forehead. "You're here. That's all that matters."

"But the baby…" I choked, panic rising in my chest. "Did I—?"

They looked at each other.

Harmony nodded, and the look in her eyes shattered me.

"You're still pregnant," she said. "They said it's a miracle. The baby's okay. Strong heartbeat."

And I broke.

Everything inside me cracked open.

I sobbed, loud and ugly, my body shaking with relief and fear and something I hadn't felt in a long time—hope.

"God… oh God… I thought I lost it. I thought I lost everything…"

Tia leaned over, holding my hand tighter. "You didn't lose anything that matters, baby. You're here. That baby is here. And we're not letting you go through this alone."

I clung to her hand like a drowning girl grabbing driftwood.

Tears ran down my face in thick rivers.

I looked up at the ceiling, still sobbing, still shaking.

And I whispered through the pain and the gratitude—

"Thank you, God… thank you for not leaving me."

The room eventually stilled.

Harmony had drifted off in the corner chair, arms crossed, her chest rising and falling with that soft, steady rhythm I used to fall asleep to at sleepovers.

Tia sat beside me, dozing lightly, her hand still wrapped around mine like she was afraid to let go.

I could still feel the bruises on my body, deep and burning. I could still taste blood at the back of my throat if I breathed too deep. But something had shifted. I wasn't alone anymore.

Not in the hospital.

Not in the world.

Not even in my pain.

I had a life inside me.

A baby.

A second chance.

And maybe—even after everything—I still had a future. That thought scared me more than anything. Because now I had a choice. I could stay here—in this place of pain and silence and shame—and keep pretending

I didn't deserve more.

Or…

I could trust in something bigger than me. I could trust that God hadn't just saved me out of pity… but because He still had a plan for me. I could heal. I could rebuild. I could try. I wasn't sure how. I wasn't even sure I was ready.

But for the first time in years…

I wanted to be.

## 15.  ROOM TO BREATHE

*"Peace doesn't knock. You have to leave the door open." – Cassandra Wade*

**The first night out of surgery was the longest of my life.**

The painkillers dulled the edges, but I still felt everything. I tried not to use them because of the baby, but sometimes I had no choice. They assured me it wouldn't be harmful—they were giving me medication approved for pregnancy.

The aching. The soreness. The heaviness in my chest that wasn't just from the bruises—it was grief. Shame. Fear. It clung to me like fog.

I drifted in and out of sleep, lost in the rhythm of beeping monitors, the low murmur of nurses, and the constant hum of fluorescent lights overhead.

And then she came in.

After Tia and Harmony had stepped out to grab something to eat, the door opened, and a nurse I hadn't seen before stepped inside. She looked older—maybe in her sixties—with silver curls pinned neatly under a lavender cap and soft, coffee-colored skin. Her presence was quiet. Gentle. She moved around the room, checking my IV, adjusting the monitor. She didn't ask what happened. Didn't ask how I'd ended up like this. She just worked quietly.

When she finished, she stood at the foot of my bed, folded her hands, and in the gentlest voice I'd heard in years, asked—

"Can I pray with you, baby?"

I didn't speak. Didn't nod. But I didn't say no either.

That was enough.

She bowed her head.

"Father God," she began, her voice thick with warmth, "I thank you for this child. I thank You for sparing her life. Lord, I don't know what brought her here last night, but You do. And I know You've kept her for a reason. I ask You to comfort her, to guide her, to heal her from the inside out. Let her know she is not forgotten. Not abandoned. Not unloved. You are there. You have always been there, Lord."

She paused, and her voice lowered even more, thick with grace.

"...Remind her that this is not the end. It's the beginning. In Jesus' name, Amen."

When she finished, she touched my foot lightly through the blanket and whispered, "Rest now, sweetheart. You're not alone anymore."

And then she left.

But the prayer stayed. It lingered in the air, in my chest, in my bones. That was the first—and only—time I saw her that day.

Later, I asked the next nurse about her. She frowned, confused. Said she was the only one assigned to my room. And no one matching that description worked that floor. I started to wonder if I'd dreamed it. But I hadn't. I was wide awake. And that encounter stayed with me.

That night, after Harmony and Tia left to get some sleep, I lay in the dark, staring at the ceiling, tears sliding into my ears.

And for the first time in years... I prayed. Really prayed. Not out loud. Not fancy. Just a whisper from somewhere buried deep,

*God, if You're really still there... help me. Help me work through the hurt, work through my faith, work through all the darkness I have seen. Lord, I need you more than ever. In Jesus' name, Amen.*

Something shifted. Not like thunder. More like a crack. Just enough light to slip through. But I felt it. And for the first time in a long, long time... I didn't feel dead inside. I felt something else.

I felt hope.

The next morning, I was awake before the sun rose. The light from the hallway crept under the door in a soft line. The hospital room was still. Monitors hummed. My IV drip clicked. Outside, the city hadn't stirred yet. No footsteps. No voices. Just the hush of a world not quite awake.

I hadn't slept much, but it didn't matter. Something inside me had shifted. Not just the pain meds. Not just the prayer. Something else. A quiet resolve settling into my bones.

When the door opened, I knew it was Harmony before I saw her. She padded in quietly, a hoodie over her pajamas, hair wrapped up, slippers soft on the tile. She didn't say anything at first. Just walked to the chair and sat down beside me.

I looked over, and our eyes met.

"Couldn't sleep?" I whispered.

She shook her head. "Didn't want you to wake up alone."

A silence stretched between us—not cold. Not tense. Just full. She stared at my face, eyes swimming with things she couldn't say yet. I saw the questions there. The ache. The anger.

"I'm sorry," I said softly.

Her jaw clenched. "You don't have to keep saying that."

"Yes, I do."

"No, you don't." Her voice broke, and she stood. Started pacing the tiny space between the bed and the wall. "You think we didn't try to find you? That we didn't look, and pray, and drive around wondering if we'd see your face on a corner or the news?"

"I didn't want you to find me like that," I whispered. "I didn't want you to see what I'd become."

Harmony turned, eyes flashing. "You didn't become anything. Someone did that to you."

I looked away.

"I should've known," she said, softer now. "I should've figured it out sooner. I was your best friend. I saw you pulling away. I knew something was off. I just didn't know it was that."

Her voice cracked.

"I'm so sorry, Div."

That broke me.

Not the softness. Not the grief. But the way she said it like she should've been the one to carry my pain.

I blinked through tears. "It wasn't your job to protect me."

"Wasn't it?" she asked. "Because I would've. I would've taken every hit. Every scar. Every moment you had to spend pretending you were okay."

I reached for her hand.

She took it.

And for a moment, we just sat there. Breathing. Holding on to the thread between who we were and who we were becoming.

"I'm trying," I said.

"I know," she whispered. "I'm here while you do."

The door opened again, and Tia stepped in with a fresh change of clothes folded neatly in her arms. She stopped when she saw us—hands clasped, tear-stained faces.

She smiled.

The kind that said I don't need to know what was said. I just needed to see this.

"Morning, baby," she said, walking over and kissing my forehead.

And for the first time in a long time, the word baby didn't sting. It soothed. I didn't say it out loud, but I think she felt it.

I'm still here.

I'm still trying.

And I'm not running anymore.

Later that afternoon, a woman came into the room with a clipboard pressed to her chest and a soft, practiced smile.

She wasn't wearing scrubs. Her cardigan was cream. Her voice was kind. Her badge read, K. MARTIN, Trauma Social Worker.

"Hi Divinity," she said, closing the door behind her. "I'm here just to talk. Nothing heavy if you're not ready. I just wanted to check in. May I sit?"

I glanced at Tia and Harmony, who both looked at me. I nodded.

The woman sat in the chair across from my bed, legs crossed, pen clipped to her folder, though she didn't write a thing.

"I know you've been through more than most," she said gently. "And I'm not here to ask for details. I'm here to ask what you need."

I didn't answer right away. Because what I needed wasn't something she could give me. I needed the year back. I needed my body to feel like mine again. I needed time to rewind to the day I stood on Chris's porch and chose the streets over safety.

But none of those were real options.

So I said the only thing I could.

"I don't know."

She nodded. "That's okay. 'I don't know' is a starting place."

She didn't push. She just explained that I could get free therapy through the hospital's survivor program. That there were safe housing options for young mothers. That I didn't have to talk to police if I wasn't ready. That I had rights—even now. Especially now.

She handed me a packet, but didn't pressure me to open it.

When she stood to leave, she looked me in the eye and said, "When you're ready to speak your truth out loud—whatever that looks like—there are people ready to hear it without judgment. Just... don't silence yourself anymore to protect the people who hurt you. That's not your job."

Her voice didn't shake. But mine did.

"Thank you," I whispered.

She nodded once and walked out.

I stared at the folder on my lap for a long time. Didn't open it.

I turned toward the window.

The sky had shifted again—soft blue, hints of gold near the horizon. A new day easing toward dusk.

And for the first time in my life, I was starting to believe that healing didn't mean forgetting. It meant naming what hurt. So it wouldn't own me anymore.

The next morning, sunlight spilled through the hospital blinds like a soft apology. I sat propped up with pillows, sipping slowly from a cup of watered-down apple juice while the IV tugged gently at my arm.

My body still hurt—but my spirit wasn't as crushed. Not like before. There was something different in me now. Something small but strong. Like a seed breaking through the dirt.

Harmony came in first, carrying a bag of clean clothes and a small bottle of my favorite cocoa butter lotion. Tia followed close behind with her usual calm presence, though her eyes looked like they hadn't rested all night.

"Good morning," Tia said softly.

"Hey," I whispered, my throat still scratchy. "Thank you… for being here."

Harmony came to my side, setting the bag down.

"You scared us," she said, her voice already cracking.

"I know."

"And you didn't have to go through this alone."

I nodded, but I couldn't meet her eyes yet.

Tia sat down beside my bed. Her hand wrapped around mine—firm, warm, familiar.

"I want you to come back with us, baby," she said gently. "Me and Harmony… we'll take care of you. You don't have to do this by yourself."

I felt the sting behind my eyes again—but I held it back this time.

I took a breath.

"I… I love y'all," I said slowly. "More than I can say. And if I could rewind time, I would've never left."

Harmony's hand found my shoulder, squeezing.

"But I can't go back," I whispered. "Not because I don't want you there. I need you. I just… I need to figure out how to stand on my own two feet. For me. For this baby."

Tia looked down, her lips pressed together.

"I want to find a women's shelter," I said. "Somewhere that can help me get on my feet, teach me how to live… not just survive. I need to get my life together."

"You don't have to prove anything to us, baby," she said.

"I'm not trying to prove something," I replied, wiping at a tear. "I'm trying to heal. And this time, I need to learn how to do that from the ground up. I want to be ready to give this child a life better than the one I had."

They were both quiet.

But then Tia nodded.

"And we'll be here," she said. "However you need us. You don't have to disappear again."

"I won't," I promised. "I won't shut you out anymore."

Harmony finally smiled through her tears and leaned in to kiss my forehead.

I didn't deserve them.

But God gave them to me anyway.

Later that day, the knock came on the door.

Tia stood up first, assuming it was a nurse, but when she opened it, her body went still.

A tall woman stepped into the doorway—mid-forties maybe, in slacks and a navy blazer, clipboard in hand. Her badge caught the fluorescent light.

"Good afternoon," she said gently. "I'm Ms. Porter. I work with the city's Victim Advocacy and Youth Outreach Division. The hospital filed a report regarding your assault, and I'd like to speak with you. Just you, if that's okay."

Tia turned back to me, waiting for my answer.

I nodded.

Harmony and Tia stepped out, closing the door behind them.

Ms. Porter pulled a chair to the side of my bed. She didn't open her clipboard right away. Didn't ask any questions.

She looked at me—not past me, not through me. At me.

"I read the intake report," she said. "But I want to hear from you. Whatever you're ready to tell me."

I hesitated. My fingers twisted in the blanket. "How much do you know?"

She folded her hands in her lap. "Enough to be angry. Not enough to help yet."

I looked away. "I was with a man named Kyson. I thought he was helping me. He wasn't."

She didn't flinch. Didn't press.

I took a breath.

"He put me out there. Had people watching me. Controlling me. I wasn't... free."

"Did he ever threaten you?"

I nodded. "More than that."

She paused. "Do you want to press charges?"

That question settled heavy between us.

"I don't know," I whispered. "If I do... what happens?"

"Well," she said carefully, "If you choose to file a formal statement, we can open an investigation. You won't be alone. We can help place you in a transitional housing program—one that protects women escaping trafficking. Full support services. Medical. Legal. Therapy."

"But if I don't?"

She hesitated. "You still get help. You'll still be protected. But Kyson? He'll keep doing this to other girls. Girls like you. Maybe younger."

That thought pierced something in me.

Not just the pain.

But the responsibility.

Because I knew what it was like to be that girl.

"Can I think about it?" I asked.

"Of course." She stood, gently placing a business card on the side table. "But don't wait too long. We'll help you either way, Divinity. We're not here to take your power—we're here to give it back."

She paused at the door.

"You survived. That's a beginning. Not a burden."

Then she left.

I stared at the card for a long time.

Victim Advocate. Survivor Services. Emergency Safe House.

A phone number.

And a name.

Ms. Porter.

I didn't reach for it.

Not yet. I wasn't against talking to her.

That meant something.

That meant... maybe... I was almost ready to fight back.

Tia and Harmony had just returned with soup when another knock came at the door.

Two police officers stepped in—a man and a woman, both with calm, deliberate movements and faces trained not to flinch.

"Ms. Rivera?" the woman asked, voice soft.

"That's me," I said, my voice still scratchy.

"We'd like to speak with you, if you're up for it," the male officer added.

I nodded. "I already spoke to Ms. Porter."

"We know," the woman said gently. "We're here to walk you through the legal side of things. What happens next."

Tia glanced at me protectively. Harmony reached for my hand.

The officers pulled up chairs. The man flipped open a notepad.

"We know you were left at a street corner unconscious," he said. "Surveillance footage from a nearby building caught a partial angle of the car—and a clear image of the man in the passenger seat."

He looked at me carefully.

"When we ran the face through the system, we got a match. His name came up—Kyson Dominguez."

I went still.

The name hung in the air like a toxin I couldn't stop breathing.

"We were hoping you could confirm that name," the woman added.

I swallowed.

"Yes," I said. "Kyson Dominguez. That's him."

The name landed with a weight that settled in the silence.

"He beat me," I continued. "He controlled me. He trafficked me. I wasn't his girlfriend. I was... I was his property."

Tia's hand squeezed mine gently. Harmony sat forward, her eyes wet but locked onto me.

The officers exchanged a look—sad, grim, confirming something between them.

"We've been tracking reports," the woman said. "Girls with similar injuries. Same M.O. Same type of control. A few tried to come forward. Most disappeared. One... didn't survive."

I swallowed hard.

"We brought photos," she added. "We'd like to show them to you— see if you recognize anyone. Only if you're willing."

My chest ached. I felt the tears building already.

But I nodded. "Yes. I need to see them. Their families deserve to know."

Tia leaned close, her voice barely above a whisper. "You don't have to carry this alone."

"I know," I said, stronger now. "But I still have to carry it."

The officer opened a manila envelope and began sliding the photos across the tray in front of me, one by one.

Some were recent. Some older. Some faces I didn't recognize.

And then—

My breath caught.

A single sob cracked out before I could stop it.

I pointed to the seventh photo, trembling.

"That's Sam," I choked. "Samantha. She… she was the first person who helped me. Taught me how to survive when I left home. She disappeared months ago. I looked everywhere."

Tia's hand gripped mine like an anchor. Harmony covered her mouth, tears falling.

"Did she ever mention Kyson by name?" the officer asked.

"No," I said. "But now… now her rules make sense. She always said—'People will offer you things. Most of them will cost you later.' She must've met him before me. She just… never got the chance to warn me."

The officers were silent for a beat.

Then the man said, "When we bring him in—if we do—you willing to identify him in a lineup?"

I hesitated, the fear flickering again at the edges of my thoughts.

But I nodded.

"I have to."

The officers stood slowly, nodding with respect.

"We'll stay in touch," the woman said. "Thank you for your courage, Ms. Rivera. It matters."

After they left, the door clicked shut behind them, and the room went quiet again.

Tia sat back down, eyes shining. Harmony leaned in, gently pulling her chair closer to the bed.

She didn't speak at first.

She just sat there beside me, her eyes searching my face like she was seeing me for the first time in a long time—not as the broken girl who left, but the one who fought her way back.

Her hand found mine under the blanket.

"You did the right thing," she said softly. "You're brave, Div. You always were."

I turned my head toward the window, the evening light falling gold across the sheets.

And I whispered,

186

"I hope Sam knows."

"I just… I wish someone had done the same for me," I said quietly. "Back then. With Darnell."

Tia's eyes filled instantly.

She didn't try to blink it away.

Her voice cracked. "We failed you."

"No—"

"I did," she insisted gently, gripping my hand like she was holding the truth in it. "I should've known. I should've seen. I should've protected you."

Harmony's voice joined her, thick with grief. "I knew something was off… with how he acted around you. The way you tensed when he was near. But I didn't know what to call it. I didn't push."

I shook my head, slow and firm. "Don't. Don't carry that."

"But—"

"He was careful. He was good at hiding. At twisting things so no one questioned him. And I…" I paused, throat tightening, "I wasn't ready to speak. I didn't even have the words yet."

Silence washed over us, but it wasn't hollow.

It was full.

Of pain.

Of truth.

Of love still present in the wreckage.

Tia leaned closer, squeezing my hand tighter.

"But you're speaking now," she whispered. "And that's what matters."

Harmony nodded. "You're not alone anymore. And we're going to walk this with you. All of it."

I closed my eyes, let the warmth of their hands anchor me.

This wasn't a full healing.

But it was the beginning of it.

Three days later, the doctor came in with my discharge papers.

"You're stable," he said. "Still healing, but strong enough to go home. You'll need follow-ups for the pregnancy and therapy for… everything else."

Everything else.

The words sat heavy in the air, unspoken but understood.

I nodded. "Okay."

Tia and Harmony were already in the lobby when the nurse wheeled me out. It was sunny. Clear skies. The kind of day that felt like a fresh page.

Tia helped me into the car, then slid behind the wheel, her smile laced with something she was clearly trying to hold in.

"What?" I asked, easing back gently against the seat.

"I have good news," she said. "I made a few calls. There's a women's shelter in the city—not far. They have a room open, and they're ready for you. Today, even."

I blinked. "Seriously?"

She nodded. "They help young mothers. Give them time to get on their feet. Help with job training, prenatal care. All of it."

My heart swelled—equal parts gratitude and nerves.

"But," she added carefully, "they're flexible on your arrival. So I was hoping… maybe you could come home with us for one night?"

I looked at her.

"Just one night," she said softly. "Let us feed you. Let us thank God for keeping you alive. No pressure. Just love."

Harmony leaned forward from the back seat, her smile shining with tear-bright eyes.

"Please say yes. I already picked the movie. And I made that chocolate cake you like."

A laugh burst from my throat before I could stop it. It startled me, how good it felt to laugh again.

"Okay," I said, smiling. "One night."

They both exhaled like they'd been holding their breath for months.

I turned to the window as we pulled away from the hospital. I wasn't the same girl who had run from that house. But for the first time in a long time, I wasn't running from myself either.

That evening, stepping into Tia's house felt like walking into a memory.

The familiar scent of lavender and vanilla wrapped around me like a blanket. The walls, adorned with family photos and warm hues, whispered stories of love and resilience.

Harmony stood just inside the doorway, arms open, her smile stretching all the way to her eyes. She hugged me carefully, like something sacred.

Tia stood behind her, a soft smile trembling on her lips, her eyes glistening.

"Welcome home, Divinity," she said, her voice thick with emotion.

I looked around the room—same couch, same rug, same light spilling

188

through the windows like hope.

And I managed a small smile.

"Thank you for having me."

Dinner was a spread of comfort foods—baked macaroni and cheese, collard greens, fried chicken, and cornbread. The kind of food that felt like home. The kind that made silence okay.

The flavors danced on my tongue, each bite a reminder of the love poured into this meal. It wasn't just food—it was restoration, one forkful at a time.

After dinner, we settled in the living room. The soft hum of a gospel song floated from the radio, low and steady. The couch cushions still sagged the same way. Harmony sat beside me, her hand resting gently over mine.

"Divinity," she began softly, "we want you to know how proud we are of you. Standing up. Speaking your truth. That takes a kind of courage most people don't have."

Tia nodded, her voice thick with emotion. "We're sorry we didn't see the signs earlier. Sorry we didn't protect you from Darnell. We failed you then. But we're here now—and we're not going anywhere."

Tears welled up in my eyes, a mix of sorrow, relief, and something brighter that I hadn't felt in years—being seen.

"Thank you," I whispered. "Your support means everything to me."

That night, I lay in the guest room—my old room—wrapped in a soft blanket, the gentle creak of the ceiling fan above me lulling me toward sleep. The air smelled like lavender.

I turned toward the small dresser, its top still cluttered with a few childhood remnants. And there, tucked in the edge of the mirror, was a faded photograph. Me and Harmony, maybe thirteen or fourteen, arms slung around each other's shoulders, laughing with mouths wide open. I didn't even remember the photo being taken—but I remembered that laugh. That version of me. The girl who trusted the world a little more.

Harmony stepped into the doorway, leaning against the frame. She'd changed into sweats and wiped the makeup from her face. Her eyes were puffy from crying earlier, but when she saw me holding the picture, she smiled.

"You kept this?" I asked.

She shrugged. "I tried to throw it away once. Couldn't do it."

I held the photo against my chest. "I don't even recognize that girl anymore."

Harmony stepped closer, voice low. "I do. She's still in there. Just

189

bruised."

I looked up at her. "You've changed too."

Harmony gave a soft chuckle. "Yeah. Life doesn't give you a choice sometimes. But you made it back. And that means something."

She walked over and gently placed the cocoa butter lotion on the nightstand. "Sleep good, D. You're safe."

The shadows still lingered in the corners of the room, soft but real. But they didn't chase me anymore. Not here. Not tonight.

With Tia and Harmony just down the hall, with their love holding me steady, I felt something new settle in my chest.

A quiet strength.

A whispered promise.

A future.

The next morning came too fast. I barely slept, though not from pain this time. It was the kind of restlessness that comes with change—the weight of a new beginning pressing on your chest like both a warning and a promise.

Tia made breakfast—something light, just toast and fruit and tea—but I couldn't eat much. My nerves twisted every bite into knots. Harmony tried to fill the silence with small talk, but I could feel her emotions swaying under every word.

Only this time, I wasn't disappearing.

I was walking toward something better.

When the car pulled up to the women's shelter, I gripped my bag tighter. The building wasn't much—a modest brownstone with chipped paint and flowerpots lining the steps—but something about it felt safe. It didn't promise perfection. It didn't demand healing on a timeline. It just asked me to show up.

Inside, a woman with salt-and-pepper braids and calm eyes greeted me with a clipboard in one hand and a hug in the other.

"We're glad you're here, Divinity," she said. "This is a place for healing, not shame."

Her name was Ms. Hightower, the shelter coordinator. And in less than a minute, she made me feel more seen than most people had in years.

Tia and Harmony didn't follow me inside. We said our goodbyes on the steps.

"I'll call you," I promised, my voice tight.

"You better," Harmony said, laughing through tears. "And send belly pics when that bump shows up."

Tia hugged me so tight I almost didn't let go.

"Take this time," she said. "For you. For that baby. But don't forget—you still got a home. Always."

I nodded, my throat too full to speak.

Then I turned, climbed the steps, and walked into my next chapter.

The room was small but clean. A single bed with new sheets. A window overlooking a patchy garden. A dresser with three drawers and enough space to feel like mine.

There were other women too—older, younger, some with babies on their hips, others quiet with eyes that said, I've seen what you've seen. A few nodded when I passed, like we already understood each other.

That night, I sat on the edge of my bed, one hand resting over my stomach. I didn't know how to be a mother. I barely knew how to be myself. But for the first time, I wasn't running. I was staying.

And in that stillness, I felt it again.

That gentle nudge.

Not a voice, but a knowing.

A call.

And this time… I was ready to answer.

The next morning, Ms. Hightower helped me schedule my first prenatal appointment at a nearby clinic partnered with the shelter. She handed me a folder with my name on it, a transportation voucher, and said, "They're expecting you."

No charge.

No catch.

Just care.

I wasn't used to people doing things for me without expecting something in return.

But Ms. Hightower didn't want anything. Not even a thank-you. Just wanted me to show up and take care of myself.

The clinic's waiting room was painted soft yellow. Posters of smiling babies lined the walls. Across from me, a woman rocked twins in her arms, humming something sweet and low.

When my name was called, I felt my heart stutter.

The nurse was gentle. Walked me through it all—bloodwork, paperwork, all the things I didn't even know to ask for.

Then the ultrasound. Cold gel. Wand to belly. Screen lit up. And there it was. A flicker. A flutter. A heartbeat. Alive. Moving. Mine.

Tears spilled over without warning.

191

"You're about twelve weeks," the technician said, smiling. "And everything looks good."

I couldn't speak.

I just nodded.

Back at the shelter, I tucked the ultrasound photo into the drawer beside my journal and the letter from my mother—miraculously recovered and returned to me by the police after the investigation.

I sat there a long while, eyes on the door.

There was a group counseling session starting in ten minutes. My name was already on the list.

I could skip it. No one would judge me.

But I'd come this far.

And I didn't want to be silent anymore.

I grabbed my sweater, slipped my shoes on, and whispered under my breath,

"Okay, God. I'm still scared… but I'm going."

Then I opened the door.

And stepped into the next part of my healing.

As I walked down the hallway toward the group room, my fingers grazed the wall—just lightly, just enough to remind myself I was still here. Still solid. Still standing.

The voices inside the room buzzed low, soft, human.

I hesitated one second at the door.

Then I stepped through it.

And with that step, I chose not just to survive—but to be seen.

# 16.  STILL STANDING

*"After you have suffered a little while... He will restore you." – 1 Peter 5:10*

**The folding chairs formed a loose circle in the center of the basement rec room**
—just enough seats for maybe ten women. The walls were plain and beige, the ceiling low, the lights too soft to feel clinical but too dim to feel warm.

I hesitated at the threshold, hovering in the doorway like I wasn't sure if I belonged.

Ms. Hightower stood by the coffee machine, refilling a chipped mug. She caught my eye and gave me a soft nod.

"You made it," she said.

I didn't reply—just stepped in quietly and took the last empty seat. No one looked up. No one asked questions. That felt like a small mercy.

The group leader, a tall, graceful woman in her late forties with box braids wrapped in a cobalt scarf, introduced herself as Ms. Dahlia. She didn't read rules. Didn't explain the format. She just smiled gently and said, "Whoever needs to speak today... speak."

For a while, no one did.

Then a woman with bright red acrylic nails and swollen ankles said, "I found out last week I'm pregnant again... third one by a man who swore I was his only."

Another woman chimed in. "My sister said I could stay. That was three days ago. Haven't seen her since."

The stories started slow.

Until Kiara spoke.

She couldn't have been more than nineteen. Hair shaved close. Lips dry. A hoodie swallowed her whole frame. She stared down at her chipped sneakers when she said, "I thought he loved me. Said I didn't need no one else. Bought me things. Gave me weed and pretty words. Then he took everything back. Even my name."

My fingers clenched in my lap.

Kiara went on, "I still don't know when it shifted. One day I was his girl. Next day I was his product."

No one flinched. No one gasped. Because we all understood.

I didn't speak. But my silence screamed.

After the circle broke, Ms. Hightower caught me on my way to the stairs.

"You good?" she asked.

I nodded. "Yeah. I just… I needed to hear that."

"Come back next week," Ms. Hightower said. "Even if you don't speak."

I looked over my shoulder at Kiara, who was now laughing softly with two older women near the snack table.

"Maybe." I said.

But in my heart, I already knew.

I'd be back.

Later that night, I opened my journal for the first time in what felt like years. The pages were clean. Empty. Waiting.

I stared at the blank page so long, I forgot how to begin. My hand hovered. For a moment, I thought about writing his name.

Kyson.

I even started the letter "Dear…"

But the pen stalled.

And instead, I scratched it out and started over.

Then I just wrote,

*Day One. I'm still here.*

The pen didn't stop after that. The words came slow, then fast— spilling, unraveling, stitching pieces of me together with every line. I didn't write about Kyson. Not yet. I wrote about the shelter. About Ms. Hightower and her peppermint tea. The way she smiled every time she passed me in the hallway like she could see through my silence and loved me anyway.

I wrote about the woman down the hall who braided my hair without asking why I looked so tired. The laughter in the kitchen at breakfast— real, unfiltered, healing laughter.

And I ended the entry with a quiet prayer,

*God, I'm not whole. But I want to be. Show me how.*

That night, I started praying consistently. Not always out loud. Sometimes just a whisper, or a breath, or a glance at the ceiling. But I prayed. And every time I did, something inside me softened. I started waking up with less dread. Started looking people in the eyes again. Started smiling—just a little. It wasn't perfect. But it was healing.

The days began to blend together—but not in the numb, endless way they used to. Now, they passed with rhythm. A kind of peace.

Mornings were spent in counseling or group support. Afternoons brought journaling, or volunteering in the shelter's kitchen. Evenings were quiet—tea, scripture, and the occasional movie night with the other moms.

Sometimes after dinner, I'd sit on the back steps of the shelter, feeling the brick against my spine and watching the sun slip behind the rooftops. It felt like the day letting go.

And then one afternoon, everything changed again.

I was lying on my bunk, the window cracked open to let in the spring breeze. My hand rested on the curve of my belly, absentmindedly tracing the slope I still wasn't used to.

Then it happened.

The faintest flutter.

Like wings brushing against my skin from the inside.

I sat up slowly, eyes wide.

It happened again.

A soft, undeniable kick.

And I burst into tears.

"Hi, little one," I whispered, laughing through the sobs. "I feel you. I feel you."

It was real now. Not just lines on a test. Not just an ultrasound photo tucked in a drawer. A life. A heartbeat. A tiny miracle growing inside of me. And I felt… joy. Pure, uninterrupted joy.

It was like God saying, *"I'm still with you. Look what I've kept."*

A few weeks later, Tia and Harmony picked me up for lunch. It was my first real outing—outside of court dates and doctor appointments. I wore a long, flowing dress Harmony had insisted on buying me. Soft blue cotton. Loose, but graceful. For the first time in a long time, I didn't feel like a stranger in my own skin.

We went to a quiet diner downtown with outdoor seating and

mismatched mugs. The waitress called everyone "baby" and brought lemon wedges without being asked. It was the kind of place where nothing matched—but everything felt warm.

We laughed so much over lunch that my cheeks hurt. Harmony cracked jokes. Tia told stories about my mother—ones I'd never heard before.

"I remember when she found out she was pregnant with you," Tia said, her eyes misty. "She looked just like you do now—soft, glowing, scared but fierce."

I swallowed the lump in my throat. "I wish she was here."

Tia reached for my hand across the table. "She is."

"She sees us," Harmony whispered, leaning in with that half-smile she always wore when her heart was full but hurting.

We took a photo that day. Me with my hand on my belly. Harmony hugging me from behind. Tia beside us, her arms crossed proudly, like an anchor holding steady through the storm.

It wasn't a perfect picture.

But it was the first one in years that looked like hope.


Then came court.

I was nearly eight months pregnant by then. My belly heavy with new life. My spine sore from more than just the weight of the child I carried. I'd been attending court dates for months. Kyson had finally been arrested. Other girls had come forward, too. I wasn't the only one.

But I would be the first to testify.

He needed to pay for what he did.

The courthouse was cold. The bench was harder. My hands wouldn't stop shaking, but I walked in with my head high. Chin up. Shoulders back.

Kyson was already seated at the defense table. He wore a suit. Clean lines. Straight tie. But it didn't hide what he really was. He didn't look at me. Good. I didn't need him to.

I took the stand. Swore an oath. Sat in a chair that felt ten times too big and not nearly strong enough to hold the weight of what I was about to say.

And I told the truth.

Every sick, painful, gut-wrenching detail.

I told it not for revenge—but for freedom.

Mine.

And every other girl he had silenced, tricked, broken.

There were gasps in the courtroom when the prosecutor revealed the full scope—how many girls. How young. How long. How calculated.

I didn't flinch.

Because nothing in that room could match what I had already survived.

And when the judge thanked me for my bravery, I didn't feel brave. I just felt clean. Like I had finally emptied my lungs after years of drowning.

That night, I returned to the shelter and opened my journal. I wrote,

*I'm still scared. But I did it. And I'm proud of me.*
*God, thank You for never letting go of me—even when I let go of You.*

Two weeks after the trial, Ms. Hightower came to my door with a quiet smile and said, "We've got the okay—you can personalize your room now."

It wasn't much.

Just a modest space with a small dresser, a chair, and a bed that creaked if I shifted too hard.

But it was mine.

And now... it was ours.

I'd received a small payment from the victim's compensation fund. Tia had helped gather donations quietly, never making a big deal out of it. With that, I bought a few things for the baby—a bassinet with soft yellow bedding, some newborn onesies, and a crocheted blanket from one of the women in group therapy who knew what it meant to start over.

One evening, I lit a small vanilla candle, cracked the window open to let in the spring air, and played my favorite worship playlist.

Yolanda Adams' "The Battle Is Not Yours" came on.

I'd heard it before—when I was younger, when my mother used to hum it around the house.

But this time... it hit different.

The first line wrapped around my ribs like a memory I'd forgotten I needed.

"There is no pain Jesus can't feel..."

I dropped the onesie in my hand, and before I could stop myself, the tears were streaming.

My hands rose, slowly, like they remembered something my heart hadn't caught up to yet.

"Jesus…" I whispered.

Then louder, "Thank You, Jesus."

It wasn't a shout.

Not loud enough to disturb anyone.

But strong enough to shake the silence.

The lyrics carried me. Through the courtroom. Through Kyson. Through the streets. Through the blood and the hospital and the dream where my mother told me I had to choose life.

I wept.

I rocked.

I praised.

And when the song ended, I sat back down—tired, but different.

Lighter.

I picked up another onesie and folded it with care.

Talking to her. My daughter.

"I don't know if I'll be a good mom," I said aloud, smoothing the pale pink fabric. "But I promise you this—I'll never leave you. I'll never let anyone hurt you."

Above the bassinet, I taped a hand-lettered sign I'd made that morning with some markers one of the women donated,

Serenity's Corner.

And when I stepped back to look at it—bassinet, blanket, onesies folded neatly in the drawer—my throat tightened.

Because that little corner didn't just look like hope. It felt like home.

A week later, I started sleeping with the light off again. It doesn't sound like much. But for me, it was everything. The dark no longer swallowed me whole. It still hummed with memories, sure—but I could breathe in it. I could stretch out without flinching, without waiting for the floor to fall out from under me.

Most nights, I'd fall asleep with one hand on my belly and the other pressed against my chest, feeling both our heartbeats.

Mine was steady.

Hers was stronger.

But peace is delicate. And sometimes… peace has a knock.

It was a Tuesday afternoon when Ms. Hightower came to find me. Her face was serious, but not hard.

"There's someone asking for you downstairs."

My breath caught.

"Who?"

She tilted her head gently. "I told her I'd ask first. She says her name is Ms. Murphy."

I blinked.

The name opened something in me I didn't know was still sealed shut. The woman. The dog walker. The reason I wasn't dead.

"Okay," I said. "I want to see her."

I followed Ms. Hightower down the stairs, my steps slow, deliberate. Every part of me remembered that day—the sidewalk, the blood, the scream that barely made it past my lips. I wasn't sure if I was ready to see the woman who had pulled me back from the edge.

But I kept walking.

When I reached the common area, she was standing by the window. Same gentle posture. Same neat curls pulled back under a floral scarf. Her eyes met mine, and for a moment, neither of us spoke.

Then she stepped forward.

"You look stronger," she said quietly.

"I am," I replied, but my voice cracked anyway.

She opened her arms, and I stepped into them.

There was no sobbing. No dramatic collapse. Just a hug. Real. Solid. Healing.

"I didn't know if you'd want to see me," she said after a moment, stepping back.

"I've thought about you every day," I admitted. "I never got to thank you."

"You just did," she smiled. "But I didn't come for that. I came to see how you're doing."

"I'm… working on it," I said. "Still healing. But I'm better."

She nodded. "I brought you something."

She handed me a small package wrapped in brown paper. Inside was a journal, thick and sturdy, with the words, *Still Here, Still Standing* etched into the cover in gold.

"I run a small group at my church," she explained. "Women who've been through… things. Like you. If you ever want to come by. Share. Or just listen. There's space for you."

I stared down at the journal for a long moment.

"Thank you," I whispered.

She touched my hand. "You're not forgotten, Divinity. You're remembered. By God. By the people He sent. You still have so much life ahead of you."

I blinked back tears and nodded.

"I'm trying to believe that."

"Good," she said. "Because it's true."

She hugged me once more, then stepped back.

"I'll let you decide when you're ready. But you'll always be welcome."

And then she was gone. Just like that. But her presence lingered. Like her words. Like her touch.

I carried the journal back upstairs and sat at my window, the sun slipping low on the horizon.

I hadn't known I needed to see her.

But I did.

Because it reminded me that even the smallest acts of love can alter the course of a life. And that sometimes, when the darkness feels endless, all it takes is one person to remind you,

You're still here.

And that matters.

I had just closed the journal when it hit me. At first, I thought it was just nerves—maybe the emotion of seeing her again, the weight of everything stirring inside. But then the pain gripped lower in my stomach, sharp and deep, like a hand twisting from the inside.

I gasped and dropped the journal.

"Ms. Hightower!" I called out, clutching the arm of the chair as the next wave hit—stronger, longer.

She was at my door in seconds, her face instantly changing. "What is it?"

"I—I think… I think it's time."

Within minutes, the shelter transformed. Voices lowered. Footsteps quickened. One of the women grabbed a towel and gently pressed it to my forehead. Another knelt beside me, whispering calm. Ms. Hightower called the ambulance with one hand and gripped mine with the other.

"You're okay, Divinity," she said firmly. "You're not alone. You hear me? You are not alone."

I was crying now, not from pain, but fear. My whole body trembled.

"I can't do this," I whispered. "I'm not ready."

"Yes, you can," Ms. Hightower said, steady and warm. "You've survived everything else. This? This is life. This is the miracle coming through the storm."

The ambulance pulled up fast. I could hear it before I saw it—the wail of a siren splitting the quiet air.

Tia and Harmony arrived moments after.

They rushed into the room breathless. Harmony's eyes wide with panic. Tia's already brimming with tears.

"We're here," Tia said, grabbing one hand.

"I'm not ready," I sobbed again.

Harmony crouched beside me. "Yes, you are. You're stronger than anyone I know."

The EMTs came in and started working fast. Monitors. Oxygen. A stretcher.

"I want Tia," I said. "And Harmony. Please."

"We'll be right behind you," Tia promised. "We're not leaving your side."

They wheeled me out of the shelter, all the women lined up by the door, whispering prayers, offering nods of love and strength.

The contractions came harder now, closer together.

Inside the ambulance, the paramedic told me to breathe. In. Out. Over and over.

But my heart wouldn't slow. What if something went wrong? What if I wasn't strong enough? What if this was the price I paid for surviving? But then I heard her voice—my mother's again, soft in my ear like it always came in dreams,

*You're not doing this alone. You never have.*

And I breathed. I let the pain roll through me. Because this time, it wasn't breaking me. This time... it was bringing something new.

The hospital lights felt too bright, like they were exposing more than my pain—like they were peeling me open.

By the time they rolled me into labor and delivery, the contractions were coming hard, fast, and without mercy. I was sweating through the gown they had pulled over me, my fingers locked tight around the rails of the hospital bed.

Tia and Harmony were there now, one on each side of me, holding my hands like they were holding me together.

"I can't—" I cried out through another contraction. "I can't do this—"

"Yes, you can," Harmony said, brushing my hair back. "You already are."

"You survived everything else," Tia added, her voice low, firm, full of knowing. "This is the part where you win."

The nurse moved quickly, checking monitors, calling out centimeters. "Almost there," she said. "She's almost here."

She.

A girl.

Serenity.

I gritted my teeth through another wave, the pain searing down my spine.

My mind flashed to Kyson.

To the fear.

To the darkness.

And then, just as quickly, I pushed his name out of my body the same way I would push this baby into the world.

He wouldn't live here anymore.

Not in me.

Not in her.

"Okay, Divinity," the doctor said. "You're fully dilated. It's time to push."

"No," I gasped. "I can't—"

"Yes, you can," Tia said, tightening her grip. "You're about to meet your daughter."

The room blurred—shouting, encouragement, counting—but all I could hear was my heartbeat and hers, beating together in that room like a new song.

I pushed.

Once.

Twice.

Then again.

The pain tore through me like fire.

And then—

A cry.

Sharp. Raw. Alive.

The whole room stilled.

"It's a girl," the doctor said, lifting her into the air.

Tears spilled from my eyes before I could stop them.

She was placed on my chest, warm and slippery, her tiny fists clenched, her lungs screaming.

I laughed and sobbed at the same time.

Harmony had to sit down.

Tia was crying too hard to speak.

And me?

I held her like she was everything I had lost—and everything I had found.

"Hi," I whispered, voice breaking. "Hi, Serenity." She quieted for a moment, like she knew my voice. Like she had been waiting for this moment just as long as I had.

The room dimmed after the nurses left. The commotion faded into stillness, like God Himself had hushed the world to make space for the sacred.

Serenity slept against my chest, wrapped in a soft pink blanket, her tiny breaths warm on my skin. Her fingers, no bigger than folded paper, gripped the collar of my gown like she never wanted to let go.

And I didn't either.

I couldn't stop staring at her.

She had my nose. My lips. But her eyes—when they fluttered open—carried something else entirely. A kind of peace I hadn't seen in years. A peace I hadn't even known I was capable of bringing into this world.

Tia sat on the couch, nodding off in the corner. Harmony was curled up in the recliner with a pillow under her head, one hand still hanging off the side of my bed like she didn't want to break contact.

I traced Serenity's forehead with the tip of my finger, watching her mouth twitch into little half-smiles only babies make.

"You're really here," I whispered.

My voice cracked.

It hit me like a wave all over again—I was someone's mother.

Me.

Divinity Rivera.

The girl who almost didn't survive. Who had given up more times than she could count. Who believed for so long that she was too broken to be loved, too dirty to be chosen, too far gone to matter.

And yet here she was.

Here we were.

"I don't know how to do this," I admitted softly, letting the words float into the room like a prayer.

"But I promise to try."

I kissed her forehead, and something in my heart clicked into place. Not perfectly. Not like everything was fixed. But like I had just met the reason I was still breathing.

The reason I didn't die on that sidewalk.

The reason God hadn't let go.

Serenity sighed against me, her little chest rising and falling in rhythm with mine.

And for the first time in what felt like forever…

I wasn't afraid.

Not of tomorrow.

Not of the pain.

Not even of the past.

Because in that hospital bed, beneath the hum of machines and the faint rustle of a blanket, I knew one thing, This was love. This was healing. This was redemption in the shape of a baby girl.

The weeks after Serenity was born were hard. There were midnight feedings and mornings I could barely lift my head. My body was still healing. My emotions still bruised. But every time I looked at her—my daughter, my reason—I found the strength.

And slowly, things started falling into place.

Tia offered to watch Serenity during the day while I looked for work. She'd pick her up with that big, warm smile and her infamous diaper bag packed to perfection.

"This baby's got a village," she always said, rocking her like she was made of glass and gold.

Harmony babysat on weekends sometimes, and when Serenity smiled at her, Harmony would melt and whisper,

"She looks just like you, Div."

That part still made me tear up.

Because I finally liked the idea that someone could.

I applied to a part-time job at a bookstore downtown—one of those little independent shops where the air smells like pages and peace. I didn't think I'd get it.

But I did.

My first check was barely enough to celebrate, but I bought Serenity a tiny stuffed lion and a rose-scented candle for Tia. Every week got better. And I started to walk with my head a little higher.

After six months of saving, budgeting, and trusting God every step of the way—I got the call. My application for transitional housing had been approved. It wasn't fancy. Just a one-bedroom apartment with a small kitchen, a little dining area, a creaky radiator, and two tight closets.

But when I opened the door with Serenity on my hip, I felt something sacred.

I dropped my bags, turned on the lights, and whispered,

"We're home."

We didn't have much. A mattress on the floor. A secondhand crib. Dishes from the dollar store. But we had love. And light. And space to breathe.

I sat in the middle of that floor, Serenity cradled against me, and cried tears of joy. Real, deep, soul-level joy. Because after all the loss, after all the wandering, after all the breaking...

God had kept His promise.

He never left me.

He had been with me the whole time.

No one tells you how hard it is. How lonely motherhood can feel in the early hours, especially when the baby won't stop crying and your body is still learning how to function again. Some nights, I sat on the edge of the bed—Serenity wailing in my arms, my shirt damp with spit-up, my eyes burning from lack of sleep—and I wondered how women did this without breaking.

I felt like I was breaking.

No—I felt like I had broken.

And now I was just trying to piece myself back together with diapers and lullabies and whispered prayers through cracked lips.

But I never dropped her.

Never gave up.

Not even once.

There were days I stared at her little face and wondered how something so pure came from someone like me. And then I'd cry.

Because I realized she wasn't a reminder of what happened to me.

She was a gift.

She was mine.

And she made me softer.

Not weaker—just... human again.

Late one night, after she finally fell asleep on my chest, I pulled out my journal. Not the one I used for daily entries—but the one I started just for letters. Letters to my mother. I didn't know if she could read them from wherever she was, but writing them made me feel close to her.

The first one started simply,

*Dear Mom,*

*You'd probably laugh if you saw me now. I have no idea what I'm doing. I hold Serenity like she's made of glass and flinch every time she sneezes. But I love her so much it scares me. I wish you were here to tell me I'm doing okay. To show me how to do this with grace.*

*I miss you more now than ever.*

Some nights, I wrote whole pages.

Others, just a line or two,

*I made it through the day.*
*I didn't cry today.*
*I held her and didn't feel like a stranger to myself.*

These letters became my therapy. They were messy. Honest. Some were angry. Some joyful. Most were both. And in writing to my mother, I started to forgive her for leaving—because I realized now, she didn't want to.

She just didn't get the chance to stay.

As the weeks passed, I got stronger. Not in the big, heroic way the movies show. But in the quiet ways that only mothers understand.

I learned how to soothe Serenity's cries faster. How to stretch twenty dollars for three days of meals. How to hold her with one hand while flipping pancakes with the other.

Each small victory was sacred. Because it meant I was still standing. Still healing. Still becoming the woman I was meant to be.

One morning, as spring leaned into summer, I sat on the small balcony outside our apartment—Serenity asleep on my chest, the city quiet for once.

The air smelled like rain and jasmine. I looked out at the sky, soft with light, and thought about how far we had come. There were still hard days. I still woke from nightmares sometimes. I still flinched at loud noises. I still double-checked the locks at night. But I no longer lived in fear. I lived in hope.

Every breath I took now was a breath I chose.

And every time Serenity opened her eyes,

I remembered why I said yes to living.

## 17.  TRUST IS A MOUNTAIN

*"I didn't know trust could feel like a slow climb instead of a leap." – Divinity's Journal*

**The first time I sat across from my therapist, I didn't speak for the first fifteen minutes.**
I watched the clock instead.
Tick.
Tick.
Tick.
She didn't rush me. Didn't push. Just sat in a soft chair across from me, her legs crossed, notebook in her lap, pen still capped. The lamp beside her cast a warm halo across the office, and for a second, I wanted to believe I was safe just because it felt like someone had thought to make the room gentle.

I had gone back to Dr. S—the same therapist I had seen years ago when things first started to unravel. She smiled softly when I walked in. Not surprised. Not pitiful. Just… present.

"I always felt like I didn't get through to you back then," she said after our initial hellos. "But I'm glad you're here now. You don't owe me anything, Divinity. But if you're willing, I'd love to hear your story."

I didn't speak.
Not that first session.
But I kept coming back. Week after week, we chipped away at the silence. She never filled it. Just let it stretch until I was ready to fold it into words.

We talked about Serenity. About the shelter. About my mother. About how hard it was to believe I could still be whole when all I'd ever known was pieces.

Some days, I shared. Some days, I just cried. But she never made me feel broken.

She just helped me gather the pieces without shame.

One afternoon, maybe three sessions in, Dr. S leaned forward slightly, her voice as calm as ever.

"Can I ask what the silence was protecting?"

The question stopped me. Not because I didn't know the answer—because I did. But saying it meant I had to revisit it. Not just what happened with Kyson. But everything. Darnell. The house. My mother's death. The girl I was before everything fell apart.

"I don't know," I murmured.

She didn't press.

But I hated lying to her. Even a soft lie.

So I tried again.

"I think... the silence kept it real. If I didn't say it out loud, I could pretend it didn't define me. That I wasn't... what happened to me."

Dr. S nodded slowly, giving the truth its room to settle.

"And now?"

"Now..." I swallowed hard, brushing my thumb against the edge of my sleeve. "Now I know it still defines me. Just not the way I thought."

She tilted her head, curious. "How so?"

I glanced toward the window, the gray sky outside somehow matching the ache in my chest.

"Before, I thought my story made me weak. Dirty. Broken. But now—" I paused, took a breath. "Now I think surviving it might be the strongest thing I've ever done."

Dr. S didn't smile. She just looked at me like I'd climbed another mile up the mountain.

"You're learning to trust your voice," she said. "That's what healing is. Not forgetting. Not erasing. But learning to tell the story from a place where it no longer owns you."

I nodded. Slowly.

Because something about that felt like truth.

Something about that felt like freedom.

I came in that day thinking I'd just talk about Serenity. How she was teething. How she'd started sleeping through the night—sort of. How she had this new habit of grabbing my nose and not letting go.

I thought it would be light.

But healing doesn't work like that.

Halfway through the session, Dr. S asked softly, "Have you been sleeping?"

I nodded automatically. "Mostly."

She tilted her head. "Nightmares?"

I hesitated. Then shrugged. "Sometimes."

Her pen moved lightly across the page.

"What happens in them?" she asked.

I blinked. My palms grew clammy. I hadn't expected that question. I wasn't ready. But my mouth answered before I could stop it.

"There's a hallway. Long. Dark. Doors on both sides. I'm running, but it's like I'm not moving. And at the end... he's there."

"Kyson?"

I nodded. "But it's not always him. Sometimes it's Darnell. Sometimes it's both. Sometimes it's me standing in front of a mirror and I look like myself, but I'm not."

My throat felt thick.

"In the dream," I added, "I scream. But no sound comes out."

Dr. S's voice remained calm, steady. "That kind of dream often means your body still remembers what your mouth hasn't spoken yet."

I looked at her. "But I already told you everything."

"Not everything," she said gently. "You told me what happened. But you haven't told me how it felt. How it still feels."

And that's when it hit me.

I hadn't.

I had described the events—the nights, the bruises, the lies—but I hadn't once said what it did to me inside. I hadn't named the shame, or the disgust, or the loneliness that still lived under my skin.

I stared down at my hands. They were shaking.

"I feel dirty," I whispered.

"You're not."

"I feel weak."

"You're not."

"I feel... ruined."

She leaned forward, her voice soft but fierce. "You are not ruined. You are reclaiming your story. That's not weakness, Divinity. That's power."

I closed my eyes. And suddenly—without warning—I was back in that McDonald's bathroom the first time I took the pregnancy test. Alone. Terrified. The image slammed into me so hard I gasped.

Dr. S didn't flinch.

She waited.

And I finally said it,

"I was going to leave that night. But I stayed. I stayed after knowing

what he was. After knowing what he'd take from me. And sometimes…
I still hate myself for that."

Silence.

Then she said the words I hadn't even known I needed,

"You didn't fail yourself. You adapted to survive. That's what you've always done. You're not here because you were weak. You're here because you were strong enough to come back."

I cried then. No holding back.

And she didn't interrupt.

She let me fall apart. Then helped me begin, piece by piece, to build myself again.

The tears didn't stop when I left Dr. S's office.

They followed me to the bus stop. Down the long avenue. All the way back to my apartment—the tiny one-bedroom I had fought to get, fought to keep.

Unlocking the door felt heavier that day. Not because the key stuck, but because I felt… hollow.

Inside, Serenity was with Tia, who had offered to keep her for the afternoon.

The silence hit me.

For a long while, I just stood in the middle of the apartment, purse still over my shoulder, jacket still on, staring at nothing.

Then I moved.

I sank down to the floor in front of the crib—the same crib I bought secondhand, the one with the little stickers still half-peeled on the side. Her blanket was folded over the edge. Her favorite stuffed lion leaned against the pillow.

I reached inside and picked it up, hugged it tight to my chest.

And I let go.

Not of the pain, not yet—but of the lie I'd been dragging around for years, that I had to carry everything alone. That if I opened up too much, I'd break beyond repair. But I wasn't breaking.

I was healing.

Piece by piece.

I cried there on the floor, knees pulled to my chest, the lion clutched in my arms like it could keep me from falling apart. The window was cracked open, and through it I could hear the rustle of the trees, the soft hum of life happening all around me.

And after a while, the ache inside started to breathe.

Later, I picked up my journal and wrote,

*I told her the truth today. The part about Darnell. About the nightmares. I thought saying it out loud would destroy me. But it didn't. It made space. Real space. I think I'm finally beginning to trust myself again. And maybe one day, I'll trust love too.*

I had taken Ms. Murphy up on her offer to come to her church. It was Sunday morning—the kind of morning that felt like a quiet promise. The sun was shining bright. A soft breeze moved through the trees like God Himself had cracked a window open just to whisper peace into the day.

Still, I showed up late.

Serenity had been fussy. I couldn't find her left shoe, and by the time I parked and unbuckled her from the car seat, praise and worship had already started. I slipped into the back row, balancing her on my hip, trying not to make noise.

I didn't even notice the man who slid down the pew to make room.

But he noticed me.

After the last note of the choir faded and the congregation took their seats, he leaned over with a gentle smile and whispered, "First time here?"

I nodded.

He smiled, warm and soft. "Same."

He looked about my age. Clean-shaven. Smooth dark skin. Kind eyes that didn't linger too long.

"Jeremiah," he whispered, offering his hand.

"Divinity," I replied, surprised I gave my name so easily.

Serenity stared at him like she already approved.

The service was so eye-opening that day, and it made me realize that if I'm trusting in God, I have to be and live like Him—and that means forgiving people even when they have done the worst thing imaginable.

The pastor's voice rose, steady and firm, his words slicing through every quiet corner of my spirit.

"Forgiveness isn't about the other person. Forgiveness is about being right with God and doing what Jesus would do. It's about freeing yourself from the chains they wrapped around you—by holding it in and not letting it go."

That hit me.

Right in the gut.

I had been holding so much. Anger at Darnell. Fear of Kyson. Guilt.

Shame. Even hurt toward people who tried to love me but didn't know how. I thought keeping it all meant I was strong. That letting it go would mean they won.

But maybe it meant I won.

Maybe forgiveness was for me. For Serenity. For the version of me who still looked for light in dark places.

I sat in the pew, Serenity quiet on my lap, and closed my eyes. And for a second, I just breathed. Not because everything was okay—but because for the first time, I saw a way it might be.

After the service, I tried to slip out quietly, weaving between hugs and handshakes. But Jeremiah caught up with me just outside, near the parking lot.

"Hey," he said, holding the folded church program in his hand. "I wasn't sure if I should say anything, but… it was nice sitting beside you."

I hesitated. My body still didn't know how to handle men being kind without a catch.

But he didn't ask for anything.

Didn't press.

Didn't pretend to know me.

He just smiled and added, "Maybe I'll see you next week."

And then he walked away. Just like that. No pressure. No game.

Just… grace.

Later that evening—after dinner, bath time, and two full renditions of the same lullaby—Serenity finally drifted to sleep in my arms. Turns out it was a nap because she woke back up in an instant. She was growing fast.

Her curls were thicker now, soft and wild like mine. Her eyes sparkled with curiosity and mischief. She had started pointing at things, babbling with such determination it sounded like she was delivering speeches no one else could quite translate.

I was folding laundry on the floor of our little studio apartment when I heard it earlier that evening.

Soft.

Clear.

Completely unexpected.

"Mama."

I froze.

My heart slammed into my ribs.

She'd been making sounds for weeks— "baba," "uh-oh," those infectious little giggles—but this?

This was her first real word.

And she said it again.

"Mama."

I turned slowly, my eyes already stinging. She was sitting on her blanket, one chubby hand lifted toward me like it had always belonged there.

My name.

From her mouth.

I dropped the laundry. Crawled to her. Pulled her against me like she was made of air and grace.

"I'm here, baby," I whispered. "I'm always here."

And then I cried. Not from sadness. But from joy. Real, quiet, holy joy. Because for the first time, I didn't feel like I was just surviving motherhood. I was living in it.

The next therapy session felt different. I sat in my usual chair, legs tucked beneath me, journal balanced in my lap like it was holding the weight I hadn't spoken yet.

Dr. S waited, patient as ever. No pressure. Just presence. When I finally looked up, I spoke the words that had been sitting in my chest since Sunday.

"I met someone."

Her eyebrows lifted slightly. "Would you like to tell me about him?"

"His name's Jeremiah. We met at church. He didn't try to do too much. Just… sat beside me."

She nodded, her smile soft. "And how did that feel?"

I hesitated.

"Terrifying."

She didn't flinch.

"But also… peaceful."

I told her about Serenity saying "Mama." How the sound of that one word had cracked something open inside me. Not in pain—but in awe. Not because it hurt, but because it healed something I didn't even realize still needed healing.

"She sees me," I whispered. "And I'm trying to see myself, too." That's how the session ended.

A few days later, Chris called. I hadn't heard his voice in months. The last time we spoke, I was still trying to convince myself I had a future.

Now, I had one.

We met at the same park where we used to sit after school. The swings

213

were still rusty. The bench still had that one screw missing from the backrest. Chris looked older. Stronger. But still him.

We talked—about life, about Serenity, about work. He already knew the edges of what had happened. But this time, I gave him the truth.

All of it.

When I told him what Darnell did, his face shifted. Not in shock—he'd always had good instincts. But in grief. Quiet, aching grief.

He didn't interrupt. Didn't shift away or fill the space with words.

He just let me talk.

And when I finished, he said, "I'm sorry I didn't see it sooner. I would've done anything to protect you."

I nodded, my eyes stinging. "I know. And you did—just by being there when I needed someone."

There weren't any sparks between us. Not anymore. But there was something deeper. A kind of love that holds you up without asking for anything in return.

The kind that says, *I believe you. Still.*

That night, I opened a fresh page in my journal. And I wrote a letter I never intended to send.

*Dear Darnell,*

*You took things from me you had no right to. You tried to make me small. Tried to make me disappear. You twisted the meaning of love and safety and home. You made me believe I was ruined.*

*But I'm still here.*

*And I forgive you.*

*Not because you deserve it—but because I do. Because dragging the weight of what you did has nearly crushed me. And I'm done carrying it. This is not for you.*

*This is for my daughter.*

*This is for the girl I used to be.*

*This is freedom.*

*Goodbye.*

*—Divinity*

I folded the letter. Tucked it into the back of my journal. And I breathed.

For real this time.

Tia and Harmony came with me to church—Serenity bundled in Tia's arms, chewing on her pacifier like she had opinions about everything.

The sanctuary buzzed with warmth and familiarity. Sunlight filtered through stained glass in soft waves, painting the pews in amber and rose. The message that morning was about surrender—the kind that doesn't look like weakness, but trust.

The pastor stepped forward, voice steady and sure. "If there's anyone here carrying something too heavy—grief, shame, trauma, fear—this is your moment," he said, scanning the crowd. "Come to the altar. Lay it down. You don't have to walk this out alone."

I didn't move at first. My feet stayed planted. My hands gripped the back of the pew. But then Tia leaned over and touched my shoulder. "Go, baby," she whispered. "We've got her."

I looked at Harmony, who nodded through misty eyes. And then I stood. Each step felt like a mile. But I walked that aisle like it was the only road that mattered.

By the time I reached the altar, my tears had already begun to fall. I closed my eyes, lifted my hands, and whispered, "God... it's all Yours. Every piece of it. Thank You for loving me. Thank You for being in the midst of the storm—even when I didn't know You were there. Lord, thank You for saving my life and giving me another chance to praise You. I'm not worthy of Your love... yet You give it anyway. Lord, I love You. Thank You."

The hands of prayer warriors surrounded me. I didn't know their names. But I felt their love.

I felt the presence of my mother in that room.

I felt Serenity's laughter echo somewhere deep inside my chest.

I felt the Holy Ghost.

I felt God—not distant, not punishing—but present.

And I gave Him everything.

When the prayer ended and I opened my eyes, I was still crying. But I was lighter.

Not fixed. Not finished.

But free.

The pastor looked out over the congregation. "And if you're ready to make this your church home," he said, "our doors—and our arms—are open."

I didn't hesitate.

I stepped forward.

And that day... I joined the church.

That day... something shifted forever.

When I returned to my seat, Tia pulled me into a hug so tight, it shook me. Harmony kissed my temple and whispered, "That's my best friend." And Serenity reached for me with both hands, babbling like she knew the moment was sacred.

I held her close. Because from this day forward? We weren't just surviving. We were covered. And we were never going back.

That night, after I tucked Serenity into her crib and sat by the window with my tea cooling in my hands, I opened my journal and wrote,

*I used to think survival was the end goal. Now I know it's only the beginning. Trust is hard. It's scarred and slow and doesn't come easy when you've been broken. But today, I trusted God enough to walk forward. Trusted myself enough to be seen. Trusted love enough to let it hold me without fear.*

*And I've never felt freer.*

*I don't know what comes next. I still have healing to do.*

*But I know this much— I was lost.*

*And now, I am found.*

*I am Divinity.*

*In motion.*

*And I will not run from myself again.*

## 18.   ONCE UPON A TIME

*"He gives beauty for ashes." – Isaiah 61:3*

**The morning sun spilled through the window of our apartment like soft honey—slow, warm, and full of promise.**

There were no alarms, no sirens, no creeping dread. Just the gentle groan of the radiator and the quiet rhythm of baby breaths beside me.

Serenity lay curled close, her thumb in her mouth, her curls wild against my arm. Not a newborn anymore, but not quite a toddler either. Almost one. That magical in-between where everything she did still felt new, sacred, and slightly surreal. She had favorite toys now. Little fits of laughter. And a tiny, fierce will that already reminded me of myself.

I eased out of bed, careful not to wake her. My feet met the coolness of the apartment floor as I moved into the kitchen. I started the kettle, part of my new rhythm—tea before the world called for too much.

The living room held the signs of our life, a secondhand swing chair, a worn blanket tossed over the couch, a board book half-open on the rug. A photo on the wall—me and Serenity at a church picnic, her head buried in my neck, my eyes soft in a way I hadn't seen in years. It wasn't perfect. But it was peace.

I opened the window, just a crack. City sounds crept in—distant horns, a neighbor's radio, laughter from a stoop somewhere down the street. The world kept moving. But for once, I didn't feel behind.

I leaned against the counter, tea steeping in a chipped mug. One hand rested on my hip, the other on the spot just above my stomach—where fear used to live. But now, there was just breath. And a quiet kind of hope.

This time last year, I'd been drowning. Today, I was floating. Not soaring. Not healed. But here. Still standing.

Behind me, soft footsteps shuffled down the hallway.

"Mama."

That word. It never got old.

Serenity stood in the doorway, half-asleep, her blanket dragging behind her, cheeks puffed from sleep.

I knelt, arms wide.

She ran to me—if you could call it a run, more like a joyful wobble—and crashed into my arms.

I scooped her up and kissed her cheek.

"Good morning, baby girl," I whispered, holding her close.

She laid her head on my shoulder, thumb back in her mouth, her small body warm against mine.

And in that moment, I didn't think about what was broken. I didn't worry about what hadn't healed. I just held my daughter and whispered a promise I was learning to believe,

"Today's gonna be a good day."


It had been years since I'd stood here. The cemetery was quiet, a gentle breeze rustling through the trees that lined the edge like watchful sentinels. The grass had grown in patches around the older stones, but the one I came for was clean. Someone had been keeping it that way.

Maybe Tia. Maybe Harmony.

Or maybe it was just time doing what it does—softening things at the edges.

Serenity sat in her stroller beside me, kicking her legs against the tray, her stuffed lion clutched tight in one hand. I reached down and rubbed her curls, needing the grounding.

The headstone read,

Naomi Rivera

Beloved Mother. Brave Heart. Quiet Strength.

1956 – 1997

The last time I visited, I was angry. Confused. Grieving something I didn't know how to hold. I remember yelling at the stone like she could hear me, asking why she left me—why the accident had to take her before I ever got to say goodbye.

But today was different.

Today, I didn't come with anger.

I came with peace.

"I brought your granddaughter," I whispered, kneeling in the grass. "Her name's Serenity. She's almost one. You would've loved her, Mommy. She laughs with her whole body. Just like you did."

I placed a small bouquet at the base of the stone—white lilies, her favorite.

"I used to think you left me," I said, tears brimming. "But now I know… you didn't want to go. You didn't get the chance to stay."

I let the silence settle.

"She's my second chance," I said finally. "And I'm doing everything I can to be the kind of mother you were to me."

I pressed my hand to the stone, soft and steady.

"I love you, Mommy. Always."

I turned the stroller toward the path and began walking back toward the car.

And behind me, the wind whispered through the trees again—like maybe it was saying it back.

The night of my 21st birthday felt like a soft exhale after years of holding my breath.

It was 2004. A new year. A new chapter.

Harmony had been planning the party for weeks. She'd called it "grown and golden" and decked out Tia's house in soft yellow streamers, gold balloons, and fresh sunflowers in mason jars. Smooth R&B floated through the air—Anita Baker, Jill Scott, old-school Mary J. Everything felt mellow and warm, like the night itself was hugging me.

Serenity walked into the room all on her own—toddling in her tiny white shoes, proud of every step. She wore a yellow tutu and had sunflower barrettes clipped into her curls. Every person in the room turned to watch her like she was royalty. And she was.

My little princess.

Tia cooked everything I loved—smothered chicken, pork chops, collard greens, garlic mashed potatoes, sweet cornbread. No one left hungry. And for dessert, there was a proper cake—round and fluffy, decorated with soft yellow icing and a single candle in the shape of the number 2 and 1 side by side.

When it came time to sing, everyone gathered close. Tia held Serenity. Harmony stood beside me.

And Jeremiah?

He was right behind me. He placed his hand lightly on my shoulder, and I didn't flinch. Because this wasn't sudden. It wasn't random.

Jeremiah had become a quiet constant over the past year.

After that first church visit, we crossed paths a few more times. Then we started sitting near each other. Then came short conversations after service, then longer ones over tea or walks with Serenity. We shared scripture. Shared laughs. Shared silence. He never pushed, never pressed. Just listened. And slowly, I let him see more of me.

Our friendship bloomed slowly—like something handled with care.

He never tried to fix me.

He just… stayed.

So yes, he was at my birthday party. Not because he was trying to win something—but because he'd already earned a place in my peace.

I closed my eyes before blowing out the candle and whispered the simplest wish I'd ever made.

*Let me keep going.*

*Let me keep growing.*

After the cheers died down, Harmony handed me a gift wrapped in sunflower-printed paper. Inside was a framed photo, me and Serenity, taken the day I moved into our place. We were sitting on the bare floor, sunlight pouring in, her curled up asleep on my chest.

Below the frame was a handwritten note,

*You are no longer who you were. You are who you've become. And it's beautiful.*

I hugged Harmony until my eyes burned.

Later that night, after everyone had gone and Serenity was asleep in her pack-and-play, I sat out on the stoop with Jeremiah. He didn't say much at first. Just sat beside me, both of us listening to the chirping crickets and soft city breeze.

"This was a good night," I said.

He nodded. "You looked happy. Whole."

"I'm working on it."

He smiled. "And it shows."

Then he reached into his jacket and pulled out a tiny box.

"Don't get nervous," he said with a grin. "It's not that kind of box."

I laughed and opened it.

Inside was a delicate silver chain with a small sunflower charm.

"Because you always find the light," he said, voice quiet. "Even when it's hard."

My chest tightened.

"Thank you," I said.

Jeremiah didn't ask to stay longer. Didn't linger. He just stood, kissed the top of my hand gently, and whispered, "Happy birthday, Divinity. You deserve all of it."

And for the first time in my life… I believed him.

Summer came slow that year—like it wasn't quite sure if the world deserved to feel warm again.

But I did.

And so did he.

Jeremiah and I never had a "moment." No dramatic kiss in the rain. No declarations under streetlights. Just time. Steady time.

We started with walks. Short ones around my block while Serenity napped in the stroller. Then came coffee dates—no fancy shops, just corners of quiet diners where we talked about everything and nothing. His past wasn't spotless either. He'd been through things. Lost things. But he didn't wear his trauma like a badge. He wore it like a teacher.

One afternoon, we sat in a park while Serenity toddled around, chasing pigeons like they owed her something. I told him about the trial. About Darnell. About Kyson. I didn't soften the edges.

He didn't flinch.

"You're not broken," he said afterward. "You're just... weathered. Like a tree that survived every storm."

"Still standing," I whispered.

"Still blooming."

He never pushed past my boundaries. Never asked when I'd be ready for more. He just stayed close enough to be felt, far enough to let me breathe.

One day, he brought over a book of poems—*The Sun and Her Flowers by Rupi Kaur*. He said, "This one reminded me of you," and handed me a folded page. The line read,

"If you were born with the weakness to fall, you were born with the strength to rise."

I didn't cry. But I felt the words lodge somewhere deep. A truth I was still learning how to say out loud.

He came to church with us on Sundays now. Sat beside me, held Serenity when she got restless. After service, we'd linger in the parking lot, just us and God and whatever was blooming between us. I wasn't sure what to call it.

But I didn't need to. Some things didn't need names. Only care. Only time. Only room to grow. And in his presence—I had all three. Jeremiah never asked for more than I could give. And that's what made me trust him. He didn't try to rescue me. Didn't rush past the barriers I kept tightly in place.

He just... stayed.

Consistent. Gentle. Steady.

We talked a lot. Sometimes for hours. Always in public places—parks, diners, the steps outside my apartment after Serenity was asleep. And he never minded when I kept space between us. Never flinched when I pulled away from hugs too soon. Never pushed when I didn't want to be touched.

"I'm not ready for anything serious," I told him once, sitting on the hood of his car as the summer heat shimmered off the pavement.

"I know," he said. "I'm just glad I get to know you—whatever that looks like."

That was the thing about Jeremiah. He didn't make me feel like I had to perform. Or be whole. Or explain every scar. He learned me slowly. With intention. He remembered what books I liked. He never forgot that I hated when people raised their voices—even in laughter.

He learned how to be quiet with me on hard days. And how to make me laugh on the light ones.

One night, after Serenity fell asleep in my arms, he texted, "You're the strongest woman I know. Not because you survived... but because you chose to live again."

That text stayed on my phone for weeks.

Because in his presence, I never felt owed.

I felt honored.

And for the first time since my life cracked open—I allowed someone to see me.

Not the mother.

Not the survivor.

Just me.

And he never looked away.

One afternoon, we met at the park. The same one where Chris and I used to talk after school. Only this time, the conversations were different.

Softer. Slower.

Woven with moments of quiet that didn't feel awkward, just real.

Serenity toddled ahead in her pink overalls, still slightly wobbly on her feet, chasing the breeze with outstretched arms.

Jeremiah brought juice boxes and apple slices in a little cooler like he'd done it before. He didn't hover. Didn't try to impress. Just laid out the blanket and sat cross-legged beside me, letting the late afternoon sun warm our skin.

Serenity tripped once, landing with a soft thud in the grass. Before I could move, Jeremiah was already up, crouched low, hand outstretched.

"You okay, little lady?" he asked gently.

She blinked at him.

Then reached for his hand.

She didn't cry.

She didn't whimper.

She just held onto his fingers, like she'd always known him. He lifted her to her feet, brushing grass from her knees. She looked up at him for a moment, then leaned forward and rested her head on his shoulder.

It was brief.

But it stopped time.

I watched, heart thudding, as he held her—quiet, careful, like she was the most important thing in the world. Then, with her thumb in her mouth, she reached out her free hand toward me. We sat like that for a while.

The three of us.

No pressure.

No promises.

Just presence.

And I realized then—she saw what I saw. Something safe. Something steady. Something we weren't quite ready to name yet. But maybe… one day, we would.

## June 2004

Summer arrived quietly. It wrapped itself around our little apartment in golden mornings and long evenings where the sun lingered like it didn't want to leave. By the time June 21st came, I'd been marking the date on my calendar with a pink highlighter like it was a countdown to something holy.

Serenity was turning one.

Twelve months.

Three hundred and sixty-five days.

One whole year of surviving. Of healing. Of growing. Together.

I didn't plan anything big—just a simple gathering at Tia's backyard. A few close friends from church. The women from the shelter. Some of the moms I met at the clinic. Harmony helped string up soft pinks and lavender decorations, and Tia made her famous lemonade and baked chicken that fell off the bone like it had a plan. We had hot dogs and burgers for the kids.

Serenity wore a white sundress with tiny embroidered flowers and pink barrettes clipped to the sides of her soft curls. She didn't understand what the day meant—but her smile never stopped. She waddled from lap to lap, giggling like the air was lighter than usual, like she could feel the joy clinging to everything.

We had one cake.

Vanilla with strawberry filling.

A single candle that bent slightly to the left.

I held her on my hip when we sang "Happy Birthday."

Her eyes were wide the whole time—like the sound of everyone singing just for her was magic. When we helped her blow out the candle, she clapped, and we clapped with her.

There were no expensive gifts. No elaborate games. Just laughter, love, and peace.

Jeremiah came, too. He didn't bring a crowd or make a scene. Just showed up with a small, soft-wrapped present in one hand and flowers in the other—for me.

"Not trying to steal your shine," he whispered. "But she wouldn't be here if it weren't for you."

He handed Serenity a plush elephant that squeaked when she squeezed it. She squealed and hugged it tight like it was already her favorite. Then, she reached for him again. No hesitation. No second-guessing.

And when she was done climbing into his arms, she rested her head on his chest like she belonged there.

I stood back for a moment, watching.

Harmony nudged me and whispered, "She doesn't do that with just anybody."

"I know," I said.

And I did.

Because I'd been watching, too. Watching how he never rushed. How he showed up, stayed quiet, and made space for me to breathe.

Later that night, after the guests had left and Serenity was tucked in at Tia's, I walked Jeremiah to his car.

"I didn't know how much I needed this," I said softly.

He looked at me, all serious eyes and quiet strength.

"You deserve soft things, Divinity," he said. "You always have."

And I didn't say anything else.

I just nodded.

Because maybe—for the first time in my life—I believed him.

### Late 2004

Six months passed after Serenity's birthday. Fall rolled in with amber leaves and crisp mornings. Life was steady—soft, sacred. The kind of peace that didn't demand to be noticed but wrapped itself around you anyway.

And somewhere between the laughter and quiet dinners, between morning texts and evening devotionals, between long walks pushing Serenity's stroller under December skies and slow talks about nothing at all—I let my guard down.

I told Jeremiah, one night after Serenity had fallen asleep on his lap, that I was scared. That men had taken things from me I'd never get back. That I didn't know if I had anything left to give.

He didn't try to fix it.

Didn't offer a solution.

He just nodded. "I know. And I'll wait as long as you need."

And that was the moment I knew. It wasn't the flowers he brought to my job on slow Tuesdays. It wasn't the way Serenity beamed every time she saw him.

It was the fact that he saw every broken part of me—and didn't flinch. He prayed with me. Not just for me. Not just over dinner. But in the quiet, sacred corners of my doubt. He held my hand and asked God to bless what we were building. To protect it. To keep it pure.

We went to church together every Sunday. Read scripture over tea. Fasted through the hard things. Praised through the breakthroughs.

And six months after Serenity's first birthday—after countless small yeses and late-night conversations and long-held prayers—we made it official.

Jeremiah wasn't loud. He wasn't flashy. But he was consistent. And kind. And godly. And when I finally said yes to him, I wasn't saying yes just to romance. I was saying yes to healing. Yes to peace. Yes to love that didn't ask me to shrink or forget what I'd survived.

I was still growing.

Still rebuilding.

But now, I wasn't doing it alone.

And that changed everything.

That night, after Serenity had drifted off and Jeremiah had gone home, I stood by the window of our small apartment.

The moon was high, casting silver ribbons across the floor. I watched the city breathe—cars passing, lights flickering, distant laughter spilling from a nearby stoop—and I thought about how far I'd come.

From the girl who ran away with nothing but a journal and a broken heart...

To a woman standing tall in her healing.

A mother.

A believer.

Still learning.

Still becoming.

I thought about my daughter—how her name, Serenity, had become more than just a prayer. It was a promise. One that was unfolding in me with every sunrise, every whispered prayer, every honest step forward.

And as I looked at the road ahead—college applications half-filled, speaking invitations unread, a testimony not yet told—I felt it, that same quiet voice from all those years ago, when I was laid up in a hospital bed, clinging to breath and hope.

*You're not done yet.*

No, I wasn't.

And as long as I kept saying yes to God,

Yes to growth,

Yes to love that looked like Him—

Then this story—my story—was just getting started.

## 19.  THE CALL

*"You don't need a stage to be called. Just a voice, and the courage to use it." –*
*Cassandra Wade*


### The year was 2012

I was 29 years old. So much had changed, all for the good. Turns out Jeremiah was my Boaz. We got married last year—quietly, beautifully, surrounded by people who had seen the worst and stayed for the best. Since then, life had moved with an urgency that felt like a wind at my back. Not rushed—just steady. Purposeful. Directed.

We bought a Brownstone—an actual Brownstone, the kind I used to stare at from corners and bus stops. It wasn't perfect, but it was ours. Serenity had a pink and lavender room with windows that caught the morning light and shelves lined with books she picked out herself. She was nine now. Brilliant. Kind. Funny in ways I never expected. And healing, too—her own kind of healing. Even though she didn't know yet all the things I had walked through to get here.

Jeremiah worked full-time as a computer technician, steady and strong in every way he promised to be. I had moved up at the bookstore. I was the store manager now. Not my dream job—but it paid the bills. It let me be home for dinner. It gave me quiet moments to read to Serenity, to make lunch on Saturdays, to breathe.

But still—I knew I was called for more. God's timing is His timing. So I waited. I stayed obedient. I listened.

And one day, the call came. No, not the kind with ringing.
The kind you feel in your chest. The whisper that grows into a roar.

Ms. Hightower invited me back to the shelter. Just for a small group. Just to "share your journey," she said gently, as if it were a favor I could decline. I almost did. But something in me whispered,

*This is why you survived.*

I sat in a metal folding chair in a circle of women, many of them younger. Some already mothers. Some still in disbelief that they were even still alive. The air smelled like lavender cleaner and cafeteria spaghetti. My hands trembled in my lap.

But I spoke anyway.

I started with three words,

*"Once upon a time…"*

The room went still.

And I told it.

Not every gritty detail. Not every scar or bruise. But the truth—the spine of it.

My mother.

Darnell.

Tia.

Harmony.

Kyson.

The shelter.

The hospital.

The night I nearly died.

The day God woke me up.

By the time I finished, I couldn't stop the tears. But they weren't alone. Other women cried too. Not because they pitied me—but because they saw themselves in the story. They heard the echo.

One woman walked up slowly after everyone had dispersed. She was maybe twenty-one. Her hand shook when she reached for mine.

"I didn't know how to tell my story," She said. "But now I think I can."

That was the moment. Right then, right there. When I realized, my pain had become purpose. My voice had been redeemed. And after that, the doors kept opening.

One of the counselors at the clinic asked if I'd speak at a local youth group. Just a few girls, she said. Nothing formal. Just share. I almost said no—again.

But that same still whisper from before stirred in my chest, *this is why you survived.* So I said yes. And then it happened again. A women's ministry invited me to their conference.

A little church on the West Side filmed my testimony on a grainy camcorder and uploaded it to their YouTube channel. And it took off. The views multiplied. The comments poured in.

"I thought I was the only one."

"You gave me courage."

"Thank you for not staying silent."

I kept every message.

Printed some.

Prayed over others.

I wasn't trying to be a speaker. I wasn't chasing stages or spotlights.

I was just showing up. Saying "yes."

Each time, I stood behind a mic or sat in a circle or leaned into a trembling hand and told the truth. And every time, I felt God—stronger. Not just in my story. But in the healing that followed. I started recognizing the shift in the room before I even opened my mouth.

Classrooms filled with teenage girls wearing sarcasm and silence like armor. I saw myself in all of them. The one who rolled her eyes when I mentioned God. The one who leaned forward when I mentioned pain. The one who looked down at her shoes when I said the word "survive."

I never preached at them. I just spoke.

About shame.

And silence.

And healing.

About how I said His name again after years of silence— and He still answered.

Eventually, a youth outreach center asked me to mentor a group of girls. Every Thursday night, we met in the back room of a church. Nothing fancy—just folding chairs, Styrofoam cups of juice, and hearts cracked wide open.

We talked about,

Boundaries.

Self-worth.

God.

Guilt.

Forgiveness.

Love that doesn't have to be earned.

One night, a girl broke down in the circle. Whispered, "He touched me too."

And nobody flinched. Because they had seen me survive. Because they believed it was possible. And in that moment, I knew something deeper, this wasn't just what I'd been through. This was who I was called to be.

People asked me all the time— "How did you find the strength?" And I always said the same thing, "I didn't. God gave it to me. I just stopped running from it."

It was the week before my thirtieth birthday. Serenity was nearly ten now taller than I expected, curious about everything, and fiercely protective of me. She danced barefoot in the living room to old-school R&B while Jeremiah watched from the couch, one hand on his coffee, the other resting against his jaw like he didn't want to miss a second of her joy.

And me?

I stood in the kitchen, staring at a letter I never expected. It came from a women's leadership network I had quietly admired for years— one I never thought would know my name.

An invitation. To speak at a national conference. Not a small group. Not a classroom. A stage. A microphone. Thousands of women. The theme? "From Surviving to Leading."

I pressed the letter to my chest and let the moment settle around me. For a second, it felt too big. Too loud. Too soon. But something in my spirit whispered, *You asked for this. You prayed for this. Now walk in it.*

When I handed the letter to Jeremiah, he read it quietly, then looked up with that same calm assurance that steadied me on my worst days.

"Div," he said, "this isn't a surprise. This is harvest. You've been sowing for years."

I blinked at him, throat tight. "Aren't you nervous for me?"

He smiled. "Always. But I'm more in awe than anything. You're walking in what God built you for."

Serenity burst into the room just then, a notebook in her hand. "Can I come hear you speak?"

I bent down to kiss her cheek. "One day. When the time's right, I'll take you with me. But this one… this one's just for me and God."

That night, after the dishes were done and the house had quieted down, I sat at my small writing desk with my journal open. The same one that had carried every version of me over the years.

And I wrote,

*I'm scared. But I'm not small anymore. And I'm not alone. I didn't need a spotlight to feel chosen. I just needed to say yes.*

The conference was held in a sprawling hotel ballroom downtown— rows of white chairs lined with gold trim, floral centerpieces on each table, and a stage that looked like something out of a dream I was once too scared to have.

Tia and Harmony came early, dressed sharp and radiant. They found their seats in the front row like proud mamas watching their baby walk across a stage for the first time.

Backstage, I paced. My hands were cold. My stomach flipped. The program director tried to brief me on timing, but her voice faded into the background.

Then I heard it,

The emcee introducing me.

"...survivor, mentor, mother, and woman of God—Divinity Rivera."

Applause filled the room.

I stepped into the light.

And I told my story.

Not from shame, but from strength.

I talked about my mother. About how love sometimes leaves you too early and still finds a way to echo through your life.

I talked about Darnell. Not to reopen wounds, but to show that healing doesn't mean forgetting—it means reclaiming.

I talked about Kyson. About how trauma doesn't always look like bruises. Sometimes it looks like false love. Like promises wrapped in chains.

I told them about the baby I almost lost.

The girl I used to be.

The God who met me in the silence.

I watched tears stream down faces—some young, some older. Some women held hands. Some bowed their heads.

But what grounded me most? When I looked to the front row and saw Tia and Harmony watching with tear-filled eyes, I could feel Serenity's presence in my heart. Even though she wasn't there in that moment, her spirit was threaded through every word I spoke.

She was the reason I stood tall. The reason I fought. The reason I answered the call.

When I finished, the room rose to their feet in a standing ovation. But the loudest applause came from within. Because I had done the impossible. I had walked through fire. And still stood whole.

Two weeks after the conference, I got the call. It was early evening. Serenity was finishing her homework at the kitchen table while Jeremiah flipped through channels, half-watching the news, half-waiting on dinner. I had just sat down with a cup of chamomile tea when my phone buzzed.

Unknown number.

I almost let it go to voicemail. But something tugged at me.

"Hello?"

"Hi, is this Divinity Rivera?"

"This is she."

"My name is Rachel Greene—I'm calling on behalf of the National Faith & Resilience Coalition. We saw your testimony at the Women's Hope Conference. One of our board members was in attendance."

My heart skipped.

"I... okay," I said, cautiously.

She continued, "We're building a new initiative. A mentorship and advocacy program for young women coming out of abusive environments. Faith-based. Community-driven. We believe your voice could help shape it. Would you consider joining our national leadership board?"

I didn't respond right away.

Serenity glanced up at me, her pencil paused mid-sentence.

"Ms. Rivera?" Rachel said, gently.

"I'm here," I whispered.

She gave me more details. They wanted me to attend the first meeting in Atlanta in the fall. Flights and accommodations covered. No pressure, she said. Just pray on it.

After I hung up, I sat in silence. Jeremiah turned off the TV.

"What's wrong?" he asked, standing.

"Nothing," I said, stunned. "Something... big. I think God is asking me to say yes again."

He stepped closer, kissed my forehead.

"Then say yes," he said. "I've seen you move mountains. It's time to climb one."

I looked over at Serenity, who had gone back to her homework, legs swinging beneath her chair.

I thought of every step it took to get here. Every night on the street. Every scar. Every tear. Every whisper of surrender and mercy that carried me forward.

Before I could sit down again, my phone rang a second time. I blinked at it.

Another unknown number. Another door cracking open.

I answered.

"Ms. Rivera?" A woman's voice. Excited. "This is Kimberly Price with Lifetime Television. I don't know if you've seen the online video of your speech at the conference—it's gone viral. Millions of views. We've received dozens of inquiries from our audience about your story."

I said nothing, stunned.

"We'd love the option to do your life story for a film. Something real. Something redemptive. We believe this could reach countless women. It's early stages, of course. We'd want you involved in the process."

My mind spun.

Lifetime.

A movie.

The world hearing my story—my pain, my darkest moments—on screen?

I swallowed hard.

"That's... a lot," I managed.

"I know," Kimberly said gently. "And we respect whatever your decision is. But we'd be honored to help share your story with the world."

When the call ended, I sat down on the edge of the couch, silent. This was different than speaking to a small group. This wasn't just testifying. This was giving the world a key to every door I once tried to keep locked.

Jeremiah kneeled in front of me, took my hands.

"You okay?"

I nodded slowly.

"I think so," I whispered. "But this is big, Jer. Bigger than I ever imagined. What if I'm not ready for that kind of light?"

He smiled, the kind of smile that held years of love and faith.

"You don't shine because you're perfect," he said. "You shine because you kept going in the dark."

I pressed my forehead to his, tears slipping free.

"I want to say yes," I said. "To all of it. But it scares me."

He kissed my hand. "That means it's probably God."

And I believed him. Because I remembered what it felt like to be voiceless. And now... people were listening. Not for drama. But for healing. And if my story—my survival—could set someone else free? Then I had to tell it. No matter how hard it was.

It was quiet in the house.

The kind of quiet that only comes after a long, full day. The kind where peace and purpose sit beside each other in the silence.

Serenity was in bed, already asleep. Smart-mouthed, bright-eyed, and curious about everything. She had started writing her own journal, asking questions about faith and family, about the world and where she fit in it.

She had gotten so big. Her favorite color changed monthly. She played soccer. She loved spicy chips and hated brushing her hair. She was mine. And somehow, she was already becoming her own person.

That night, I sat at my desk and opened my journal. The words came easily.

*Dear Mommy,*

*It's been almost two decades since you left me. I was a little girl the last time I heard your voice outside of a dream. But I've carried you with me every step of this journey.*

*Serenity's grown up so much. You'd laugh at how she bosses me around. She wears your sass like armor and your kindness like perfume. Sometimes I watch her when she sleeps and wonder how a girl like me ended up raising a girl like her.*

*I wish you could see me. Really see me. I think you'd be proud.*

*I went back to church. I found love again—safe love. I use my voice now, Mommy. I tell the truth. And people are listening. Not just because of what I went through... but because of what God brought me out of.*

*I forgave Darnell.*

*I forgave Kyson.*

*I even forgave myself.*

*Because I realized holding onto all that pain meant I wasn't making space for the life God was trying to give me. But now? I'm living. Fully.*

*I got the call today. Lifetime. They want to turn my story into a movie. Mommy... it feels so big. So unreal. But maybe it's time. Maybe this is what God's been preparing me for all along.*

*I've told my story to rooms of people, but this? This would mean millions. Billions. This means letting the world see me—raw. Broken. Redeemed.*

*I'm scared. But I know what you'd say. You'd say to trust God. And to never forget why I started.*

*So tonight, I'm praying on it. Asking Him to speak. Because if I'm going to do this, I need to do it with full obedience. Full faith. And full fire.*

*I miss you. Always.*

*Love,*

*Divinity*

I closed the journal gently. Set it on the dresser. Climbed into bed with a heart full of questions and a mind too full to rest. But I did sleep.

And in that sleep—He came.

234

Not in blinding light. Not in thunder.
But as her.
As my mother.

She stood in a room full of sunlight, wearing the same soft yellow blouse she had on the last time I saw her smile in a photo. She looked exactly how I remembered her—strong and beautiful and warm all at once.

I didn't speak.

I couldn't.

She walked toward me, reached for my hands.

"It's time," she said softly.

"Mommy…"

"I've been watching. Every step. Every stumble. Every rise. You've done more than survive, Divinity. You've walked into your name."

Tears streamed down my face.

"I don't know if I'm ready."

My mother smiled. "Baby, you were born ready. You just had to remember who you are."

She motioned to a long, open road behind her. "Say yes. Say yes to the story. Say yes to the world. Say yes to the call. Not because it's easy. But because you're chosen. And chosen doesn't mean perfect. It means prepared."

I reached for her—but she was already fading.

And with one last look, she said, "He's with you. I've always known."

I woke up with tears on my pillow and peace in my chest.

No doubt.

No fear.

Just yes.

I whispered it into the morning light as Serenity stirred in her room.

"Yes."

To the film.

To the story.

To the call.

And the journey—still in motion.

## EPILOGUE

*"...to bestow on them a crown of beauty instead of ashes,*
*the oil of joy instead of mourning,*
*and a garment of praise instead of a spirit of despair.*
*They will be called oaks of righteousness,*
*a planting of the Lord for the display of His splendor."*
*—Isaiah 61:3 (NIV)*

People still ask me where I found the strength. The strength to survive. To walk away. To speak. To forgive. To keep going.

And the answer is simple, I didn't.

God gave it to me.

I had every reason to give up. Every door had closed. Every hand had let go. Every mirror told me I was too broken to be whole again. But every time I reached the edge, He pulled me back with whispers of— Not yet. You still have work to do. There's someone else who needs your story.

And I listened. This time, I listened. The pain didn't vanish. The scars didn't fade. But they stopped being chains.

They became keys.

Keys that unlocked doors for other girls like me— Girls who think silence is safer than truth. Girls who believe survival is the end of the story. It isn't. Survival is the start.

Today, I still speak.

Still write.

Still walk into rooms where people expect shame— and give them testimony instead.

My daughter, Serenity, is ten now. Her laughter fills our home. Her questions stretch my heart. Her prayers remind me, faith is taught best by example. She is not a symbol of my past. She is the proof of God's promise.

I still wear the name Divinity like a declaration. Not because I'm holy—But because I'm His.

And now, when God calls?

I don't run.

I don't hide.

I answer.

And I stay in motion.

## A Letter from Divinity

To the girl still hiding her pain.
To the woman carrying shame that was never hers.
To the survivor who doesn't feel strong enough to claim that word—

This is for you.

I didn't write this story because I'm perfect. Not because I've figured it all out. Not because I'm fearless now. I wrote it because I survived. Because I was broken in places I thought would never heal. Because I once believed God had forgotten me. But He didn't. He was there—in the silence, in the mess, in the midnight cries and whispered prayers. And He's there with you, too.

You don't have to tell your story today. You don't have to know what healing looks like yet. But I need you to know this, There is hope. You are not ruined. You are not alone. You are not disqualified from love, purpose, or peace. Healing is not linear. Forgiveness is not weakness. And your voice is not too small to matter.

I pray that somewhere in my words, you found a mirror. Or a doorway. Or the courage to take one more step.

Thank you for walking with me.
And if no one has told you lately,
 I'm proud of you. Keep going. Keep healing. Stay in motion.

With love,
Divinity Renee Destiny Rivera

*A Letter from the Author*

Dear Reader,

Thank you.

Thank you for walking through the pages of this journey with Divinity. Thank you for staying through the heartbreak, the darkness, the breakthroughs, and the light. Thank you for seeing her—not just as a character, but as a mirror of someone you may know... or maybe even yourself.

Though Divinity's story is not my own, it is the story of many. Too many. Teenagers who have cried behind closed doors. Young women who have survived what they were never meant to carry.

People who have questioned their worth, their purpose, and whether God had forgotten them.

This book was born from a deep desire to say, You are not alone. And in my obedience to say yes to God. This is a story he gave me to tell because it is meant to reach someone or many. Even in your biggest storm—even in the silence—God is there. He has not left you. He has not forsaken you.

Sometimes, the noise of our pain is so loud we can't hear His voice. But He's still speaking. Still guiding. Still walking with us, even when we stumble. My prayer is that this story reminded you of that.

That in brokenness, there can still be beauty. That in trauma, there can still be transformation. That your voice matters. Your healing matters. Your life matters.

Keep moving.

Keep praying.

Keep believing that peace is possible.

Because it is.

With all my heart,
  *-Cassandra Wade*

# ABOUT THE AUTHOR

**Cassandra Wade** is a storyteller and woman of faith whose writing is rooted in truth, healing, and resilience. As the founder of Wade Designs, she has used her creative gifts to uplift others through custom journals, planners, and digital content—tools designed to inspire intentional living and personal growth.

Divinity in Motion... When He Calls is Cassandra's debut novel—a deeply personal and powerful reflection of survival, faith, and transformation. Though fictional, the story carries the emotional truth of many real-life journeys. Cassandra's passion is giving voice to the unspoken and reminding others that brokenness is not the end of the story.

A proud mother and widow, Cassandra honors the memory of her late husband, Tony, in every step of her journey. She continues to write, design, and serve, all while walking boldly in her God-given purpose.

Made in United States
Orlando, FL
15 July 2025

62982995R00144